"Erin Bartels has a gift for creating unforgettable characters who are their own worst enemy, and yet there's always a glimmer of hope that makes you believe in them. The estranged sisters in *All That We Carried* are two of her best yet—young women battling their own demons and each other as they try to navigate beyond a shared painful past and find their way to a more hopeful future."

Valerie Fraser Luesse, Christy Award–winning novelist

"*All That We Carried* is so much more than just a beautiful novel—it's a literary adventure of both body and spirit, a meaningful parable, a journey of faith. Erin Bartels creates amazingly realistic characters in two sisters wrestling with their past and with one another. Not only did this story make me want to pull on my hiking boots for my own adventure, it propelled me to search out a deeper faith. Simply stunning. A novel not to be missed!"

Heidi Chiavaroli, award-winning author of *Freedom's Ring* and *The Tea Chest*

Praise for *The Words between Us*

"*The Words between Us* is a story of love found in the written word and love found because of the written word. It is also a novel of the consequences of those words that are left unsaid. Bartels's compelling sophomore novel will satisfy fans and new readers alike."

Booklist

"*The Words between Us* is a story to savor and share: a lyrical novel about the power of language and the search for salvation. I loved every sentence, every word."

Barbara Claypole White, bestselling author of *The Perfect Son* and *The Promise between Us*

"If you are the kind of person who finds meaning and life in the written word, then you'll find yourself hidden among these pages."

Shawn Smucker, author of *Light from Distant Stars*

"Vividly drawn and told in expertly woven dual timelines, *The Words between Us* is a story about a woman who has spent years trying to escape her family's scandals and the resilience she develops along the way. Erin Bartels's characters are a treat: complex, dynamic, and so lifelike I half expected them to climb straight out of the pages."

Kathleen Barber, author of *Are You Sleeping*

Also by Erin Bartels

We Hope for Better Things

The Words between Us

All That We Carried

a novel

ERIN BARTELS

Revell

a division of Baker Publishing Group
Grand Rapids, Michigan

Published by Revell
a division of Baker Publishing Group
PO Box 6287, Grand Rapids, MI 49516-6287
www.revellbooks.com

Printed in the United States of America

Library of Congress Cataloging-in-Publication Data
Names: Bartels, Erin, 1980– author.
Title: All that we carried: a novel / Erin Bartels.
Description: Grand Rapids, Michigan : Revell, a division of Baker Publishing Group, [2021]
Identifiers: LCCN 2020019550 | ISBN 9780800738365 (paperback) | ISBN 9780800739607 (casebound)
Subjects: LCSH: Domestic fiction.
Classification: LCC PS3602.A83854 A79 2021 | DDC 813/.6—dc23
LC record available at https://lccn.loc.gov/2020019550

21 22 23 24 25 26 27   7 6 5 4 3 2 1

For Alison, naturally

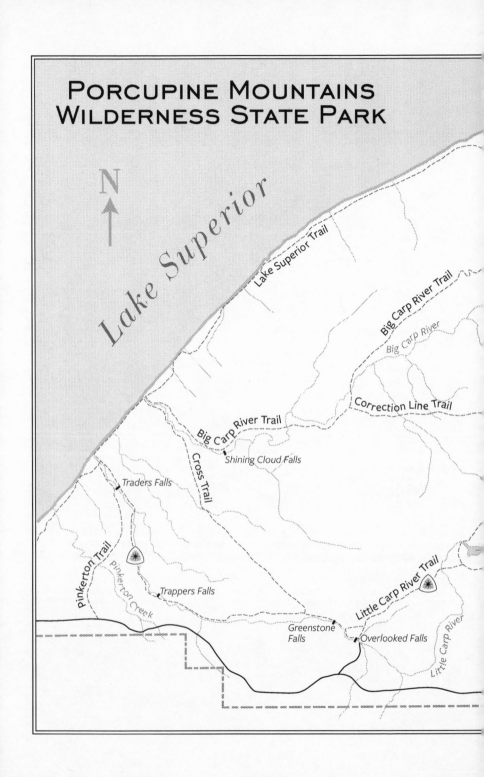

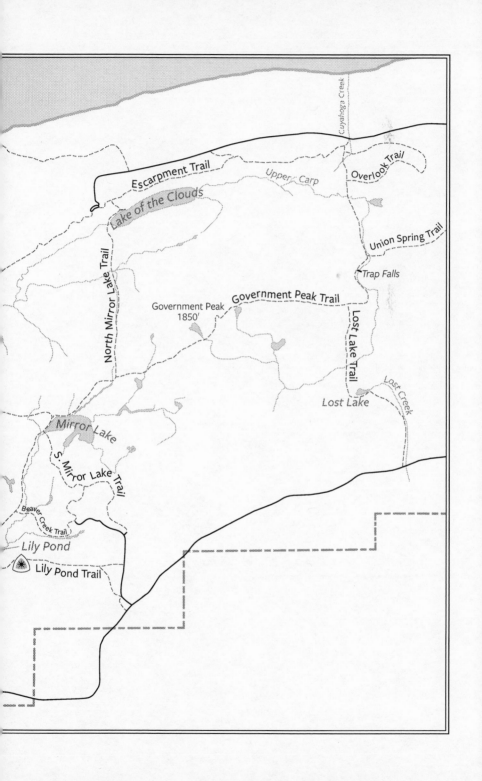

One

MIDWESTERNERS DO DUMB THINGS on the one nice day in March. The thought that winter might indeed have an end makes them giddy, unpredictable, and more than a little bit stupid. They wear shorts, make big plans, believe that this—finally—will be the year they get in shape or go to Paris or write their screenplay. And much like you wouldn't hold a friend to a promise they made while emerging from the effects of anesthesia after surgery, Olivia Greene felt that her sister had no right to hold her to the promise she'd made on that unseasonably warm day seven months ago.

Melanie had called at lunchtime when Olivia would not be in court and would therefore have no excuse for letting the call go to voicemail as she normally would. The sun had just broken through the rushing clouds, lighting the towering smokestacks of the power station south of downtown like columns of a Greek temple. Mists lifted from the low places along the road that were still cradling crusted snow. And at that moment, after an unsatisfying lunch at a mediocre restaurant with two colleagues she didn't much care for, Olivia had felt just restless enough to agree to a weeklong backpacking trip with the younger sister she hadn't seen in a decade.

That Melanie chose a hike, she couldn't quite understand. Hiking had long been ruined for her.

Now as she pulled off the highway and into the gas station lot where they had agreed to meet in Indian River, Olivia wished that day had been as miserable as the rest of March always was. If it had been sleeting, she never would have agreed to this nonsense.

She didn't know what kind of car her sister drove, but she didn't bother looking for her either. Melanie wouldn't be there yet, despite living only a half hour away. Instead, Olivia got out of the car, rubbed her hip, which was sore from the long spate of sitting, and went into the gas station. The sprawling shop had the normal gas station fare—pop, beer, candy, salty snacks—but it also sold accoutrements for three distinct, though at times overlapping, markets: veterans, hunters, and those passionate about right-wing politics.

She made haste to the bathroom, sure that everyone she passed knew she was out of her element. She'd done her hair that morning and put on makeup because that's what she did every morning, and while she was dressed in jeans and a hooded sweatshirt, she suspected they were brands you could not get at any store Up North. She washed her hands and wondered if she should buy a camo baseball cap to fit in. Of course, where she was going it wouldn't matter. She wouldn't be seeing many people, and of those she did see, she guessed that at least half would be young professionals like her, dabbling a bit in nature, thinking that a walk in the woods would solve their problems.

Olivia knew better. Problems like hers couldn't be solved.

She snagged an iced tea out of the cooler and passed a rotating case of hunting knives on her way to the counter. A knife. She'd forgotten to buy a knife at the sporting goods store at the mall when she was stocking up on gear for the trip. She didn't know exactly what she might need one for. She only knew that if she didn't have one, a need would present itself. She looked over the knives on offer, eliminating those with Confederate flags, divisions of the Armed Forces, or nationalist sentiments on the handle, until all that was left to choose from were animals. Whitetail deer, black bear, turkey, wolf, fish. A fish would do.

"Excuse me," she said to the woman behind the counter, "could I get the knife that says brook trout?"

The woman opened the case and extracted the knife Olivia pointed out. "You should get the one with the salmon," she said. "Salmon run's started."

Olivia just smiled and held out her credit card. She'd never cared for that half-crazed look of a spawning salmon—the eyes desperate, the scales turned a bloody red, the upper jaw looking for all the world like the thing would be screaming if only it had vocal cords.

"I guess you want the one with the state fish," the woman said, then she narrowed her eyes. "Where are you from?"

"East Lansing."

She nodded. "Heading to the cottage one last time for the year?"

"Hiking."

The woman looked her up and down and sort of shrugged, as if to say that the fact some suburban girl in designer jeans was going hiking wasn't her business, but she wouldn't be surprised

11

when the front page of next Sunday's paper sported a headline about a dead hiker. Natural selection and all.

"Around here? Or are you headed to the Upper Peninsula?"

"The UP, yes," Olivia said. She wished the woman would just ring up the knife and be done with it. A line was beginning to form behind her, though the clerk didn't seem to notice.

"Pictured Rocks?" the woman said.

Olivia winced. "No." She lowered her voice. She didn't really want to announce to a bunch of strange, burly men what remote place with no cell service she was headed for. "My sister and I are hiking the Porcupine Mountains."

"Hoo! The Porkies!" she all but shouted. "I hope you're ready for that." Then she gave Olivia a look that told her she was clearly not ready for that.

"We know what we're doing," Olivia said more tersely than she meant to. "We've hiked before."

The woman shook her head and finally rang her up. Olivia snatched up her things and headed for the exit.

"Watch out for bears!" the woman yelled.

Back at the car, she tucked the knife into a small compartment in her pack and looked at her smartwatch. 12:18. Melanie had not called or texted. She pulled both packs out and leaned them against the car, carefully so as not to scratch the finish. Though the trip had been Melanie's idea, Olivia had thought it best if she did the planning and the packing. It took her much of the summer, fitting it here and there into the cracks in her frenetic schedule. Mel's pack was lighter for the moment but would weigh more once she added her clothes and food, both of which Olivia would inspect before they set off, to ensure that

Melanie had adhered to the list she'd sent her back in July. She was about to lock the car when she spied the corner of something beneath the seat. She pulled it the rest of the way out.

The map. She had almost left the map behind.

Sure, they would have trail maps at the welcome center, but not like this one. Olivia had ordered it months ago. It was waterproof and tear-resistant, and she'd augmented it with additional details, clearly marking the trails they were going to take in pen. She'd emailed a scan of the map to her boss because she'd read that you should always make it known to others where you plan to hike and when you plan to return, so that if for some reason you *didn't* return, people would know where to look for you.

Her stomach churned at the almost oversight, and she had to sit down. Maybe the woman behind the counter was right to be skeptical.

"Ollie!" came a chipper voice, and Olivia looked up to see her little sister, strawberry blonde curls bouncing as she all but skipped up to the car. "I'm so excited to see you!"

Olivia stood to give Melanie a hug, keeping the map clenched firmly in her hand. Melanie squeezed her so tight her back cracked.

"Yikes!" Melanie said as she pulled away. "We need to take care of that!" She spun Olivia around and began to knead her shoulders. "You're all tied up."

Olivia shrugged away. "No point in fixing it now. I'll feel a lot worse in a few days."

Melanie dropped her hands for just a moment before crushing Olivia in a second hug. "I just can't believe I finally get to see you! It's been way, way too long."

Olivia felt her throat tighten. The last time she'd seen Melanie was during the funeral and the week of dazed shock afterward. Now all of the emotions of that time—the fathomless grief, the exhaustion, the enormity of their shared loss—rushed in like a dammed river reasserting itself against the puny will of humankind. She gripped her sister with a ferocious possessiveness that surprised her—then she remembered the reason she'd avoided Melanie for so long. She let go and took a step back. "Let's get these in your car. Did you already get gas?"

"I've got plenty of gas. I'm only twenty miles from here."

Olivia looked at her watch but said nothing. They lugged the packs over to Melanie's car, and Olivia started pawing through a reusable grocery tote in the back seat. "What's all this?"

"What?"

"This." She dug around. "Where's the cheese? Where are the little packages of chicken salad and tuna I put on the list? And no jerky? How are you going to get enough protein?"

Melanie started tucking things back into the bag. "I'm a vegan. You know that."

"A vegan? No, I didn't know that." Olivia felt herself looking at her sister the same way that dubious clerk had looked at her. "Did you at least stick to the clothing list?"

"I have what I need."

"And everything's in Ziploc bags?"

"No."

"No?"

"I didn't want to use all that plastic. It's wasteful."

"What if it rains?"

"I checked. It's not supposed to rain. Anyway, aren't the packs waterproof?"

14

"They're water-*resistant*. But if they're outside all night, they're going to get damp. Even if it's just with dew."

"It'll be fine."

Olivia took a deep breath. "Let's just get going. We still have a six-hour drive ahead of us, and we're behind schedule as it is."

"Okay," Melanie said. "I just have to use the ladies' room."

She walked off—no, *ambled* off—toward the gas station. As unhurried as ever. When they were kids, Melanie was forever lollygagging behind, interested in a puddle or a rock or her own belly button. Olivia would be waiting on her little sister to catch up all week.

It felt like an hour before Melanie reappeared, but that was probably just because Olivia checked the clock so many times.

"Okay, let's go," she said when Melanie finally got in the driver's seat. "Just head north on I-75 and I'll tell you where to go from there."

"I know how to get to the Upper Peninsula, Olivia."

"I know you do. Sorry." Olivia shrugged. "Once a bossy big sister, always a bossy big sister."

Melanie pulled out of the parking spot and clicked on her left blinker.

"The highway is right," Olivia said, pointing. "It's right there. You can see it."

"I thought we could go to the Cross in the Woods shrine first," Melanie said, eyes gleaming and expectant.

"Why on earth would you ever want to go there?" Olivia said. "Did you become a Catholic?"

"No, but I try to make it a point to do something Catholic every couple months."

"What? Why? No, never mind. It doesn't really matter. We don't have time for it."

"But it's just three minutes away," Melanie said. "I passed it on the way here."

"Well, maybe you should have gotten on the road earlier so you could see it before you were supposed to meet me, which was at noon, by the way, not 12:45. You obviously didn't even leave your house until *after* noon. Now it's almost an hour later than I had us scheduled to get on the road. And we still have to stop for dinner, and we're not going to get to the motel until after eight o'clock, if we're lucky."

A car honked behind them. Melanie switched to her right blinker and turned right.

"Besides," Olivia said, "there's no popping in with Catholics. You're either in or you're out. No in between. Remember when we'd sleep over at the O'Neils' and have to go to Mass with them? We never knew what was going on, and we weren't allowed to do the bread and wine thing because we weren't Catholic."

Melanie pulled onto the highway and drove in silence for a moment. "I did leave before noon," she finally said. "I had to stop on the way to get a turtle out of the road. And then I had to upload the video to my YouTube channel."

Olivia bit her tongue. While she had been waiting, Melanie had been uploading a video of herself saving a turtle?

"It's already got a bunch of comments," Melanie continued.

And that was why she had taken so long inside the gas station. She'd been checking to see how many people liked her.

It didn't matter, Olivia told herself. What's done is done and can't be undone—the phrase her mother used to say any time

Melanie broke one of her toys or ruined one of her books or tore one of her shirts. The phrase Olivia repeated to herself whenever she thought of what happened to her parents. What's done is done and can't be undone.

"I'm glad the turtle is okay," she said.

Melanie smiled. "Me too."

Two

MELANIE'S HEART QUICKENED when the first tower of the Mackinac Bridge came into view. This would be her seventh time over the bridge, a significant number. Seven days of the week. Seven notes in the diatonic scale. Seven letters in the Roman numeral system. The seven in the Tarot deck was the card of the chariot—the symbol of overcoming conflict and moving forward in a positive direction. Lucky number seven. She'd need luck on this trip if she hoped to move forward in a positive direction with Olivia.

She hit her sister's upper arm with the back of her hand. "There's the bridge!"

To her surprise, Olivia smiled. A good sign. Maybe it would all work out. It had to. Because they couldn't go on as they had for the past ten years. Something had to change. Only time together would do it. Time with no distractions. Time in the forest. Time for Melanie to explain herself. She had seven days to make it work. Seven days was enough. Her seven-day spiritual detox program was her most popular offering on *Meditations with Melanie.* And nothing needed detoxing like her relationship with her sister.

"I know a bailiff who refuses to cross big bridges," Olivia said. "He'll drive miles out of his way to avoid it. If he were going to the UP, he'd have to drive all the way around Lake Michigan and come in through Wisconsin."

"Why doesn't he just use the assistance program?" Melanie said. "Someone who works for the bridge authority will drive your car across for you if you're uncomfortable with it."

"I guess he's too afraid for even that. It's weird. He can't remember anything bad that ever happened to him on a bridge, he's just always been scared of going over them."

"I wonder if he's tried hypnosis to cope with his fears."

Olivia laughed. "No, I don't think he's tried hypnosis."

"It works for a lot of people."

"I'm sure it does." Olivia shifted in her seat. "Man, my hip is killing me."

"What's wrong with it?"

"Nothing. Just sore from sitting so long. It'll be fine."

Melanie slowed to forty-five miles per hour and pulled into the left lane. She would have preferred to drive in the right lane closer to the breathtaking expanse of blue water beneath her, but with big trucks required to go no faster than twenty and with Olivia already touchy about the time, she decided it was better to be fast than fascinated. If she got stuck behind a semi for five miles at twenty miles per hour, Olivia would probably have a stroke.

"You know, bridges are an important symbol in a lot of different belief systems," Melanie said. "They can be about crossing over from life to death. They can be about finding connection with one another. In a Tarot deck they can symbolize spanning the gap between misery and harmony. And they work either way. So if bridge cards start showing up in readings, it doesn't necessarily mean something bad or something good. It all depends on where your life is moving. Either we are moving toward misery or toward harmony in our lives."

"Yeah," Olivia said, "or they can be about the fact that we need one piece of land to connect to another piece of land so we can get a car across it."

Melanie bit the inside of her cheek. "How about some music?"

"Sure."

Olivia punched the button for the CD player. After a moment of silence, the sound of a solo acoustic guitar rang out, joined a moment later by a cello. Then a powerful female voice singing about rain and wind and absence and regret. Mel glanced over at her sister. Olivia's eyes were closed, just the way their father's had always been when he listened to loud music in the living room after a hectic day at work. But the face Mel saw was their mother's. Broad forehead, sensible nose, strong jawline. Olivia had their mother's straight brown hair and solid build. She had her no-nonsense attitude and her drive. She was in all ways fierce and formidable. The ultimate big sister.

Well, almost. The ultimate big sister wouldn't have left when Melanie needed her most.

As the last bittersweet notes of the song rang out, the car left the metal grate of the suspension bridge and the tires hit the concrete. Melanie and Olivia reached out to turn off the CD player at the same time and shared a smile. There were some songs that just needed to ring in your ears for a while.

"I haven't heard that since . . ." Olivia trailed off.

Melanie lowered her window to pay the toll. She handed the clerk four dollars, beat him to saying "Have a nice day," and pulled back out into traffic. She had driven perhaps a quarter mile before she realized Olivia never finished her sentence.

"When was the last time you heard that song?" she prompted.

"Do you have other CDs in here?"

Melanie allowed the deflection. She could guess the answer. "Back of your seat."

For the next forty-five minutes, Olivia played DJ as they drove west along the north shore of sparkling Lake Michigan. The CDs she put into the player had all once been part of their parents' collection, parceled out between the two sisters along with the photo albums, the jewelry, the books, and some of the furniture. Melanie relaxed into the soundtrack of her childhood and entered an almost meditative space, adrift in memories of times lost.

The road continued straight, the lakeshore curved away south, and they headed into the alternating pasturelands and scrub forest of the interior. Here the trees had more color than they did in the northern reaches of the Lower Peninsula. The varied green of the pines, spruces, and firs stood out against a tapestry of yellow and orange, with the occasional red thrown in like a garnish of flame. Fields of grazing dairy cows and wide wetlands playing host to migrating geese and herons occasionally broke up the monotony of the trees. Overhead a pair of sandhill cranes flew low and slow, heading south for the cold season ahead.

It was beautiful.

"I've sent a bunch of people to prison up here," Olivia said. "Not sure it's much of a punishment."

Melanie shook herself out of her reverie. "You look at all this gorgeous nature and that's where your mind goes? Prison?"

She shrugged. "It just popped into my head. It's the only connection I have to the UP."

"No it isn't," Melanie said.

"I don't like to think about that trip."

Melanie paused, picking her next words carefully. "The trip wasn't the problem."

"I don't want to talk about it. I know it helps some people to talk about things like that—I know it helps you—but that's just not me."

"I know. It's fine. We'll talk about something else."

But neither, it seemed, knew what that something else should be. They drove along in silence for a few minutes more.

"This is your turn up here," Olivia said, looking up from the paper map on her lap and gesturing at the upcoming intersection. "Turn right."

Melanie pointed the car north. Overhead, birds of prey soared on thermals. That, at least, was safe to talk about. "Look, a bald eagle. I see hawks and eagles all the time. Every time I leave the house, I see one. I think it must have something to do with my aura. Like they can sense a kindred spirit or something."

Olivia leaned forward and looked out the window. "That's a vulture."

"What? No, it's a bald eagle."

"That?" she asked, pointing.

"Yes."

"That's a vulture. If those are following you around, I think you may want to reexamine your aura. But I'm guessing you just see them a lot driving because of the roadkill."

Melanie craned her neck to keep the bird in sight. It couldn't be a vulture. She saw those all the time. They were eagles.

"Watch the road," Olivia snapped.

Melanie felt a stab of panic when she saw she had veered over the center line, and she overcorrected. She took a breath, let it out slowly, centered herself. Everything was okay.

"Do you want me to drive so you can look at the scenery?" Olivia said.

"No," Melanie mumbled. How could they be vultures? Settling her eyes back on the horizon, she saw a bank of gunmetal gray approaching from the northwest. "I think it's going to rain."

Olivia looked up from the map again. "Yep. Let's gas up at Seney so we don't have to do it later in a downpour."

"How far is it?"

"Not more than ten minutes, I should think."

Melanie looked at the gathering storm. "I hope we make it."

Three

IN ADDITION TO GAS at fifty cents more a gallon than downstate, the little gas station on the outskirts of Seney offered a wide selection of animal pelts slung over the railing by the door. Olivia ran her hand over each one as Melanie pumped the gas. No matter what the animal—deer, coyote, fox, raccoon, skunk—they all had a rough overcoat for protection and a soft undercoat for warmth. Like her and her sister. Melanie the soft and loving, she the stiff and repellent. No matter how she had tried to change that about herself, she always came up short.

She warned the clerk inside about the coming rain. He snapped his fingers at a young man, who sprang into action gathering up the furs and disappearing with them into a back room.

"Sorry," the clerk said to Olivia, "did you want to buy any?"

Olivia politely declined and asked where the bathroom was. When she walked back outside, Melanie was walking in.

"I'm glad he took those pelts away," she said. "I have to go so bad, but I wasn't getting within ten feet of those poor things."

24

Olivia rolled her eyes, then looked at the sky. "Hurry up. We're going to get dumped on any minute now."

She got into the driver's seat as Melanie disappeared inside the store. The first drops of rain hit hard and fat on the windshield and were quickly followed by more. Minutes later, Melanie ran out and tried to get in the driver's seat before realizing Olivia was already there. She ran around to the other side, shoulders hunched against the steady rain, and practically fell into the passenger seat and slammed the door.

"Sheesh! That came on fast. I'm already soaked."

Olivia looked at her. "It's not that bad."

Melanie shook a shower of water out of her curls.

"Hey!" Olivia said. "You're getting the map wet."

"Relax." Melanie laughed. "We've got GPS."

"Not for long. Can't depend on it where we're going."

"You're driving?"

"What's it look like?"

"Looks like you're driving. Better you than me. I hate driving in the rain."

"Me too, but it's better than having to ride when someone else is driving." Olivia headed west into the storm. Maybe they would get lucky and drive through it rather quickly. "Can you get a radar map on your phone right now?"

"I can try." Melanie started tapping at her phone as the rain intensified. "Not much for a signal."

"See?" Olivia squinted into the curtain of rain and slowed the car. "Never mind. We have to drive through it either way." She looked at the speedometer and sighed. So much for making up time lost to Melanie's turtle.

The CD player remained off as Olivia concentrated on the road. Which was fine with her. It had been pleasant at first to hear all of those songs from when she was a kid and a teenager. From before everything in her life changed irrevocably. But after Melanie mentioned that trip—the last trip she'd taken to the Upper Peninsula, and the last one she had ever meant to take until that stupid warm day in March—she knew she couldn't listen to any more old songs and keep her composure, which she was determined to do. Other people might burst into nostalgic tears at the drop of a hat, but she was not one of those people. What's done is done and can't be undone.

The storm gave her something else to focus on. The closer they got to Lake Superior, the worse the weather got. Olivia could feel the wind trying to nudge the car off the road. She considered stopping to wait it out, but the numbers on the clock had her pressing on.

Not long after they passed through Munising, Olivia saw flashing lights in her rearview mirror, though she couldn't hear any sirens over the pounding rain. She pulled to the side of the road and let a state trooper pass. A minute later it was followed by another. Then an ambulance, then a fire truck. With each emergency vehicle, Olivia's stomach dropped a little further and the lump that had formed in her chest rose up her throat until it was sitting on her voice box.

"Something awful must have happened," Melanie finally said.

Olivia stared straight ahead and put all of her energy into focusing on the gray line of the road that could just be distinguished from the varying grays of the skies above, the lake to their right, and the rain all around. The colorful drive had turned dark and dull, and the only bright spots were the headlights and taillights of other cars and the spinning lights of the first responders.

On a fairly straight stretch of road along the Lake Superior shoreline, Olivia slowed to a crawl of less than five miles per hour. A cluster of flashing lights marked the spot where all of the emergency vehicles had converged. In the center of it all was a motorcycle on its side and a man facedown in the street. Olivia gripped the wheel tighter. Melanie covered her mouth with her hand. Was this what the scene had looked like at their parents' accident? It had been raining then too.

A drenched police officer held up a hand. Olivia stopped the car and waited for clearance to go. With every second that eked by in view of the man in the street, she felt her heart rate tick up, up, up. She risked a glance at Melanie, and the panic left in a whoosh. Her sister was looking into her phone and fixing her hair.

"What are you doing?" Olivia said, incredulous.

"Shh. Just be quiet a minute." Melanie tapped the screen, waited a beat, then started to talk. "Hello out there, my Mellies. This is Melanie Greene at a moment of crisis, coming to you on behalf of a fellow sojourner who needs your help. As I film this, a man lies in the street in the pouring rain. There's been an accident. First responders are on the scene, but it's not clear from where I sit if the man is dead or alive. If he is alive, he is most certainly unconscious. He does not have a helmet on. I'm asking you right now, wherever you are, to stop what you're doing and start to pray. Send your prayers up to heaven, send your good vibes and warm thoughts to this man. Whatever goodness and positive feeling you have, project it out toward Michigan's Upper Peninsula, which is where I am right now, and I'll help channel it all into this man. We may never know the outcome—the officer is telling us to move ahead—but the Universe will. And the Universe works in mysterious ways."

Olivia stared open-mouthed as Melanie made a peace symbol at the camera and then blew it a kiss.

"Remember, my Mellies, you control your destiny. Peace, love, and life to you." She clicked off the camera and started swiping at the screen.

"What. Was. That?" Olivia said.

"Go," Melanie said, motioning to the officer who was now approaching the car.

Olivia waved an apology and crept forward past the flashing lights. Melanie continued to fiddle with her phone.

"We need to get somewhere with better reception," Melanie said. "How far are we from Marquette?"

Olivia struggled to keep her tone even. "What were you doing just now? Were you just using a quite-possibly-dead man to up your YouTube numbers? What is wrong with you?"

"Of course not," Melanie said, obviously offended. "I was using my already very high number of viewers to help *him*. I would have thought that was obvious."

Olivia let out a skeptical little puff of air. "Good vibes and warm thoughts? That's what you think will help this guy? Whatever hope he has of ending this day in a hospital bed rather than in a locker in the morgue is standing around him in uniform. Positive energy from your Mellies, whatever those are, has nothing to do with it."

"Look, I don't want to argue about this right now. Can you please just get us to Marquette? I need to upload this as soon as possible."

"I can't believe you of all people could think that thoughts and prayers have any effect at all."

"I said I don't want to argue about it," Melanie said with more force.

Olivia bit off her next reply. When they were children, she knew just how to get a rise out of her little sister. She'd always loved an argument. It was why she became a lawyer. But she didn't want to fight with her sister now. She wished they got along better, and she knew that a lot of their problems were probably her own fault. She was really the only person she knew who didn't get along with Melanie, the most get-alongable person in the world.

For now, she would put all her energy into getting them to Marquette. For dinner, which she suddenly realized was way overdue, and for whatever flaky purpose Melanie had in perpetuating the archaic belief that there was a god or a force or some greater meaning to the universe, something that cared about what happened to the billions of inconsequential humans walking around on this indifferent planet.

But mostly for dinner.

Melanie sat on the living room floor, hugging her knees in her plaid flannel pj's and staring intently at the glittering pile of reds and greens, golds and silvers. Outside, the world was still dark. Inside, the room glowed with light and anticipation.

"Just tell me one," Melanie said to Olivia, who was seated in the wingback chair, pretending to read the newspaper, pretending not to care about the presents beneath the tree.

"No."

"Come on, Olivia," Melanie pleaded. "If you tell me one of mine, I'll tell you one of yours."

Olivia turned the page. "No."

Melanie picked up a box and shook it. Olivia put the newspaper down on the coffee table and knelt next to her sister. "I know what that one is," she teased.

"Tell me," Melanie said, eyes alight with that special mania that comes over children on Christmas morning.

"No," Olivia said with a smug smile. "You're going to find out soon anyway."

Melanie flopped onto her back. "They're taking forever!"

Olivia tucked the box back under the tree and picked up one of her own.

Melanie sat up. "I know what that one is."

Olivia had her own suspicions, but she was trying not to get her hopes too high. If she was wrong and the box didn't contain a Tamagotchi—if it was the cheaper knock-off Giga Pet that would solidify her status in her friend group's second tier, for instance—she'd still have to act pleased when she opened it. She handed Melanie the box she'd just been shaking.

"Okay," Olivia said, her voice as official and older-sistery as she could make it. "I won't tell you what it is, but I will answer three yes-or-no questions about it. And then you have to do the same for this one."

Melanie spun to face her, sitting as close to her as possible without actually landing in her lap. Olivia scooted back a few inches. Melanie scooted up.

Olivia put her hand out to stop her: "Okay, ready?"

"Ready."

"Ask me a question."

"What is it?"

Olivia rolled her eyes. "No, a yes-or-no question. Like, can you wear it, or something."

"Can you wear it?"

"No."

Melanie frowned in thought. "Is it a toy?"

"Yes."

She bounced up and down on her flannel-clad butt. "What is it?"

"No, that's not a yes-or-no question," Olivia said, exasperated. "Ask if it has batteries."

"Does it have batteries?"

"No. That's three. My turn."

Melanie collapsed onto her side and bounced back up again. "No fair!"

"It is so. We said three questions. That was three questions."

"But—"

"My turn."

Melanie scowled. "Fine."

Olivia held up the gift in question. "Is it electronic?"

"Yes," Melanie mumbled.

"Is it Japanese?"

"What?"

"Is it Japanese?"

"I don't know."

"What do you mean you don't know? You said you knew what it was."

"I don't know that."

Olivia huffed. "Fine, that question doesn't count."

"Do you want to know where it came from?"

"Yes!"

"Oh, it came from Meijer."

"Not the store!"

"Yes, I was there when Mom bought it at Meijer."

Olivia put her face in her hands. "Never mind. Forget that one."

"Okay, you get one more."

"Two more."

"No, I told you it's electronic and it came from Meijer." Melanie ticked off the short list on two fingers.

"Fine." Olivia thought hard. She needed to ask a question that her little sister would actually know the answer to. "Can it die?"

Melanie laughed. "No! It can't die. It's electronic, silly."

"What's going on in here?" Olivia and Melanie's father shuffled into the room, followed by their mother. They were both in robes and slippers, hair mussed, eyes half closed.

"I'll make some coffee," their mother said.

Their father flopped onto the couch. "Do you girls know what time it is?"

"It's Christmastime!" they shouted in unison.

Melanie leaped on top of him. He shot an arm out and wrapped it around Olivia, dragging her into the pile. Both girls squealed and giggled and tried to get away. He let them go and called out to his wife in the kitchen. "Excedrin?"

"On it," she replied.

A few minutes later, Mom and Dad were snuggled up on the couch, steaming mugs in hand, while Olivia and Melanie scrambled around on the floor, finding and distributing presents, setting aside the ones that would be brought to their grandparents' house later that day. When the piles were all made, the girls looked expectantly at their parents.

"Okay," their dad said. "One at a time. Starting with . . ." He moved his finger slowly across the room. "Mom."

The girls deflated for just a moment. Then Olivia grabbed a present off her mom's pile. "Do this one first."

Melanie jumped up. "Yes, we made that one for you!"

Their mother plucked the bow from the box and tore the paper away. Inside the small, square box sat a pinecone stuffed with cotton and adorned with an orange triangle and two black and yellow circles of construction paper.

"It's an owl!" Melanie said.

"I see that. It's lovely!" Their mother held it aloft by the string attached to the top, and it turned slowly in the air.

"It's for the tree," Olivia explained.

"I found the pinecone," Melanie said.

"And I cut out the eyes and the beak," Olivia said. "And I tied the string."

Their mother handed it to Melanie. "Hang it on the tree for me."

Melanie bounded across the room and hung the owl directly in front of another ornament.

"Come here," their mom said, and she gathered them into her arms. "That was so thoughtful of you two. Thank you. I love it."

For just a moment, all four of them were on the couch in a tight, warm ball.

"Okay," their dad said. "Who's next?"

Four

MELANIE SAT IN THE BATHROOM stall and finished uploading her video. Whatever Olivia thought of her motives, she
knew they were pure. If Olivia had devoted her life to justice,
Melanie had devoted hers to encouragement. And for every
criminal Olivia had sent to prison, Melanie could count hun-
dreds of people she'd helped through hard times. For all she
knew, one of those people her sister had prosecuted now watched
Meditations with Melanie to cope with their new situation in life.

Upload complete, she returned to the table where Olivia was
perusing the menu.

"Might be a good idea to eat big tonight," Olivia said. "Last
chance for real food for a while."

Melanie searched the menu in vain for the V for vegan symbol
and then started back with the salads. She was used to building
her own vegan meals at restaurants. Even though most chain
restaurants were quite accommodating nowadays, local joints
Up North were still hit or miss unless they were run by Millen-
nials. After Olivia ordered a steak, medium rare, with buttered
mashed potatoes and green beans, Melanie started in on her

order: garden salad, no croutons, olive oil and vinegar on the side, with a couple lemon wedges and a plain baked potato. Yes, plain, thank you. No, no butter, no cheese, no sour cream. Yes, just plain.

"I can bring you butter on the side," the waitress said. She had a concerned look on her face, as though she was responsible somehow for Melanie's well-being and the only thing that would ensure that well-being was some sort of dairy product.

"No, thank you."

The waitress left, shaking her head, and Melanie was sure that she would bring butter anyway.

When Mel looked back across the table at Olivia, her sister was already looking at her.

"Hey," Olivia said, "I'm sorry I freaked out a bit back there."

Melanie nodded. "It's fine. I know we don't see eye to eye on stuff like that."

"Yeah, but I shouldn't have made that big of a deal about it. You've never come into a courtroom during a trial and given me your two cents about how to do my job, and I shouldn't have put my nose in where it didn't belong in your job. That is your job, right?"

"Partly," Melanie said. "I do make money off the YouTube channel from ads, but mostly it helps me market my detox packages and my life coaching services."

Olivia nodded, but Melanie had had enough experience with this to tell when she was being judged. Her sister thought she was a flake or a hippie or maybe even just garden-variety dumb. But Melanie had seen how her words changed people's lives. She made people happy, and that was all that mattered.

"So is being vegan a part of the detox or something?" Olivia asked.

"It's what I advocate in my program. Some people just do it for a span of thirty or sixty days. Some make a permanent lifestyle change because they lose weight and they just feel so much better and more energetic."

"That can't be why you do it though. You've never needed to lose weight."

"No." Melanie fiddled with her utensils.

"Okay, so is it a moral thing? Like an animal cruelty thing?"

"Not exactly." Melanie smoothed her napkin on her lap. "I started thinking about reincarnation, and I got . . . anxious. About Mom and Dad."

Olivia's eyebrows practically met above her narrowed eyes. "What do you mean?"

Melanie looked her plain in the face. "I didn't want to accidentally do anything to Mom or Dad."

"You mean . . . eat them?"

Olivia was looking at her like she was the dumbest person she knew. She should have listened to the voice inside her that had been telling her to just lie to her sister. But lies brought negative energy and bred more lies, like how one fruit fly somehow led to dozens. It was better to tell the truth, even if it made you look foolish.

"Okay, let me get this straight," Olivia said, and she began counting off on her fingers. "You believe in reincarnation, and that good vibes and positive energy can help people you don't know miles away from you, and also in prayer, and you do Tarot readings, and you try to do something Catholic every couple months. Am I missing anything? I'm not trying to be mean here, I'm just trying to understand. What's the basis of your belief system?"

Melanie leaned back as the waitress put their food on the table. She picked up the little dish of butter next to her potato and handed it to Olivia. "The basis of it?" she said, buying time.

"Yes, what is it based on? Like, Christians base their beliefs on the Bible, Jews base their beliefs on the Torah, Muslims base their beliefs on the Quran, Native Americans base their beliefs on an oral tradition. So what are your beliefs based on? I'm seriously not trying to be mean. I just don't get it."

"No, I know you're not. Believe me, I can tell when you're trying to be mean."

They shared a hesitant laugh, and Olivia cut into her steak.

"I don't know," Melanie said, poking at her salad with her fork. "They're based on a lot of things. Things I've read and teachers I've heard and poems and documentaries and stuff like that."

"So, there's no one set of teachings or documents or traditions. You're just picking the stuff you like from everything that's out there. Like, cafeteria style."

Melanie took a big bite of her salad to give herself a moment to think. No one had ever asked her what she based her beliefs on before. It hadn't seemed to matter to any of her clients or people who attended her workshops or her online audience, her Mellies. Why did it matter to Olivia? Olivia who believed in nothing at all.

Melanie swallowed and took a sip of water. "I guess you could say that."

Olivia put down a forkful of potatoes. "But that's completely illogical. You can see that, right?"

"Why should it be?"

"Because of the law of noncontradiction. If one of those groups is correct, then everyone not part of that group is wrong. If Christians are right about having to believe in Jesus, then any other system of belief with other gods and other ways to heaven can't be right. Or if Buddhists are right about reaching nirvana, then the Christians can't be right. You see what I mean?" Olivia finally put the potatoes into her mouth, but she kept talking right around them. "You can't believe just a little bit of everything. And anyway, why bother? Why not just choose one?"

Melanie let that last question settle into her brain. "Frankly, I've never really seen the need to choose just one."

"But you can see how that doesn't work, right?" Olivia insisted.

Melanie shifted in her seat and changed tacks. "What do you think happened to Mom and Dad? Like, where do you think they are now?"

Olivia frowned. "At some point immediately following the accident, their hearts stopped, they stopped breathing, and their bodies shut down. The potential energy left in their cells after they died was used up as, well . . . as natural processes progressed."

"So in your opinion there's nothing left of them."

"Nothing." Olivia offered her a sad smile. "It's not that I wouldn't love to see them again. I just don't think I see any evidence of an afterlife."

Melanie leaned forward. "Okay, but what if you're wrong?

Then you'd miss your chance to see them again. That's why I try to follow all of these different belief systems. Because wherever they are, I want to be there someday."

Olivia's expression softened. "So, you're just covering your bases."

Melanie gave a little nod. "I guess so."

Her sister said nothing and focused on dismembering her steak.

Melanie finished her salad, the sound of her own chewing deafening in the general silence. One look at the dry baked potato made her feel ill. There was no way she could stomach all of that now. Not with her guts tied up like they were. She had always thought of herself as someone who lived life from a place of generosity and love. It had never occurred to her that something else might lie at the root of her magnanimous attitude toward the spiritual realm. Something that looked suspiciously like fear.

Five

IT WAS PAST 7:30 when the waitress finally came around
with the bill. Even though Olivia had her credit card ready,
she still had to all but shove the little plastic tray back into the
waitress's hand to get her to run it immediately. At the rate they
were going they wouldn't make it to Ontonagon until after ten
o'clock. Had they been going to a big hotel in a major city, it
wouldn't have mattered. But only a few cities in the Upper
Peninsula even had big chain hotels, and Ontonagon wasn't
one of them.

What awaited them was not room service and down pillows
and streaming TV but a tiny one-room cabin with beds that had
probably been there for forty years. Or rather, *bed*. They would
be sharing, like they used to do on the hide-a-bed in the family
room when Mom and Dad let them have a "sisters' sleepover"
and fall asleep watching a movie.

Olivia explained their weather delay to the owner over the
phone, and he graciously said that he'd be up until at least ten
but that his wife went to bed at nine. If he was too tired to stay
up, he would just leave the cabin unlocked with the key inside.

Olivia also called the park headquarters to ask about the trail conditions after the rain, but she had to leave a message.

The deluge had let up some while they were eating, and the dash to the car parked on the street outside was easier than the dash inside had been. Melanie's hair was curlier than ever in the wet air. As Olivia checked the rearview mirror for traffic, she saw that hers was flat and lifeless. She'd meant for both of them to take showers tonight so they'd be fresh for the morning and get out of the cabin as early as possible, but the long day of driving had taken a toll on her energy reserves, and she was sure she'd fall asleep as soon as her head hit the pillow.

As they left Marquette, the sky ahead was dark with clouds obscuring an early sunset.

The next two hours on the road were quiet. The rain was light yet persistent, and Olivia found it impossible to relax. She sat upright away from the seat back, gripping the steering wheel in both hands and scanning the edges of her headlights for eye-shine that would indicate a deer that might leap out in front of the car. She was used to city driving, which was never very dark and where the largest animal you might hit was a raccoon. Here in the sparsely populated western UP, even her brights couldn't illuminate enough for her tastes, and any time an oncoming car appeared, she had to turn them off.

She tried and failed to avoid thinking of her parents. It had been dark and rainy then too—for them at least. When it all happened, she and Melanie were far away, sleeping in tents along with four other friends, out of reach and out of touch on the backcountry trails of Pictured Rocks National Lakeshore. It had been warm and dry on the trail, and they were on their second of three planned overnights on the long Labor Day weekend. That day they had explored caves in the sandstone cliffs that had been carved out of the rock by the wave action on Lake Superior. They had splashed in the frigid water, baked in the warm sun, and marveled at the clear blue of the sky and turquoise of the lake. Everything was perfect.

It was sometime after they had roasted marshmallows over the campfire, Olivia figured later, that the accident occurred. That was when the six friends had coupled up—which had been Olivia's plan all along—and edged away from the firelight for a little privacy. She'd carefully chosen the group to include three potential couples with similar interests. She and Eric were both heading into their senior year of college and were into all the same bands. Melanie and Keith were both going to be sophomores and were artistic. And her friends Bryce and Lisa were both junior-year fitness nuts.

She'd never played matchmaker before, but like almost everything else she tried, she found she had a knack for it. It was all about taking what she knew about each person and projecting it into the future. What was cute and quirky now but would get nails-on-the-chalkboard annoying later? Which strengths could balance out which weaknesses? Could at least one person in every couple be reasonably expected to make a decent living? She'd thought of everything.

Before she could see her plan come to full fruition, she was found by a ranger and taken aside along with her little sister. She was startled at first to hear a perfect stranger ask her if she was Olivia Greene, but then she remembered that all of their names were on the campsite registrations for particular nights.

All a ranger had to do was look for her on the right part of the trail, which could be easily deduced by where they had slept the night before and where they planned to sleep that night.

She couldn't recall later exactly what the ranger said. The details were erased by the numb shock. All she knew in that moment was that her parents had been in an accident, that they had been taken to a hospital, and that she and Melanie needed to get home. The six of them silently followed the ranger down a two-mile access trail to his truck. They piled the packs in the back and squeezed seven people into seating for five, then he drove them back to Eric's Explorer.

The logistics of getting Olivia and Melanie home to Rockford and getting everyone else back to campus in Ann Arbor were ironed out with a few phone calls. The hikers would meet Olivia and Melanie's Uncle Craig in Lansing, and he would take them the rest of the way home. The others would continue on back to the University of Michigan. What no one told them until Uncle Craig had delivered them back to their house, where Aunt Susan and Grandma Ann were waiting, was that both of their parents had died from their injuries before they reached the hospital.

They were just . . . gone.

In the week that followed, the gray haze of grief colored everything. It obscured the faces of friends and family, dulled the sounds of conversations and eulogy and hymns. It settled into Olivia's spirit until her dreams, which were inevitably nightmares, felt more real than her waking hours. She felt as though she was slipping silently into a still pond and if she went all the way under she might never resurface.

Her solution was to get back to school as soon as possible. Her classes offered the distraction she needed. Melanie had gone the other direction. She dropped out of school, spent two years emptying and selling their childhood home with Aunt Susan's help, and then fell into a pretty severe depression that Olivia had never truly known the scope of, though Aunt Susan kept sending her emails that hinted at it and suggested that Olivia may want to get in touch with her little sister.

But getting in touch with Melanie meant having to face all of the emotions she had been avoiding. And it meant dealing with her rage over the fact that Melanie had betrayed them all by forgiving the guy who'd caused the accident and who'd walked away unscathed. Using law school as a convenient excuse, Olivia managed to avoid her family and her memories for years. Until Melanie came after her.

The move north to Petoskey helped Melanie begin to break out of the hold depression had on her, but even Olivia had to admit that it was starting a blog that really made the most difference. A blog that became a YouTube channel that became a life coaching business. Melanie got better and had apparently made it her mission in life to get other people better too.

Olivia knew that was what this trip was about. Melanie had arranged just the right combination of things to force Olivia to face the past—a long car drive, a remote hiking trip, music from their childhood in the CD player. In the end, Olivia had acquiesced to Melanie's harping. But she put her foot down on the location. Melanie had wanted to return to Pictured Rocks to finish the hike they had started ten years before. But there was no way Olivia would ever set foot on that trail again. She knew she'd recognize the exact spot where that ranger had appeared out of the trees to tell her the worst news she would ever receive. She would go hiking if it would get Melanie to leave her alone. Just not there. Never there.

They pulled up to the main-office cabin at 10:08 p.m. Though the rain had been lighter much of the way there, they'd hit another downpour a few miles from the motel.

"Stay in the car," Olivia said. "I'll check us in and get the key."

She dashed out, arms above her head to fend off the torrent, then yanked on the front door to no avail. A man of about sixty wearing a robe was rounding the front desk. He hurried to the door and turned the lock, ushering her in.

"Oh, come in, come in! I'm so glad to see you made it." He tugged lightly on Olivia's arm and shut the door behind her.

A woman, also in a robe, came out from behind the counter. "We were so worried."

Olivia wiped the wet hair from her face and was about to speak when she found that she couldn't. A lump had risen suddenly in her throat, and she felt—absurdly—like she was about to cry.

"Oh! You're soaked!" the woman said, rushing into action. She snatched a towel from the cupboard beneath the coffee maker and handed it to Olivia as the man pulled her farther into the room. "And you're limping, you poor thing."

She was?

"Where's your sister?"

Olivia pointed out the door. "Car," she managed. What was wrong with her? She stood in courtrooms with people who had done despicable things to their fellow human beings—deceptions, beatings, rapes, murders—and had never had a problem controlling her emotions. Why was it so hard to check into a stupid little cabin?

She took a deep breath. "We're here. And ready for bed."

"I bet you are," the man said. "Willa?"

The woman pulled a key from the wall behind the counter and pointed. "It's the third one down. The lights are on for you. Wanted you to be able to see it in the dark."

Olivia nodded. "I'm so sorry we kept you up. It wasn't my intention to arrive so late. I had it all scheduled out and—"

"Nonsense," the man broke in. "You can't schedule everything. Weather will have its way."

"Bernie, what about the road? Don't forget that," Willa said.

Bernie shook his head. "No, these girls are going west, to the Porkies, aren't you?"

"Yes," Olivia said, surprised to realize that she wasn't at all upset about this man referring to her as a girl. "What road?"

"It's nothing," Bernie said.

"It's not nothing," Willa protested. "Up in Houghton they've had roads washed clean away today by this storm. Had no rain all summer—dry as a bone out there—then all this rain all at once. Ground can't keep up with it."

"But they're not going to Houghton, they're hiking the Porkies," Bernie said. Willa seemed about to speak again, but her husband cut her off. "The road out there is fine. The trail may be another matter. But maybe it won't be so bad. It certainly was a dry season. Now let's let these girls get some sleep."

Willa gripped Olivia's hand. "Do be careful out there. I worry so much about hikers, especially if you don't have any men in your group."

Olivia laughed at that. "Oh, don't worry about us. We've managed so far without men. I'm sure we'll be just fine." She gave Bernie a wink, which he returned. "Well, I better get back out to my sister. Oh! When do I pay? We'll be getting out early tomorrow morning."

"We're up at six, dear," Willa said. "Now go get some sleep."

"Thank you, again, for staying up so late."

"No problem," Bernie said. He unlocked the door for her, and she rushed back into the car.

"Everything okay with the room?" Melanie said. "You were in there a long time."

"Yeah," Olivia said. "We just got talking. They're a nice couple."

At that moment she knew why she'd found it so hard to speak at first. Bernie and Willa looked to be about how old her parents would be now, and they had been up late, worried and watching for her and her sister to come in out of the storm.

Olivia quickly pulled the car away to where the floodlight could not illuminate her face and then idled slowly toward the third cabin on the left. She parked as close to the door as possible, glad she'd packed a separate bag for this overnight stay so she wouldn't have to lug her pack in through the rain. In less than a minute, she and Melanie were inside with their things, shaking the water out of their hair and taking in their new surroundings.

The room was small, only about the width of a double bed and two nightstands. Along one wall was the door to a tiny bathroom. Another wall was lined with a small refrigerator topped with a microwave, a narrow sink, a two-burner stovetop, and a petite table with two chairs, above which was a laughably out-of-place flat-screen TV. So maybe they did have streaming up here.

Olivia dumped her stuff on the table and turned on the TV. She didn't have to search for the local news and weather channel. It must be what everyone watched before they left for the day's adventures. Footage of the flooding up in Houghton was terrible, but it wasn't what she was looking for. She scanned the ticker for anything that included the Porcupine Mountains. She heard Melanie moving about behind her—using the bathroom, brushing her teeth, changing into pajamas. The ticker repeated itself three full times. Nothing new.

Finally, Olivia turned around to find Melanie snug under the covers, writing in a journal. She could read no anxiety on her little sister's face. In fact, Melanie smiled contentedly as she scribbled away.

"What are you writing?" Olivia said.

"Oh, just notes about the day." Melanie looked up. "Did the news have anything on that motorcycle accident?"

Olivia had nearly forgotten the accident. "I don't think so."

"I tried to see if I could find anything before we left Marquette, but the only articles about accidents were years old. And you know there had to be more than the one accident in all that rain. I don't understand how search engines work. Maybe there should just be one website where all accidents are reported and then followed up on, so you can find out what happened after the accident."

Olivia wished she would stop saying the word *accident*.

"It could be like the Weather Channel. But, like, the Accident Channel, you know?"

"I'm getting ready for bed." Olivia disappeared into the bathroom. Since she was already all wet, she might as well take a shower. The tiny stall was tight quarters for someone as tall as she was, and the well water smelled faintly of sulfur, but the towels were soft. She slipped into clean pj's and took a moment to savor the feeling. Soon she'd be grimier than she had been in many years.

When she came out of the bathroom, Melanie had switched from her journal to a book. Olivia got into bed and tried to look surreptitiously at the cover.

Melanie tipped the cover toward her. "It's about a man who hiked the Appalachian Trail solo after he lost his wife to cancer," she explained. "It's really good."

Olivia turned away and switched off the lamp on her side of the bed.

"Do you want me to turn this off?" Melanie said.

"No, you can read."

"Do you want me to read to you?"

"No. I'm going to sleep."

"Okay."

"Don't stay up too late," Olivia said. "I have my alarm set for seven o'clock. Enough time to check out, eat, and get to the park headquarters to check in when they open at eight. If you have to take a shower tomorrow morning, make it quick." She kneaded her pillow, laid her head down, and closed her eyes. Tomorrow would come quickly.

Sleep would not.

Six

MELANIE THREW THE CAR into park in the small dirt lot at the Government Peak trailhead and turned to her sister. "Here we are! Right on schedule."

Per Olivia's desires, they had rolled in to the Porcupine Mountains Wilderness State Park visitor center at 7:58 a.m. and were waiting outside the door when it opened at 8:00. They checked in, received their backcountry camping permit, and got an update on the weather—fine but on the cold side—and trail conditions—a bit soggy in places. The rivers and waterfalls would be running high, but nothing insurmountable. Melanie made the four-mile drive to the trailhead in silence as Olivia frowned over her map and made some last-minute notes. And then they were there.

"This is so exciting," Melanie said as they unloaded their packs and poles. Olivia had insisted they both have a set of hiking poles because they would technically be hiking in mountains, though anyone who had hiked in any major range would laugh at what Midwesterners considered mountains. According to Olivia, they'd scale one of the highest peaks in the park today, at a measly 1,850 feet.

An orange hatchback roared into the small gravel lot, parked at an obnoxious angle, and spit out three loud people and an empty beer bottle, which none of the three stooped to pick up. Two guys and a girl in their early twenties, dressed as though they were going to be Instagramming their trip.

"Day hikers," Olivia said with just a touch of derision. "Let's get moving fast so we don't have to hike near them."

The hatchback opened, revealing three brand-new packs. Not day hikers.

"Maybe we should let them go on ahead of us," Melanie suggested. "They look pretty fit."

"And we're not?"

"I mean, we're not decrepit yet, but it's not like we're running marathons or anything. And you were complaining about your hip."

Olivia approached the noisy trio. "Excuse me." No one heard her, or if they did they were ignoring her. "Excuse me!"

They stopped talking and looked at her like they'd never seen another human being before. "Yeah?" the girl said, challenge in her voice.

"Are you hiking the backcountry?"

"Yeah," one of the guys said.

"I'm just wondering if we might be going the same way," Olivia said, pulling out her map.

The guy gave his friends an eye roll and leaned in. "This where you're going? The stuff in pen?"

"Yes."

"We're going that way too. At first. Then we're skipping over this way to the lake." The other two already had their packs on, and the girl handed him his while never taking her narrowed eyes off Olivia. He pulled it on and snapped the belt across his stomach. "Why?"

"Just curious," Olivia said. She folded the map and headed back to Melanie's car.

The girl whispered something to the guys, and they all laughed. Then they headed into the forest.

"I guess that settles that," Olivia said. "We'll hike behind them and hope we don't catch up."

Melanie picked up the beer bottle and tossed it in the back of her car. "Little early in the day to be drinking, wouldn't you say?"

"Your car's going to smell like beer when we get back," Olivia warned. "But I guess there's no trash can, so . . ." She trailed off.

Packs were hoisted and straps were clicked into place, then Melanie locked the car and tucked her keys into a side pocket.

"You have your water, right?" Olivia said.

"Yes."

"And your food."

"Oh! No, wait."

Olivia sighed and dug Melanie's keys out of the pack. "What were you going to eat?"

"Calm down, we didn't leave it."

"We almost did." Olivia quickly transferred the food to the food bag and the food bag to the pack that was still on Melanie's back. "What about this box back here? What's in there?"

Melanie opened the other back door and grabbed the box before Olivia could open it. "Nothing. Just some stuff I wanted you to go through after the hike." She shoved it across the back seat, where it landed next to the beer bottle.

"What is it?"

"Just stuff. You'll see. Later. Let's get going. This trail isn't going to hike itself!"

Olivia locked the car and stuffed the keys back into the side pocket of Mel's pack. "Okay, disaster averted. Let's go." She started down the trail.

"Wait!" Melanie said, pulling out her phone. "We have to get a start-of-the-hike selfie."

"We do?"

"Yes, of course we do. Stop being so difficult. Take your sunglasses off."

"This better not end up on your website."

Melanie snatched the sunglasses off Olivia's face and positioned her by the sign for the Government Peak Trail, which indicated several destinations, including where they would sleep that night: Mirror Lake, 8 miles.

Melanie snapped several pictures, then swiftly thumbed through them. "Come on. Act like you want to be here." She snapped several more, pronounced them "workable," and turned off her phone to save the battery.

"Okay then, let's go. Sun sets at 7:32."

With Olivia in the lead, they started walking. The trail led gently up beneath a canopy of yellow birch and burnished maple. The forest floor was already littered with a mosaic of fallen leaves, and the underbrush was heavy with berries of red, white, and nearly black. Melanie took in the glorious colors, breathed in the sweet scent of decay, and felt lucky—no, blessed—to be in this exact place at this exact moment. A moment that would never come in exactly this way again.

On any other day, she would have stopped right then to record it in her journal—what she saw, what she heard, what she felt—so that she could go back to it someday when the darkness came creeping in from that place where it always lurked just outside her field of vision. Not that all of the moments she recorded were pleasant. Some were downright painful. In fact, of all the pages of the first journal she'd filled after her parents' accident, Melanie could count on one hand those that testified to anything other than complete despair. She wasn't sure she'd ever be able to return to that journal for solace, to relive those exhausting days of grief mingled with pragmatism, the bouts of crying over some item in the house and then having to decide what to do with it. Save, donate, discard. The slow dispersal of goods dragging out her grief along with it.

But then, journals weren't just about the happy days, and anything of significance got written down. Or perhaps some moments only became significant by virtue of being recorded. The particular patterns and colors of the leaves at this hour of this day probably weren't important in any sense that Olivia would understand. But to Melanie they marked the beginning of a sparkling new chapter in her relationship with her sister. The one in which Olivia would finally forgive her for the event she recorded at the end of that first journal. The unforgivable sin that had forever rent the fabric of their relationship.

Melanie hadn't noticed him at the committal service in the cemetery that day until Olivia pointed him out.

"What does he think he's doing here?" she'd said, her voice like granite.

Melanie followed her gaze to a young man standing in the

open passenger door of a car whose windshield still sported the neon-yellow price sticker typical of a certain echelon of used car lots. He was wearing sunglasses, though the day was cloudy, but Melanie recognized the wiry build, tattooed arms, and buzzed dark hair of Justin Navarro. Uncle Craig began walking toward the car, presumably to ask him to leave. But he didn't have to. Justin got into the car, and whoever was in the driver's seat drove away.

Later, on the pages of her journal, Melanie wondered why Justin had thought it appropriate to come and how long he had been there, skulking along the edges of their sorrow. She saw him the next week at the other end of the medicine aisle in the grocery store, and then at the thrift store the week after that, when she dropped off several bags of her father's clothes. He was thumbing through shirts, and she wondered if she might run into him someday in a parking lot and realize that he was wearing something of her dad's.

She'd decided right then that she needed to speak to him. That she couldn't go on seeing him in town, pretending nothing had happened when both of their lives had changed forever. Yes, it was awkward at first, and Melanie had to work hard to keep from crying, but that first tentative conversation ended with an agreement to meet for coffee the next day. One coffee led to another, which led to meeting once a week, during which the two of them would update each other on how they were doing emotionally and what was happening in their lives.

Over the course of the next few months, Melanie came to realize that she could not hate Justin Navarro the rest of her life as Olivia intended to. She had to let go in order to move on.

She told him she forgave him, and she recorded the moment later that day on the final pages of that first journal. Then she called Olivia at school to tell her and to encourage her to do the same. After a stunned silence followed by some sharp words, Olivia hung up on her. That was when Melanie knew that Justin didn't only take her parents from her, he took her sister as well.

Until now, if Melanie had anything to do with it.

The climb continued for maybe another thousand feet before it leveled out and they crossed a small wooden bridge.

"That's Cuyahoga Creek," Olivia announced. "The next bridge will be over the Upper Carp River."

From behind her, Melanie could barely make out the words, but she didn't really care all that much what the creek was called. It was sweet and talkative, and that was all that mattered. Jeweled trees leaned in toward the water, as though listening to the creek tell its particular story. She looked up to say as much to Olivia, but she was already several yards away, climbing up the next little hill.

Melanie followed, though at a deliberately slower pace. Olivia may have a schedule, but she did not. She was determined to enjoy every moment of this walk in the woods in her own way, at her own speed. It was how she had determined to live her life as well, one of the reasons she had moved north to the artsy little town of Petoskey, where she celebrated every season's unique offerings. The hot, windblown summers when the cries of seagulls mixed with the sounds of children on the beaches and the cracks of baseball bats in the park. The crisp, colorful autumns when the city emptied of tourists and the gales started out on Lake Michigan. The long, snowy winters of firelight and candlelight. And the fresh green springs when she would comb the beaches in search of the stones of fossilized coral that gave the city its name.

Here in this moment, in the Porcupine Mountains, Melanie celebrated the transitions she saw all around her, from the trees preparing for winter to the berries and seeds that would fatten up the birds and bears and stock the squirrels' larders. Everything was beautiful and magical. The only thing keeping it from being absolutely perfect was the fact that Olivia was walking too fast to notice it.

They traversed relatively even terrain for about a half mile until they came to an open space and the second bridge, where Olivia finally stopped to let Melanie catch up. "Grab my water for me?" she said.

Melanie pulled one of Olivia's two 32-ounce water bottles from the side of her pack and handed it to her, then she turned to let Olivia return the favor. Olivia drank sparingly. Melanie gulped down a third of the bottle in a matter of seconds.

"Whoa, slow down there," Olivia said. "Conserve."

"You have a filter, right?"

"Yes, but you can't get water just anywhere."

"We're literally standing above a river."

"Well, we're not stopping to filter here. We're not stopping until Trap Falls, where we'll take a short snack break, then we'll lunch on Government Peak, and you can't get water there. I wasn't planning on having to refill the bottles until we make camp tonight."

"If I need some when we stop at Trap Falls, we can just do it there."

Olivia sighed and held out her water bottle to Melanie to put it back in her pack.

"What's the big deal?" Melanie said, handing hers over. "If we're stopping anyway."

"I just don't want to spend a lot of time there, that's all."

"Why wouldn't you want to spend time at a waterfall?"

"Because it's only a quarter of the entire distance we have to travel today, and I don't want us to get off track so early in the trip. We're well rested, we're fresh, our muscles don't hurt yet. We need to make the most of that today because tomorrow we're not going to be feeling quite as good."

"Fine, but if you're not careful, you're going to catch up with those other people, and you clearly don't want to be anywhere near them."

Olivia said nothing, but her expression grudgingly acknowledged that Melanie was right. She started walking again, a little slower. Melanie retrieved her phone, took a few shots, and turned it off again. Then she soldiered on but still managed to focus on the positive. She was out in the beauty of nature with someone who sorely needed such beauty.

Not long after the bridge, they began a steady climb. The trail soon converged with the river they had crossed, which ran rushing and gurgling along in a gorge to their left in the opposite direction of their hike. The sound of it filled the air so that Melanie could no longer hear any breeze in the trees. She listened closely for patterns and variations, trying to discern what it was the river wanted to say to her. It had no schedule, no agenda. It ran and jumped and danced its days away with joyous abandon, whether anyone was there to see it or not.

Melanie felt a sudden and unexpected yearning to feel that free, to be utterly unaware and unconcerned with the results of her labors—to forget about views and likes and comments in order to make room for the sheer joy of being. It was the attitude she advocated for others but found difficult to cultivate in herself. With each step, each deepening breath that came with the effort of the constant uphill climb, Melanie felt more keenly the weight of the expectations she had placed on herself over the past ten years. The weight of being the perfect bereaved daughter, the manager of the estate, the dispenser of good advice, the bubbly online personality. She could feel her cheeks and ears getting hot, could feel her heartbeat in her temples, a trickle of sweat running down her neck. And still the top of the hill was out of sight and out of reach.

Just when she thought she couldn't take another step and would have to call out to her sister to stop so she could catch her breath, she ran into Olivia, who had already stopped ahead of her. Both of them were breathing hard, unable to speak. Wordlessly they retrieved the water bottles, and this time they both gulped, though Olivia still stopped herself before Melanie did.

"You're going to be all uneven," Olivia said. "Give me your other bottle." She reached into the matching pocket on the other side of Melanie's pack, then poured from one of the bottles to the other until the water was evenly distributed. Then she put both back in Mel's pack without asking if she was done drinking.

"Here, give me yours," Melanie said.

"No, it's fine. Just put this one back."

Melanie did as directed while Olivia consulted her map.

"We're about a third of a mile away from Trap Falls. We'll

take the packs off there and stop for a fifteen-minute break and have a snack."

"Good," Melanie said.

Olivia looked across the narrow river that was now at about the same elevation as they were. "This must be the way you go for the skiing and mountain biking trails."

"Which way?"

Olivia pointed across the river. "This way. That's Union Spring Trail across there."

"The bridge is out," Melanie said.

"No, there's no bridge. You have to ford it." Olivia turned to her. "You did bring water shoes like I told you to, right? They were on the list."

Melanie shook her head. "I didn't see the need."

"They wouldn't have been on the list if they weren't needed."

"I just figured why buy special shoes when I would never use them again. I'll just go barefoot."

Olivia squeezed her eyes shut. "I didn't want anyone slipping on slimy rocks and going down in a river, that's all. But, whatever. It can't be helped now." She hitched the pack up onto the top of her hips and tightened a strap. "Let's go."

They walked alongside the water, in and out of trees, the occasional leaf drifting down from the canopy to land on their path. Then they veered away from the river back into the woods. In a little while, Melanie could hear the waterfall—a rushing, murmuring *shhhh* off to her left that promised rest and peace and beauty. Then it was up ahead, tumbling white and black down a cascade of moss-covered rocks and ending in a swirling pool of water, foam, and yellow leaves.

Melanie quickened her pace, unbuckling her pack as she went, then dumping it next to a crude wooden bench. She stood at the edge of the pool, stretched her arms over her head, and breathed deeply, unfettered by the weight she'd been carrying. "This is gorgeous," she proclaimed, turning to Olivia. "I wish we could camp right here."

Olivia carefully leaned her pack on the other side of the bench and sat down. "It's supposed to be the best waterfall in the eastern half of the park. But we'll see lots more in the next couple days. That's how I chose our route. I wanted to see as many of them as we could. By the time we're done we'll have seen eight named falls. This will be the only one today."

She prattled on about the itinerary, but Melanie hardly heard her. She was taking off her shoes and socks and edging toward the water. Though it couldn't be more than fifty degrees out, her feet were hot and sweaty. She dipped them into the frigid flow of the Upper Carp River and closed her eyes, breathing slowly in through her nose and out through her mouth three times. Mesmerizing.

When she opened her eyes, she spotted movement up above the falls. A tawny back, a muscled leg, a long, ropelike tail. She stopped breathing. She looked again, harder. The shape was moving away. Melanie got to her feet, crouching, and put a finger to her lips to silence her sister.

Olivia stopped talking for a moment. "What?"

"Shhhh!" Melanie beckoned her with a finger, then held up a hand. A second later she straightened up. "Shoot. It's gone."

"What?"

"I think it was a cougar."

Olivia closed the distance between them. "It was probably a deer."

"No, it had a long tail."

"It was probably a deer," Olivia said again. "A cougar would have taken off running the second it heard us walking up, and if not, then definitely when we started talking."

"And a deer wouldn't?" Melanie challenged. "I know what a deer looks like and moves like, and this wasn't a deer. It was definitely a cougar."

"A second ago you said you *thought* it was a cougar. Now it's definitely a cougar?"

"It was a cougar."

Olivia looked at her a moment, then shrugged and turned back to the packs. "I guess, maybe. Anyway, whatever it was, it's gone now and we need to eat something."

Melanie looked back to where the creature had been. She had seen a tail, hadn't she? Olivia had already ruined her theory about hawks and eagles always showing up when she was around. Her sister was not going to ruin the fact that in the first hour and a half of the first day of their hike, she had been visited by an elusive big cat that had been the stuff of legends until the Department of Natural Resources finally confirmed that they were indeed reestablishing themselves in Michigan. Melanie decided to take it as an omen that her idea for the hike and for reconnecting with her sister and helping her to heal was the right one. That cougar was Olivia—powerful and solitary and elusive. Yet she was courting Melanie, slinking around the margins, wanting to be seen. All Melanie had to do was not scare her off.

She took some pictures of the falls, then put her socks and shoes back on and joined her sister on the bench. Olivia ate a little container of diced pears and a handful of trail mix while Melanie sampled from her bag of vegan granola. They sipped some water and watched the waterfall tumbling down the rocks.

"This is nice," Olivia said. She stood up and tucked her trash bag into her food bag and her food bag into her pack. "Let's get going."

Melanie reluctantly followed suit. She wished Olivia had planned less walking and more looking. That's how she would have planned the trip. But even though the hike had been her idea, Olivia had taken over the logistics. Just like when they were kids and Melanie had wanted to have a lemonade stand one summer. Olivia took over production and pricing and took all the fun out of it. Or when Melanie decided to go to the same college as her sister and Olivia took over registering her for classes and planning out what she should take each semester to get in all her requirements. Or when their parents died and Olivia took over the funeral planning, thus ensuring it would end up being embarrassingly short and strangely uncomforting. That was the one good thing about her abrupt return to college—it allowed Melanie to deal with the estate at a far healthier pace without her big sister's interference.

Soon Melanie's thigh muscles were burning again with the steady climb. The river arched to the left as they veered to the right, deeper into the golden woods. Melanie kept thinking of that cougar and all of the reasons it hadn't been a deer—the height, the heavily muscled back leg, the tail. It irritated her that Olivia didn't believe her. Did she think she was stupid? That she didn't know the difference between a cougar and a deer? Between predator and prey? Or that she was making it up entirely?

Finally, the argument got so heated inside her head that it boiled over to her mouth. "It's possible that the cougar didn't run off because it couldn't hear us over the sound of the waterfall."

Ahead of her, Olivia turned her head slightly but kept on walking. "I don't know about that. They have excellent hearing. I mean, they have to be able to hear their prey over the sound of water and wind and stuff. It seems really unlikely that if one was at that spot it wouldn't have heard us. And smelled us. And probably seen us with our completely non-camouflaged clothing."

"Okay, but a deer has even bigger ears," Melanie said between labored breaths. When would this incline end? "And a deer wouldn't have slunk away like this thing did. It would have bounded away, and I would have seen the white tail sticking up."

Ahead of her, Olivia tripped on a root but caught herself. "The deer might be used to seeing people."

Melanie pushed a branch out of the way. It snapped in the air behind her and hit the back of her pack. "In all these woods? I don't know about that."

"The wildlife use the trails," Olivia said. "Deer would likely come into contact with people, and certainly they would hear and smell them. And that loud little group had to have gone by not long before we did. I'm sure that would have scared off just about anything."

"It is completely plausible that I saw a cougar," Melanie persisted.

"Possible," Olivia corrected. "I wouldn't say plausible. More likely, if it wasn't a deer it was a coyote."

Melanie caught her foot on a rock and pitched forward, catching herself with a hand on a tree trunk. "Cougars and coyotes are nothing alike. Coyotes are dogs. Cougars are cats. You couldn't make up two more different creatures."

"Watch out," Olivia said as she pushed a branch out of her way and it came swinging back toward Melanie's face. "Man, it's getting close out here. This trail must not be used much."

Melanie stopped a moment and looked around. "Yeah, this is much narrower than before." She looked at her smartwatch. "We've gone over three miles since we started at the parking lot. Almost three and a half. How much further to this mountain peak?"

"It's 4.8 miles from the parking lot."

Melanie started walking again. "I'll definitely be ready for a break."

The trail had leveled off while they were arguing, and now as Melanie decided to let the cougar thing drop, the trail did the same, heading steeply downhill. She groaned. If they were heading up to one of the highest peaks in the park, they would most certainly be going back up just as steeply at some point. She was about to say as much when she heard Olivia far ahead of her say, "What the heck?"

Melanie quickened her pace and caught up to her sister, who was standing on the edge of a river, looking from the map to the river to the map again.

"This shouldn't be here," she said. "There's no river crossing before the peak."

Melanie took the map from her hands. "What do you mean?"

Olivia took it back. "I mean, there's no river crossing before the peak."

"Well, obviously there is," Melanie said, spreading her arms in front of her to indicate what was clearly a river they must cross.

Olivia poked at the map. "No, there is not. Look."

"That's what I was trying to do before you snatched it out of my hands." Melanie reached out for the map and Olivia handed it over. "Where did we park?"

"Here," she said, pointing. "And this dotted orange line is the trail we took to the falls. See how it leads to Government Peak? And see how it also doesn't lead us over a river?"

Melanie traced the line with a finger to where it met a dotted black line labeled Lost Lake Trail. A dotted black line that led to a river crossing a full mile south of the point at which the orange line of the Government Peak Trail turned sharply west.

"Um, we never made a right turn," Melanie said, indicating the spot where the trails converged.

"What?" Olivia leaned in.

"Right there. We should have turned right."

Olivia took the map back and stared at it, mouth open. "We're a mile off course. And it's not even lunchtime." She rubbed a hand over her face from forehead to chin and back up over her mouth. She looked like their mother did whenever they'd done something without thinking, like when seven-year-old Melanie had decided to wash the car with Brillo pads.

Melanie looked at her with a pained smile. "I think we need to turn around."

Seven

THE WALK BACK to the junction of Government Peak Trail and Lost Lake Trail was made in silence. Partly because the climb back up that last hill was arduous and putting a strain on Olivia's sore hip, and partly because she didn't trust herself to speak. She kept repeating to herself that it didn't matter—what's done is done and can't be undone—but it did matter. She should have been paying closer attention to the sign that surely had to have been there. She shouldn't have argued about what Melanie thought she saw because Melanie was always seeing things that weren't there—spirits and ghosts and miracles and signs, of what, Olivia was sure Melanie decided completely arbitrarily.

When they finally got back to the junction, there was indeed a sign. In fact, it was embarrassingly obvious.

Olivia tried to put a smile on her face. "Well, here we are. Back on track." She avoided looking at her watch, though she'd stolen glances at it over the past mile. "Let's get as far as we can before we stop for lunch."

Melanie merely nodded. She didn't apologize. There was no reason for her to; Olivia had been leading the hike so far, so it was her responsibility to keep them on the right path, no matter how distracted her sister might have made her.

Thankfully, the ground was fairly level here, with only gentler rises and falls over ridges and small creeks that were probably dry during the summer but were flowing with rainwater now. There were soggy spots, but the hiking poles helped them navigate without too much trouble.

Still, they weren't going quite as fast as Olivia would have liked. The underbrush leaned in close, scraping at their arms and packs and slowing them down. For nearly a mile, Olivia saw nothing but the ground in front of her feet as she watched for roots and rocks and focused on forward movement to the exclusion of all else.

They'd already gone nearly six miles that day, and Olivia was getting hungry. If Melanie felt the same way, she did not say. In fact, she said nothing at all for so long that Olivia began looking back over her shoulder every so often—hard to do with a pack—just to make sure she was still behind her. She was— right behind rather than lagging, as she had been before their unfortunate detour.

Just when Olivia was starting to feel her energy wane, the trail relaxed and came to a marshy area surrounding a lake. She paused and took out her map. "There," she said, pointing to a little red triangle by the pond. "We can eat there if no one has set up camp yet. I don't know about you, but I need to eat before I climb a mountain."

"Yes!" Melanie proclaimed. "I'm so glad you said that. I'm starving."

"Why didn't you say something?"

Melanie raised her eyebrows. "Seriously?"

Olivia shifted her footing and folded the map. "You can say when you're hungry or thirsty or have to stop and pee, you know. This isn't the army." Melanie made a "yeah, sure" face that made Olivia equal parts angry and ashamed. "I'm just trying to get us where we need to go."

"Okay, well, where I need to go right now is anywhere I can sit down and eat."

"Right."

Olivia led the way to the campsite, which was indeed empty at the moment, though the warmth coming off the fire ring suggested it had been occupied earlier. They dumped their packs against a couple tree trunks and stretched their shoulder muscles. Olivia cracked her neck. Melanie caught her ankles in turn behind her back and stretched the muscles on the front of her thighs, then she looked at her watch.

"No wonder I'm so hungry. It's nearly two o'clock!"

"Yeah, I know," Olivia said.

"How much further do we have to go from here?"

Olivia examined the map. "The peak is right here behind us. After that it's about three and a half miles more."

Melanie dug around in her pack. "That doesn't sound so bad."

"Well, I don't expect we'll make great time climbing the mountain."

"Oh, it's barely a mountain," she said, pulling out her food bag. "How hard can it be?"

"With packs? Plenty hard." Olivia retrieved her own food bag and pulled out a stick of cheese and a stick of beef jerky, which she alternated eating bite by bite.

Melanie chomped off the end of a carrot stick. "Why don't we just leave them behind and pick them back up when we come down?"

Olivia almost laughed out loud. "Melanie, the trail goes *over* the mountain. It's not, like, a side excursion. When we come down, we'll be on the other side."

"Oh."

"And I hope you're eating more than just that."

Melanie polished off the carrot stick and followed it up with another. "I told you, don't worry about my food. I've got it covered."

They both chewed quietly for a few minutes, the silence of the famished. Olivia savored the taste of the meat and cheese and followed it up with a few dried apricots. She watched her sister consume some nuts and dried cherries and another carrot stick and marveled that anyone could willingly give up meat and dairy products. And who in their right mind would give them up because they were worried that they might accidentally eat their own parents?

"How does reincarnation work?" she said before she could stop herself. "I mean, isn't it, like, if you're bad you come back as some lower life form, and if you're good you come back as a higher one?"

"Sort of. It's more like you accumulate good and bad karma throughout your life, and then what you have when you die would determine if you were going to be born into a higher or lower caste if you're Hindu. Eventually the goal is to reach moksha, but you have to not want it in order to attain it. For Buddhists, you attain enlightenment through the eightfold path—correct view, correct intention, correct speech, correct action, correct livelihood, correct effort, correct mindfulness, and correct concentration. Until you get it right, you are continually reborn."

"Sheesh." Olivia took a drink of water. "So, you think that Mom and Dad accumulated enough bad karma to come back as subhuman? They always seemed like pretty good people to me."

"Well, no. I wouldn't think so."

"Though, I guess if you have to get everything perfect, no one would make the cut." Olivia regarded her sister. "Actually, you always seemed like you'd rather come back as an animal than a human."

Melanie laughed and pushed the air out of her food bag. "Yeah, probably."

Olivia chewed on an apricot. It made some sense that human beings had developed religious systems that had such high standards they were impossible to reach in practice. Scare people with the thought of eternal damnation or continual rebirth as a slug or a centipede and they'll work hard to avoid it, which in turn would make for a more ordered society.

But then, not everyone who broke the law meant to. Justin hadn't. Even so, Olivia wished there were some kind of eternal consequences awaiting him. He ought to come back as a mosquito or a fly, something universally despised and likely to get swatted.

"So," she continued, "for someone who's not Hindu and not living where there's a caste system, what's the next step up? Being born into a richer family? That's basically the higher class in America. But then that doesn't seem like something the Buddhists would be real into. Kind of materialistic."

"I don't pretend to know how it all works," Melanie said. "It's just a nice philosophy to live your life by. It keeps you mindful of how your actions and attitudes affect others."

Olivia stood up and stuffed her food bag back into her pack. "Fair enough. But if you're doing good things so that you'll be freed from the cycle of death and rebirth, aren't you doing it for selfish reasons? Doesn't that kind of negate your altruism?"

Melanie crossed her arms. "Why do you do good things? If it's not because a spiritual belief system requires them or encourages you to do them, then why do them?"

Olivia had to think for a moment. "Because it's good to help people."

"Why?"

"Altruism makes for a kinder and more unified society, which is good for everyone."

"Oh, come on. You don't do good things for the sake of society. You do them because it makes you feel good to do them, doesn't it?"

Olivia furrowed her brow. "I guess, ultimately, you could say that."

"And what evolutionary purpose does that serve?" Melanie said. "If we're all just a collection of atoms and molecules and chemical reactions concerned solely with our own survival—which is your view, right?"

Olivia nodded slowly, unsure of where Melanie was about to take this.

"Then what do we have to gain by, say, helping an old lady with her groceries? If she isn't fit to carry them, she shouldn't eat. She should be picked off by natural selection. Or what about people who train seeing-eye dogs? They're training a natural predator to help the blind rather than eat them like they would in the wild. How does that make sense in your worldview? How do hospitals make sense? Or food banks? Wouldn't you have a better chance to pass your genes on to the next generation if there were fewer people to compete with?" Melanie swung her pack onto her back. "When you can answer those questions, then you can criticize my beliefs." She started walking.

Olivia snatched up her own pack and hustled to keep up. "I wasn't criticizing."

"Yes, you were."

"I wasn't, honest. I was just trying to—hang on a minute, would you? I have to get my straps snapped."

Melanie stopped, hip out of joint. Olivia quickly buckled her straps, then reached out to grab Melanie's arm.

"I didn't mean for that to come off as combative. I just don't get it, is all. It just doesn't make any sense to me."

"It doesn't need to. It just needs to make sense to me."

Olivia put her hands up in a "you win" gesture, but she wasn't really ready to let it drop entirely. "All right, I'm sorry." She raised her eyebrows. "Friends?"

Melanie smiled thinly. "Of course."

They started up the path with Melanie in the lead. The going was steep much of the way, and by the time they reached the top, Olivia was sweating. Up there the breeze off Lake Superior was no longer blocked by land or trees. It wicked the moisture from her neck and hairline, and she put her arms out. She turned slowly around, taking in the view: rolling hills as far as she could see, covered with orange, brown, red, yellow, and green. Above, the sky was blue with a few clouds drifting by. Below, the earth was a carpet of leaves. This was the best of what Earth had to offer. And it was plenty.

Melanie spoke up. "Hey, why don't we just camp here tonight?"

"We can't camp here."

"I saw some of those triangles here on the map, so there must be campsites."

"There are, but we didn't reserve a campsite here. You can't just pick any site you see. It's not first come, first serve. I reserved our sites months ago."

Melanie stepped off the stones. "But we could share with someone else if they came."

"No, we can't. Those are the rules. What if, when we got to the site we reserved, those people from the parking lot had already set up camp?"

"So?"

"And they took the flattest spot for their tent and left us only slopes with a bunch of roots for our tent. And they were loud and annoying. And they left a mess. And you came out in the woods so you could be alone, but instead you're forced to spend the night with strangers. Anyway, if we camp anywhere closer than where I reserved for tonight, it will make tomorrow's hike that much longer."

"I don't think any of that would bother me."

"Well, it would bother me, so we're not going to do it. Come on. We need to keep moving."

Without waiting to see if Melanie was ready, Olivia started her descent.

"Race you to the top!" Olivia blew by, a flurry of swishing snow pants and trailing turquoise scarf, dragging the sled behind her.

Melanie trudged on, slower than she had to. You can't rush climbing Mount Everest. She'd already been on the climb two days. Her Sherpa kept on, a few paces behind, but the rest of the team had fallen away, one by one, unable to take what the mountain threw at them. The blinding snow, the biting wind, the thin, cold air, the emptiness—ah, the horrible emptiness.

"Come on!" Olivia screamed from the top. "I'm not waiting for you much longer!"

Melanie sighed behind her bright pink scarf. Imagining was so much easier without Olivia around. She focused back on the task at hand, digging one spiked boot and then another into the icy path, stepping over the frozen body of some poor soul who didn't make it up and now wouldn't make it down.

"I'm going!" Olivia shouted. She knelt on the two-person sled and heaved herself off the top of the hill.

Melanie watched her sister shoot down, narrowly missing two other kids on saucer sleds, then faced the looming summit with renewed determination. The mountain would not defeat her. Not this time.

"You really are the slowest person alive," Olivia said, coming up from behind her and matching her pace. "It does not take this long to climb a hill. Do you want to go home?"

"No," Melanie said.

"Are you too cold?"

"No," she said again.

"Then what is taking you so long?"

"I'm climbing Everest."

Olivia threw back her head. "Ugh. Just walk up the stupid hill and get it over with. At this rate you're only going to get to go down it a couple times before we have to go."

"Mountains are hard to climb."

Olivia huffed out a sigh and started running up the hill. At the top she yelled down, "I scaled Mount Everest before you did!"

But to Melanie the sound was just some strange groaning on the wind. She pushed on through the storm, finally reaching the summit on the third day. After that triumphant moment, Everest seemed to shrink. The rocky ground smoothed into slick snow packed down into ice. And she joined her sister on a two-person sled, careening down to where her father sat on top of a picnic table, sipping hot cocoa out of a Styrofoam cup.

"Three more times and then we're done," he said. "Mom's got chili on the stove and it's starting to get dark."

Eight

THE LIGHT WAS JUST BEGINNING to falter when Melanie caught the first sight of Mirror Lake. Seeing it ahead, she felt her spirits rise for the first time since Trap Falls. She was more than ready to stop walking. The trail from Government Peak was muddy much of the way, and the close underbrush made a constant scraping sound on their nylon packs. And though she took walks on most days, rain or shine, Melanie hadn't realized just how different it would feel to walk all day, up and down many inclines, with fifty pounds of gear on her back.

"We made it!" she said, quickening her flagging pace a little. "Where's our site?"

"It's not too far. Maybe just another half a mile or so."

Melanie stopped. "Half a mile?"

"It's on the other side of the lake."

Melanie groaned. Of course Olivia had chosen one on the other side. She always had to make things more difficult than they needed to be.

"I just figured that it would give us a leg up tomorrow morning if we were already a little further along the trail."

"I'm not going to be able to even lift my legs if I don't get this thing off my back soon."

"Then I guess we better keep walking."

They passed a cabin. And then another. And, cruelly, another. Why couldn't they have stayed in the cabins? The forest around them dimmed as the sun slipped down the other side of the modest mountains. Melanie struggled to keep up with her sister's pace. Finally, they came to a little wooden bridge across a river that drained slowly out of the lake.

"It's just on the other side," Olivia said.

But just on the other side, the first site they came upon was already occupied. Had someone done what Melanie had wanted to do and just picked a site? Olivia kept walking right on by. Where was this stupid campsite?

Thankfully, she stopped at the next numbered spot and unbuckled her pack straps. "Let's get the tent up quick."

The moment Melanie got her pack off she realized how badly she needed to pee. "Where should I go to the bathroom?"

"Wherever you want." Olivia looked around and pointed. "I suggest that way, away from our neighbors. The toilet paper and the shovel are in the front pocket of my pack, and there's hand sanitizer in there too."

Melanie hurriedly retrieved the items and started picking her way through the trees. But no matter how far she went, she could still see Olivia unrolling the tent. Using a large tree trunk as a shield, she bent down and started to dig a hole. The ground was thick with fibrous roots, and it took her a moment to realize that she had to stab the plastic trowel straight down to cut through. She had dug little more than a depression in the dirt when she just couldn't hold it any longer.

She piled leaves over the spot, used the hand sanitizer, and then tucked everything back into the plastic bag. When she got back, Olivia already had the tent up and was unrolling the fly.

"Okay, what do you want me to do?" Melanie said.

"I'm almost done with this. Why don't you go gather firewood and I'll get the sleeping pads inflated and the bags laid out."

"Don't you need to go to the bathroom?"

"It can wait."

Melanie dutifully walked back into the trees in search of firewood. But coming as they had at the end of a long summer season full of hikers, the pickings around the campsite were slim. She managed several handfuls of sticks for kindling, but larger branches were nonexistent. She dumped her meager offerings into the fire ring and said to Olivia inside the tent, "I'm going to have to go a little further afield for wood."

"There's a flashlight in the bottom left pocket of your pack."

Melanie looked around at the darkening woods. "I shouldn't be that long."

She walked out past the pee tree, as she decided to refer to it, and up a small rise, marking her path by taking note of particular saplings and bushes. She found a long stick next to a rotting log, another caught in the branches of a bush covered in clusters of tiny blue-black berries. One here, one there. Steadily the bunch grew until it took two hands to hold them. She'd have to go drop them off, then come back out for more.

Melanie turned back to where she had come from and

scanned the trees. She could see her breath. She couldn't see Olivia or the tent. Suddenly she realized that she had stopped making a point to mark her progress. And even if she had continued to purposefully notice this tree or that, she was surrounded by trees. Trees that had all started to look the same, especially as the light, which had seemed sufficient when she left without a flashlight, began to fade. She felt a spike of panic stab up her spine and almost called out to her sister—she couldn't have wandered out of earshot—but no. She was an adult. She should have been more careful. Olivia should never know that she got herself all turned around and quite possibly lost.

She'd been moving so slow she couldn't have gone far. And she had been going slightly uphill. The campsite, therefore, had to be downhill. Keeping a firm grip on the sticks and branches she had gathered, Melanie walked swiftly in the direction that felt the most downhill. The long branches trailing behind her caught themselves on a bush. She wrenched them free, stepped into a sudden depression, and nearly twisted an ankle. When she stopped for a moment to right herself and pick up a dropped stick, she thought she heard movement to her left.

Olivia? Or something else?

Sudden fear froze her to the ground. What was it? A bear? A wolf? Had the cougar from Trap Falls been tracking them all this time?

Melanie's breath came in little white clouds of vapor, puffing out of her open mouth in swift succession. What was she doing out here? She didn't know anything about the woods. She'd been on just one hike—the one—and it had been led by Olivia's friend Eric, who had been an Eagle Scout. That trail had been in a far more populated area and was visited by many more hikers and tourists. On that hike, a ranger had found them easily. Out here in sixty thousand acres of wilderness covered in a blanket of trees, who would find her? Who would find her if she really was lost?

Melanie nearly screamed as something leaped across the leaves right in front of her feet. She breathed once, twice. A chipmunk. Just a chipmunk rushing to get ready for winter. She had to get ahold of herself. And she had to get back to camp.

"Mel?" Olivia's voice came from a little ways away, behind Melanie's right shoulder.

She'd been going the wrong way.

She rushed in the direction of the voice. "Coming!" After a minute, she could just see the blue and gray tent through the trees, and relief flooded her body. She broke through the underbrush back into the campsite, dragging her sticks and branches behind her.

"Nice job," Olivia said, taking in Melanie's haul. "How far did you have to go?"

"Not far," Melanie said with a carefully placed smile.

"You should have taken a flashlight."

"I needed both hands to carry the wood."

Olivia and Melanie set to work breaking the branches down into sticks for the fire ring.

"I found the bear pole so we can hang the food bags after we eat," Olivia said.

At the word *bear*, Melanie stiffened. "Maybe we should eat in the tent so bears won't be attracted to the smell of food out here."

Olivia leveled a look in her direction. "That's absolutely the worst thing anyone on a hiking trip can do—other than start a forest fire. You never, *ever* bring food into a tent."

"Okay."

"Not even gum or mints in your pockets. Nothing. Understand?"

"Yes."

"A tent isn't going to mask the scent of food to a bear. That's why there are bear poles, so you can store your food far away from your tent and up off the ground where bears can't get to it."

"Okay."

"Melanie, I'm serious. Don't ever bring food into the tent."

"Okay! I got it!" Melanie snapped a large branch under her heel. "You don't have to talk to me like I'm an idiot."

Olivia began making a tepee of sticks in the fire ring. "I'm not trying to make you mad, but the people you read about getting attacked by wild animals, usually they *are* idiots. They do dumb things that could easily have been avoided if they'd just educated themselves a little. I'm not saying you're dumb," she hastened to say as she struck a match, "but bringing food into a tent is dumb."

"Yes, I'm well aware of that now. Thank you."

It took a few tries, but the fire finally caught. They stood on either side of it, alternately warming their hands and the backs of their legs, and eating their supper in silence. Melanie didn't know what Olivia was thinking about, but she could not stop the thought that was rampaging through her own brain over and over and over—that were it not for her sister saying her name, she would have been lost in the woods in the cold at night with no food, no water, no shelter, no compass, no flashlight.

She *was* dumb. She *was* one of those idiots who might end up on the news someday. She, quite simply, had no idea what she was doing. She never really had. She'd been walking through life dealing with each day as it came, never planning, always reacting. She'd stumbled onto some things that made her happy, at least on the surface—but she'd always admired how Olivia set about conquering a task, how she always seemed to know what was coming next and what to do about it. Melanie would give almost anything for that kind of certainty.

When they were done eating, Olivia hung the food bags on the bear pole and went out into the woods with the trowel and the toilet paper—and a flashlight. The fire had died down, and after they brushed their teeth and washed their faces, Olivia smothered the remaining embers. They took turns in the tent changing into their pj's—not so much for modesty's sake but because changing clothes in a small tent required so much contortion that only one person could comfortably do it at a time. Once they were both inside, Melanie could feel Olivia assessing the level to which she'd adhered to the command on the packing list to bring warm pj's, but to her credit Olivia said nothing.

Melanie brought her journal and a pen into the tent, but once she'd crawled into the downy sleeping bag, a wave of exhaustion overtook her. She set the book aside, turned off her flashlight, and snuggled down into the reassuringly constrictive warmth of the mummy-style bag and zipped it up from the inside.

Day one was done, and it hadn't gone as well as she'd hoped.

Tomorrow was a new chance to connect with her sister. A new chance to help her heal. A new chance to gather enough courage to tell Olivia what she could no longer avoid telling her.

Melanie closed her eyes and listened to the silence outside the tent. And within minutes, she was asleep.

Nine

OLIVIA LAY ON HER STOMACH, flashlight trained on the map in front of her. Compared to today's, tomorrow's walk looked easy. The black dotted line of the Little Carp River Trail led south and west of Mirror Lake on what looked to be fairly level ground much of the way. Two and a half miles to the bridge at Lily Pond, where they would break for snacks. Another half mile to the spot where they would ford the Little Carp River. Two more miles to Greenstone Falls, where they would eat lunch. Then a pleasant afternoon along the river until they forded it again and made camp at Trappers Falls.

Or should they eat lunch earlier?

A small snore from her sister told Olivia that Melanie was not about to be engaged in conversation about when and where to lunch the next day. She glanced at her watch. 9:30. Today had been kind of a mess, but they had managed to deal with the unpleasant surprise of going the wrong way. The tent had been up before dark. They were fed and safe and warm in the sleeping bags she had purchased expressly because they were rated for five degrees Fahrenheit. She folded the map, clicked off the flashlight, and zipped herself snugly into place, pulling the bag's built-in hood over her head and cinching it shut until only her eyes, nose, and mouth were showing.

It felt good for a moment to lie so flat on the ground, which was hard despite the sleeping pad beneath her. Within the confines of the mummy bag, she rotated her feet to stretch her leg muscles and pulled her shoulders down and in, stretching her upper back. Her spine decompressed, her bones settled into place, her breath came slow and regular.

But she didn't fall asleep. It was too quiet. Too dark. Too still. She opened her eyes but could see nothing at all. Wrapped as she was, flat on her back, hands crossed over her stomach, she began to feel as though she were in a casket. Like she was not *on* the ground so much as *in* the ground.

Olivia sat up with effort, bringing the sleeping bag with her. If she could sit up, she was not in the ground. She tried to think of something else, anything else, before her mind could go to the last caskets she saw—those of her parents. But trying not to think of them only made her think of them all the more.

It had been a closed-casket funeral. They hadn't had a will that specified end-of-life matters, so circumstance chose for them. The accident had been bad. Their bodies were not in good shape. Olivia wanted them to be cremated and the ashes scattered—no keeping them in a jar on the mantel or in a box in the closet. She didn't want the memory hanging about. Melanie wanted them buried so there would be a place to visit them and to bring their grandchildren someday.

In the end, Olivia conceded, and her parents were given a Christian funeral at the church they had attended for Christmas and Easter and at which her father had tutored refugees in read-ing and writing in English. The service, though well attended because of the tragic nature of the accident and the relatively young age of its victims, offered Olivia little comfort. Her parents had never talked about their religious beliefs. They had never prayed before meals or before bed. Never taught their daughters to. She knew they'd both grown up going to church, but other than the holidays, they'd never taken their own children. If God hadn't mattered all that much to them, why should they matter all that much to God?

And yet the minister seemed to say that they did matter and that they were safe with God and all the saints who'd gone on before. Did he know something about them she didn't? Or was this just the standard thing he said at all funerals? She'd wanted to ask him then, but there was no time. Over the years she'd thought about calling up the church to talk to him, but the longer she waited the less it seemed to matter. Until one day she realized it had all been for show. Nobody knew what happened after death except what you could observe from this side of it—that the organs shut down and the body broke down into its component parts according to predictable patterns. Re-ligion was just there to give people something to do, to keep their minds off death, or at least to make death seem not so permanent.

The only thing, in fact, that had stuck with Olivia from the service was a snippet of Scripture the minister read. Something about doing justice, loving mercy, and walking humbly. He'd said her parents did those things, and she guessed that at least was true. But so what? It hadn't kept them from harm.

Olivia lay back down and twisted herself and the mummy bag onto her side like a worm. Oof. Not that side. She turned over. That was better. She could fall asleep like that. She lay there listening to Melanie's soft breathing and tried to match hers with it, to slow her body down and trick it into sleep. Whether she actually did fall asleep before she heard the scream was anyone's guess.

It came from somewhere back in the forest, back where Melanie had been searching for wood for the fire. Every hair on Olivia's body stiffened, and she stopped breathing for a moment, listening intently to the silence. Listening for some other sound to make sense of the first one. But there was nothing.

"Melanie?" she whispered. But Melanie was asleep. How? How could someone sleep through that unearthly scream?

Olivia wrenched her hand up inside the sleeping bag and unzipped it enough to get her arm out. Outside the bag the air was cold. She turned her wrist and her watch glowed out the time. 11:45. Had she really lain there awake for two hours? She must have slept. Must have been dreaming.

But there it was again. It had to be an animal. Maybe a screech owl? Didn't they make terrible noises? Or maybe it was a rabbit that had gotten caught by something. She'd heard that terrified rabbits screamed. And weren't cougars said to scream? Hadn't she read that in some book as a child? Whatever it was, Olivia now understood why the woods used to frighten people, why so many fairy tales involved witches or creatures of malice lurking in the shadowy spaces between the trees at night.

A third scream rang out, exactly the same as the others. It was an animal, she decided. A person being attacked wouldn't scream three separate times in exactly the same way. This was an animal noise, whatever it was.

"Melanie?" she tried again. But still her sister slept soundly.

Olivia zipped herself back into the mummy bag and listened, but there were no more screams. Eventually the adrenaline that had been coursing through her body dissipated and she was able to breathe normally again. She shut her eyes and tried to settle her heart. She tried not to think of how tired she was going to be the next morning if she couldn't get some sleep.

Somehow, miraculously, she did manage to drift off. And she could only be sure of it because she was definitely awakened sometime later by another sound. If the scream had been loud and sharp and distant, this sound was low and lumbering and close. This sound was breathing. And footsteps. And it was right outside the tent.

Instantly Olivia's mind pinpointed the exact location of the knife she had purchased back at the gas station in Indian River. It was in the little zippered compartment on the front of her pack. Outside. Her pack was outside, hanging from the broken branch of a pine tree about six feet off the ground. Why hadn't she brought the knife in with her?

More footsteps. More heavy breathing. Olivia waited for the sound of a zipper, the sound of their tent being opened. Those screams had been a person. They might have been three people. Someone was going campsite to campsite, murdering people. She struggled to get to the zipper of her bag again, to get an arm free, to get out of the bag so she could protect her little sister. But what could she do? She had no gun, no knife, not even one of her hiking poles. And if somehow she survived whatever was about to happen, she couldn't call for help because there was no cell signal. She felt her heartbeat tick up another notch. Her breath was coming faster. She had to keep her head. Had to stop herself from hyperventilating. She braced herself and waited for something to happen.

But the sound of the tent being unzipped never came. The footsteps had stopped.

The breathing had not. In fact, it was closer than ever, just inches away from her face on the other side of a few microns of nylon. Something was there, outside the tent. It was not leaving, but it also was not coming in. In fact, it sounded like it had lain down.

It wasn't a deer. The heavy footfalls and heavy breathing weren't in the least deerlike. It wasn't a porcupine or a raccoon—they slept in trees, and this sounded bigger than that. The footfalls were too loud to be a fox, a coyote, or even a wolf. And a cougar, if there were any around as Melanie believed, would have been completely silent. The only thing left was a bear.

There was a bear on the other side of the tent fabric. Its head had to be less than a foot from her own, because she could clearly hear it breathing, deep, capacious breaths.

Had Melanie brought food into the tent despite Olivia's stern warning? Did her own fingers smell like beef jerky? She snuck a hand to her face. It just smelled like hand sanitizer.

Olivia waited another minute for something to happen. But the breathing outside the tent never changed, except perhaps to get slower. She settled back down into her mummy bag as quietly as possible, drawing the zipper closed again. Even if there was a bear outside, it wasn't doing anything. It wasn't nosing at the tent, wasn't scratching at the food bags. Maybe it was just chilly, and their tent, with its two warm bodies inside, was a smidge warmer than the cold black woods. Maybe it was lonely and just needed a friend. Someone with whom to share the dark night.

Olivia slowed her breathing to match the pace coming from outside the tent. And finally slept.

Ten

"RIGHT HERE, SEE?"

Melanie bent over the spot that Olivia pointed out.

"You can see the lines where his claws dug into the ground," Olivia said. "Maybe when he was getting up."

Melanie studied the marks while Olivia got out her phone and took a few pictures.

"If it was a bear, it was a small one," Melanie said.

"It sounded big," Olivia said. "Well, it sounded heavy and slow, and that says big to me."

Melanie stood up and poked through the ashes in the firepit, looking for any leftover heat. It was cold. She could see her own breath, and her hands and nose were freezing. "And what about the scream?"

"Oh," Olivia said, standing straight, "that was just unearthly creepy. I've never heard anything like it before. I'll have to look it up later. I can't believe you slept through all of this."

Melanie couldn't believe it either. She wasn't allowed to have her cougar, and now Olivia got a bear and a . . . whatever that was? The double standard was irritating enough, but what really needled Melanie's mind was the fact that the bear had gone to Olivia's side of the tent rather than hers. She'd always prided herself on her connection with the animal world. Animals could tell she was a kindred spirit. They were drawn to her. They weren't drawn to Olivia. Olivia who once pushed a pony away at a petting zoo. Olivia who had said her eagles were vultures.

"I'm going to get the food bags," Melanie announced.

"I'll start rolling up the pads and bags, and then we can break down the tent," Olivia called after her.

"I'm eating breakfast first."

Melanie stalked off to the bear pole. The long, hooked pole with which she was supposed to get the bags down was surprisingly heavy and hard to maneuver into the loop of the bag ties. Once the first bag was finally on the hook, Melanie lost control, sending it to the ground with a thud. She hoped it was Olivia's. The next one came down more softly, but Melanie's arms were so tired it took her three tries just to hang up the hook.

She retrieved the bags from the ground. It had been Olivia's that fell so hard. It was significantly heavier than her own bag, and she wondered for a moment if she hadn't brought enough food along. Or maybe vegan food was lighter than Olivia's jerky and cheese and whatever else she had in there.

Olivia had the pads and bags rolled, stuffed, and strapped to the packs by the time she got back, and was already breaking down the tent. Melanie sat on a half-rotted log and pulled a vegan protein bar out of her food bag.

"Just have something to eat first," she said.

"I'd rather be ready to go once we've eaten," Olivia said.

Melanie retrieved one of her water bottles. It was full. She checked the other one, also full. "You already filtered our water?"

Olivia shook out the tent fly and laid it on the ground. "Yeah. I did it this morning while you were getting dressed."

"And you did the pads and the sleeping bags."

"I want to get started early. We'll be going by some really nice features this afternoon, and I don't want us to feel rushed when we get there."

Melanie stopped chewing and tried to swallow the lump of protein bar. She hated protein bars on a good day. As she saw now how childish she was being, this one was making her feel ill. She swished some water around in her mouth and swallowed the chunks like a mouthful of pills. "You could have woken me up earlier. I must have gotten way more sleep than you."

"I feel strangely okay," Olivia said as she slowly and tightly rolled the fly, brushing off every speck of dirt with a dry wash-cloth as she went. "I'm actually kind of excited about tonight. We'll be camping near a waterfall, and we'll be the only ones there. And, I don't know, there's something about knowingly going to sleep next to a bear that's just kind of invigorating."

Melanie frowned. She put the rest of the protein bar back in her bag and stood up. "What do you want me to do?"

Olivia pointed. "Grab those ties for me?"

Melanie retrieved two strips of nylon fabric and handed them to her sister.

Olivia swiftly tied the rolled fly and set it aside. "Can you pack up the tent poles and pegs? The rubber bands are in the bag there."

As Melanie did as directed, Olivia straightened, folded, and rolled the tent in the exact same manner as the fly. Then she strapped tent, fly, and hardware bag to the top of her pack.

"I'll be right back," she said, retrieving the toilet paper and shovel.

When she disappeared behind a tree, Melanie picked up Olivia's pack with her right hand and her own with her left hand.

"Why is your pack so much heavier than mine?" Melanie asked when Olivia returned.

"They're about the same."

"No, they're not. Yours is way heavier."

"Maybe a little."

"How much does the tent weigh?"

Olivia shrugged. "I don't know."

Of course she knew. Melanie could all but guarantee Olivia had added up the weight of every item on her calculator app as she walked around the sporting goods store. "Shouldn't I carry at least part of it? Or if you carried it yesterday, I should carry it today?"

"No, it's good. I'm trying to lose some weight. This will help me."

Melanie didn't argue further. It was never profitable to argue with Olivia when she had her mind made up—she pitied the defense lawyers who had to face her in the courtroom. She'd just have to find a way to even out the load later.

Once they'd eaten, they headed out. The ground was level, but that was about the only good thing one could say about it. The rains had turned many low spots into bogs that sucked at Melanie's hiking shoes, and even once she got moving at a good clip she just couldn't get warm. The sleeping bag Olivia had gotten was great for the cold night, but her leggings, tee, and fleece jacket just weren't cutting it in the crisp morning air.

Every few hundred feet, Olivia veered off to the left or right of the trail to avoid mud or standing water. Melanie followed. They struggled through the brush, up little hills, around fallen trees, and then they were back on the trail, looking for the next reassuring blue blaze painted on a tree trunk. A bit farther and the whole process repeated itself.

Melanie poked her hiking poles into the sludge and tried to step on rocks or rotting sticks or logs rather than in the muck, but every surface was slick with mud and she slipped off about half the time. Off trail, she tripped over everything in her path. She cursed and growled under her breath. Her brand-new vegan hiking shoes looked like the feet of a filthy extra in a documentary about the spread of the plague in medieval Europe.

When they stopped to pull out each other's water bottles, Melanie looked up at the blank gray sky that had been so blue the day before and released a bitter sigh. Even the colorful foliage on the trees seemed dry and dim, where yesterday it had felt like she was walking through a million suncatchers. By the time they reached the bridge over the river at Lily Pond, Melanie was in what she had always thought of as a brown mood—her signal to herself that she needed to change things up before she sank further down into black.

"After lunch, why don't we see who can spot the most varieties of mushroom," she said.

Olivia raised her eyes from her pack. "Wouldn't the person in the lead have an unfair advantage?"

"We'll switch on and off every fifteen minutes, how's that?"

Olivia shrugged. "Okay."

They sat on a bench built into the wooden bridge and faced the pond. It could have been so beautiful in the sunshine. For about a minute neither spoke. They just stared ahead at the trees mirrored in the still water and framed with browning cattails. A young couple with a friendly shepherd mix approached from the right, the direction they would soon be heading.

"Morning," the man said.

"Morning," they said in unison.

Melanie wished they would stop so she could pet the dog, whose paws were as muddy as her shoes—not a promising sign about what they were soon to face—but the couple didn't even slow down. She retrieved her bag of carrot sticks. Olivia pulled out a can of SpaghettiOs.

"What. The heck. Is that?" Melanie said.

Olivia turned the can's label toward her. "SpaghettiOs."

"Yes, I can see they're SpaghettiOs. But why? Why on earth would you bring SpaghettiOs hiking?" Melanie gagged a little. "You're not eating those cold, are you?"

"Do you see a microwave out here?"

"Blech! Gross!"

"Settle down," Olivia said as she peeled back the aluminum lid.

"That is so disgusting." Melanie turned away. "Ugh. I can't even look at you."

Olivia started laughing. "You sure you don't want some?"

"Sick. No."

Olivia leaned closer and waved a spoonful of the cold canned pasta in Melanie's face. "Hmmm?"

Melanie swatted her away, sending SpaghettiOs flying over the bridge and into the water.

"Hey!" Olivia said, still laughing. "Man, you are just as easy as ever to annoy."

"Well, you're just as annoying as ever."

Olivia snickered. "So sensitive."

Melanie knew Olivia was just giving her a hard time, but the word *sensitive* got under her skin. Because she wasn't being sensitive. She was just being herself. And she didn't like being told that she was somehow more delicate than everybody else. It wasn't her who was sensitive—it was everyone else who was callous. Especially Olivia, who'd never given Melanie the satisfaction of falling for a prank or doing anything but shrugging when criticism was leveled at her. If anything, Olivia could stand to be more sensitive.

"That explains why your food bag is so heavy," Melanie said. "How many cans are in there?"

"Just two. I had a hankering for SpaghettiOs when I went shopping."

"Weirdo."

Olivia kept smiling and shoveling SpaghettiOs into her mouth. Melanie foraged around in her bag for a few more morsels. She was already missing salads and roasted veggies and smoothies and almond milk protein shakes and pan-fried tofu with rice and lentils. She chewed on a granola bar and followed that up with a handful of almonds. Eventually she wasn't hungry anymore, but she wasn't satisfied either.

It was the first time she went to dinner with Justin that she'd decided to become a vegan. Right there in a dark corner booth of a Mexican restaurant on East Paris Avenue in Grand Rapids. It was a terrible place in which to become a vegan. Even the bean dip wasn't vegetarian. She and Justin had been emailing each other for weeks, talking about what had happened the night of the accident and what happens after you die—what might have happened to her parents, what might eventually happen to him. He was reading a New Testament someone had given him at a support group, even though he admitted to being a scoffer in the past. But now it felt like he really had something for which he needed to be forgiven. They'd covered a lot of ground in those emails, and Melanie had started thinking through the ramifications of reincarnation. Seeing the couple at the next table chowing down on tacos, ground beef spilling out the other side, she felt almost sick. That night she'd eaten a salad of just lettuce, tomatoes, and onions.

"Ready?" Olivia said when they had both tucked their food bags back into their packs.

"Sure."

"You want to lead first?"

"Hmm?"

"The mushroom thing. You want to be in front first?"

"Oh, yeah. I guess so."

Olivia caught her eye. "Hey, what's wrong?"

Melanie shook her head. "Nothing. I'm just . . . it's just kind of gray today, you know?"

"Yeah. Not as nice as yesterday."

"And I can't seem to get warm. All I can think about is getting back in that sleeping bag." When she saw the concerned look on Olivia's face, she added, "For the warmth."

Olivia nodded, but Melanie worried she had tipped her hand. When she'd been in the throes of depression after the accident, she'd spent most days in bed. Olivia wasn't there, but Melanie knew that her aunt had tattled on her. It was good she did. If Melanie had been left to herself, she'd probably still be in that same bed. It was good to have people who cared about you. Though, if she was honest, it wasn't either of them who'd gotten her out of it. It was Justin.

"Why don't you go first," Melanie offered. "And you can't just say 'there's one' when you see it. You have to describe it. Like 'the one that looks like white oyster shells' or 'the one that looks like earwax.'"

"Lovely," Olivia intoned. "All right. Let's get a move on."

For the next fifteen minutes, Olivia led the trek and the mushroom count. It was a silly game, but it helped Melanie focus on something other than her brown mood. She did manage to spot some that Olivia had missed, including a rather phallic purple mushroom that looked nearly black against the leaf litter. When they got to the spot where the Little Carp River Trail met the Lily Pond Trail, they switched off, Melanie leading the way west toward the first place they would have to ford the river. As she searched out mushrooms, she saw not only the seemingly endless variety of fungi—tall and short, skinny and fat, ones that looked like open umbrellas and ones that looked like closed umbrellas, red, orange, yellow, white, solid and spotted and striped—she also saw so much she might have otherwise missed. Lichens and ferns of various types, and so many different and delightful varieties of mosses.

Melanie was fully entranced. She'd never dreamed her

manufactured distraction would be so good for her soul. What-ever creative force was behind this world, he/she/it never seemed to run out of ideas. There was no real reason for so much variety, was there, other than that it was meant to enchant those who looked upon it?

Behind her, her sister snagged a mushroom she hadn't seen as she was musing. What did Olivia see when she looked at the multitude of species in just this small parcel of land? No doubt there was a scientific explanation for it all. Something that didn't want a divine designer. But Melanie just couldn't understand how anyone could think there was nothing more to this life than survival of the species.

"Why is it you don't believe in God? Or some kind of higher power?" Melanie asked when they came to the Little Carp River crossing and started to change out of their hiking boots and socks.

Olivia shoved her feet into her water shoes. "I guess I just don't see any evidence for it. Or need for it."

Melanie rolled up her pant legs and slipped her hands through the loops on her hiking poles. "I see evidence everywhere I look."

"Believe me, I know," Olivia said. "Don't forget your boots."

Melanie silently chided herself for nearly leaving the most essential part of her hiking gear behind and decided to drop her line of questioning until she'd thought of a better response.

"Ready?" Olivia said.

Melanie nodded. "Want me to go first?"

"I can. That way if there's a problem you can avoid it."

"Why should you have to find the problem?"

Olivia stopped at the water's edge. "I don't know. Maybe

because I'm the one who remembered water shoes. Plus I'm the oldest. Just used to doing things first."

Melanie stepped up beside her. "I don't think that's necessary anymore." Without waiting for Olivia's response, she stepped into the water. She sucked in a breath at how cold it was but didn't hesitate to take the next step. The water was fast moving but shallow, not even reaching to Melanie's calves. The poles helped her brace and balance, but she immediately regretted not purchasing the water shoes. The submerged rocks were slimy beneath her bare feet. Even so, she was across in less than thirty seconds and turned back to give Olivia a triumphant look. But Olivia was right behind her, looking down at her own footing, totally missing Melanie's conquest of the watery obstacle.

Melanie dried her feet on the hand towel Olivia had instructed her to bring, put her socks and shoes back on, and shoved the towel back into her pack without much thought to where it should go.

"My turn in front," Olivia said. "How many do you have now? I have twenty-four."

"I don't know. I wasn't really counting."

"What? This was your game, Melanie."

Melanie took a sip of her water and looked around. "Is this a campsite?"

Olivia took out her map. "Yes. Two of them."

"Too bad we can't just camp here. My feet are freezing."

"Well, we can't. We've barely gone three miles anyway. Hey, what is with you today?"

Melanie felt herself fighting back sudden tears. She would not cry, not in front of Olivia. Especially when she had no idea what she would be crying about. It had been so long since she'd felt this way. Was it simply being with her sister that had yanked her back?

"Do you need a break?" Olivia said, not unkindly.

Melanie whipped her emotions into submission and put her water bottle away. "No, I'm fine. Moving will help me warm up." She wrenched her pack—which was getting heavier by the moment—onto her back and shoved her arms through the straps.

"Okay, if you're sure."

"Totally. Let's go. And I have thirty mushroom species. So I'm winning."

Olivia smiled. "How about we say you won. I don't think at this point I could tell the difference between what I see and what I've already seen. So you win the mushroom game. We'll have to think of something else for the next leg."

Melanie scowled. She knew she must look like a petulant child who'd been put off by a playmate who was tired of the game. But she couldn't stop herself. "Don't patronize me, Olivia. If you don't want to play, that's fine. I'm fine." With that, she found the next blue blaze on a tree and started walking away.

They walked in silence for ten minutes. Twenty. The ground got wet again, and Melanie was now the one who had to look for the driest route around the muck. Small puddles alternated with what in some cases looked to be a hundred yards of sludge pockmarked with the soggy footprints of hikers who had gone before. It was slow going and frustrating. Kind of like recovery. Good days and bad days. Serenity and struggle. Wanting to quit but pressing forward because that was the only way out.

After quite some time focused only on the ground directly in front of her, Melanie looked up and stopped. Where was the next blue blaze? And when had she last seen one?

"What's wrong?" Olivia said behind her.

Every fiber of Melanie's being wanted to lie, wanted to keep walking and miraculously stumble back upon the trail. Yet overriding her fear of looking stupid for leading them astray was the greater fear of being lost in the woods where no one would find them.

She turned to her sister and said in a calm voice that belied the mounting anxiety within, "I think we've lost the trail."

Olivia gripped Melanie's hand tighter. "Stop pulling."

Melanie pulled harder. "I see it!"

Olivia yanked back on her arm. "It's not going anywhere. It's bolted to the ground. And Mom and Dad said we have to stick together."

The Ferris wheel loomed up ahead, lights flashing, music singing from tinny speakers. A sea of people lay between them and it, a sea in which Melanie seemed determined to be lost.

Pulling her like the husky she kept asking for but never received, Melanie propelled Olivia forward, slamming her into strangers, who wheeled and yelled things like "Hey!" and "Watch it!" and a few things she knew she was not supposed to say—ever.

They made it to the entrance, but the line stretched back twenty feet or more.

"Do we have to do the Ferris wheel?" Olivia asked as they tacked themselves onto the end of the line.

"Yes!" Melanie whined. "It's my favorite part and Mom and Dad said I could and they said you had to take me, so there."

"Fine, but then you have to come with me to play some of the games."

"Dad says those are fixed and a waste of money."

"He said the whole fair is a waste of money."

They waited as the current group of riders exited out the little gate and then shuffled forward as the line did. The conductor emptied and filled four seats, sent the wheel around three times, then repeated the process. Finally, it was their turn to board. Olivia handed their tickets to an unsmiling woman who never looked at them and led Melanie to the open seat. A scruffy man smelling of cigarette smoke secured the bar across their laps, and the wheel began to spin, slowly lifting them higher and higher above the crowd.

"Olivia!" came a shout from below.

She waved to the figure on the ground.

"Ooooh," Melanie teased. "There's your boyfriend."

Olivia punched her in the arm. "He's not my boyfriend."

"I bet he is. I bet you kissed him." Melanie puckered her lips and closed her eyes.

Olivia punched her again.

"Hey! Knock it off. I'll tell Mom."

"And I'll tell her how annoying you're being and she won't blame me."

Melanie crossed her arms but could only maintain the sulk for a few seconds before she pointed and screamed, "There's Mom! There's Dad!"

Olivia joined Melanie in waving maniacally for a moment, and then they were making the next circle. When they next reached the top, the wheel stopped. The sun was setting and the moon was rising, and Olivia could see for miles in each direction. Farm fields and clusters of trees and long, straight roads leading off to the horizon. It felt like . . . possibility.

"Melanie, what do you want to be when you grow up?"

"I want to work at the fair."

"You want to be a carny?"

"Yeah. It would be so fun. I bet they get to ride all the rides for free."

Olivia rolled her eyes. "Yeah, they all look like they're having loads of fun."

"What do you want to be?" Melanie asked.

Olivia looked west toward the brilliant setting sun. "An explorer."

Eleven

OLIVIA GAZED OUT into the unending parade of tree trunks, her eyes searching for a spot of blue amid the brown and orange and yellow. She wasn't really concerned just yet. They couldn't have gone that far off the trail in their quest for dry ground. But as each slice of forest was ruled out, her mind clicked into problem-solving mode.

She was prepared for this. She had the map. She had a compass. She had her instincts. She'd simply formulate a plan and everything would be okay.

"I'm so sorry, Ollie," Melanie said.

"It's fine. Don't worry. It will all be fine. Just let me think."

Olivia examined the map. She looked again at the lay of the land. Had they been going mostly uphill or down?

"Well, do we know which side of the trail we're on?" she said. "Did we last go right or left to get around the mud?"

"Right," Melanie said. "Wait. No. Maybe left? I don't know. We've been weaving all over the place. I don't know why they don't keep up this trail more."

"Mel, it's wilderness. That there's a trail at all, wet or dry, is pretty much the only thing they could do. They can't control the weather."

Olivia chewed her lip. If they'd gone to the right, getting back on track should be rather simple. If they went south, they'd hit the trail. But if they'd gone to the left, going south would bring them farther away from it. They'd eventually hit the river, but they'd be miles off course. At that point they might be better off crossing the river to get to South Boundary Road so they could hitchhike back to their car. The hike would be over and they would have missed all the best features of the park—most of the waterfalls, Lake Superior, the escarpment, and the Lake of the Clouds.

"The compass is in the bottom right pocket," Olivia said, turning. "Can you get it out for me?"

Melanie dug around a bit, then she started removing things and handing them to Olivia—flashlight, a skein of thin rope, a baggie with matches in it, the ridiculous brook trout knife. "Let me try the left side."

But Olivia knew it wasn't in the left side. The left side was for first aid, not tools. She unbuckled the straps on her pack. "Let me look."

For the next few minutes, Olivia carefully removed every single item in her pack, one by one, and then put them back. With every pocket she emptied, she felt just a bit more panic tickle the back of her neck. Where was it? She knew she'd bought it along with all the rest of the gear. She remembered the price, the label. She remembered throwing the packaging into the recycling bin. She remembered puzzling over what seemed like needlessly complicated instructions and bringing it to bed with her to watch YouTube videos of how to properly use it.

And then she could see it clearly, sitting on her nightstand the night before she left. She'd already packed the car. She told herself she'd remember to grab it in the morning, repeated her mantra for the next day: keys, cell phone, compass, keys, cell phone, compass. Only, while she had remembered the first two items, she had forgotten the third. It was still there, sitting on the nightstand, completely useless.

"I don't have it," Olivia said.

"Did you put it in my pack?" Melanie said.

"No. I mean I left it at home. On my nightstand."

Melanie began unstrapping her own pack now. "Are you sure? Don't you think we better just check mine?"

Olivia agreed, but she knew they would not find it. And they didn't. They were lost in the woods with no compass. With the sun hidden behind a blanket of soft gray clouds, they couldn't even tell what direction they were facing. They put everything back into place in their packs and stood up.

"Now what?" Melanie said.

Olivia looked at the map again. The squiggly lines marking off the changes in elevation blurred. She pulled herself together and wiped at her eyes. "Okay, here's the deal. Wherever there's water, you're going to be going down to it, right? The river cuts through and wears away the rock below. So we need to go downhill to get to the river. You see all these lines really close together?" Olivia pointed to two unnamed peaks on the map. "If we get to this steep incline, we're going the wrong way." She pointed to another set of lines. "And I don't remember going up any areas like this. Now, being that we're both right-handed, I think it's likely we're on the right side of the trail."

"I'm left-handed."

"What?"

"I'm left-handed," Melanie said again. "How could you not remember that?"

Olivia frowned. "And you were in the lead."

"Yeah, thanks for pointing that out. I had forgotten how this whole mess was my fault."

"I didn't say it to point that out. I just said it because it might mean that you tended to go around things to the left rather than the right. It matters to the solution, Melanie. You need to stop being so sensitive."

Melanie threw up her hands. "There's that word again! Sensitive. I've always been too sensitive. Well, sorry, but I don't think I'm being too anything. We all know this is my fault. We all know you're going to fix it. And then you'll have something else to be smug about, some other story to tell about your flaky little sister and how you always have to get her out of scrapes."

Olivia stepped back and waited for Melanie to exhaust the geyser of words that had obviously been hovering near the boiling point for a while. It had been so long since they'd spent concentrated time together, she'd forgotten how volatile her sister's temper could be. Melanie spent so much energy trying to get along with people and agree with them that she never opened the tension valve until she was at the point of exploding.

"Are you done?" Olivia asked. "Because that sort of thing isn't going to help this situation at all. We both should have been looking for the next blue blaze. I'm as at fault as you are. And I'm the one who forgot the compass."

Melanie pressed her lips together.

"Okay, then," Olivia continued. "Let's start moving with the assumption that we're on the left side of the trail. We'll head to our right for a bit. And if we start climbing steeply uphill, we'll assume we're going the wrong way and turn around. How does that sound?"

Melanie nodded and ran a hand over her curls, which were looking limp and greasy. Olivia was sure her hair looked even worse.

"Let's take a picture," Olivia said.

"What?"

"Let's take a picture for your blog or whatever. The time we got lost in the woods."

Melanie managed a small smile. "Okay, sure." They got her phone out of her pack and turned it on. "What face should we make?"

"I don't know. The face you were making a minute ago when you were so mad at me would do."

Melanie let out a little laugh, but Olivia knew she was embarrassed. Mel snapped a picture, then turned off the phone without looking at it.

"Now then," Olivia said, "we better move."

Melanie looked at her. "You're much calmer than I would have thought you'd be in this situation."

Olivia shrugged. "What's done is done."

"And can't be undone," Melanie finished.

"Except we're going to try to undo it now by getting back on the trail."

She started picking her way through the trees to the right, not at all confident that this was the correct action in their situation. But what else could she do? They couldn't just stand there. They had to do something with the knowledge they had, which admittedly wasn't much.

It was slow going. Neither Olivia nor Melanie said anything. All of their concentration was on feeling the ground beneath their feet and scanning the trees around them for a shock of blue. If only the sun would come out, that would be something at least, but no matter how Olivia strained her eyes against the flat gray sky between the treetops, she could not discern any difference in the light.

Every time she felt that the ground was leading them down, it would begin to go up, and every time she felt it going up, it would begin to go down. Looking again at the squiggly elevation lines on the map, she could rationalize this pattern no matter what side of the trail they might be on. She could also see that it would be better for them to be lost on the left side, closer to the road and eventual rescue, than the right side with its mountains and trees that stretched on for miles until they ended abruptly at Lake Superior.

She looked at her watch. They had been walking for twenty minutes or more. Surely if they were going the right direction they would have hit the trail by now. But without a compass or the sun, they couldn't even be sure that they were going in one direction rather than in circles.

Unbidden, thoughts of news stories of lost hikers and lost children crowded in. People who had wandered off a trail and over a cliff, who'd gotten stuck in canyons or attacked by wild animals. She remembered a heartbreaking story about a toddler who'd wandered away from his grandmother's house only to be found dead weeks later, less than a mile from where searchers had been on the first night of the search. That story had haunted her for months after she'd read it, and now it was back, running rampant through her mind.

That would be them. They would run out of food. Someone would be injured and leave a delectable little trail of blood behind them. They'd be tracked by Melanie's cougar. They'd eat poisonous wild mushrooms in a doomed bid to stay alive, or they'd freeze under the first snowfall, which wasn't that far off.

"Hey, doesn't moss grow on the north side of trees?" Melanie said.

Olivia shook herself back to reality. "What?"

"Moss grows on the north side of trees, right?"

"That's not just an old wives' tale?"

"I don't know. I don't think so." She walked around and looked at several of the larger tree trunks nearby. "Well, these have moss on both sides, but there's more on one side than the other."

Olivia examined the trees. "Yes. Maybe."

"We don't have anything better to go on, do we?"

Olivia shook her head and looked again at the map, hoping, she supposed, that everything would all suddenly fall into place and make sense. "If that's true, I think we've been going west, more or less. And we haven't hit the trail. If we were on the left side, we probably should have hit it by now. We could be going along right here where there's not a lot of elevation change overall."

Melanie leaned over the map, and Olivia ran her finger along a short section.

"If we kept going this way—if this is the way we're going—we would eventually start going downhill, but we wouldn't reach a trail for miles, and it would be this Cross Trail here, not the Little Carp River Trail we want."

"You think we should turn south?"

"Or what we think is south, yeah."

Melanie nodded. "That sounds like a good idea."

"I think it's our best bet—as long as we're actually on this side of the trail and actually going this direction."

They shared a resigned look and then turned what may or may not have been south.

"You know," Melanie said as they picked their way through the trees and underbrush, "this all goes to show that you can plan all you like using the facts you know, but at some point you're going to run into something you just don't have the data for, and you're going to have to go with your gut and trust the Universe to send you in the right direction. Not all of life can be mapped out."

Olivia rolled her eyes, knowing Melanie couldn't see her face. "That from one of your videos?"

"No, but it will be."

"If we ever get back to civilization."

"Don't say that. You're such a pessimist."

"Experience has led me to what I think is a reasonable view of the world," Olivia said, "and it's not necessarily negative."

"Well, what would you call it?"

"Indifferent. The world is indifferent. The universe doesn't want one thing or another. It's just running along according to the natural laws that were put into motion billions of years ago when the universe started expanding. It doesn't care whether I have a good life or a bad life, a long life or a short life. I don't matter to it. You don't matter to it. And that's okay."

"That doesn't sound okay to me. That sounds horrible."

"Luckily, you are not bound to it. I'm not interested in proselytizing and getting everyone to agree with me. I'm not a militant atheist or anything. It makes no difference whether others agree or not. Believe what you want."

"So at this moment, as we wander around, lost in the woods, the only hope you have is in yourself? In your ability to find the trail again?"

Olivia didn't answer.

"That seems like a sad way to go through life, is all I'm saying," Melanie said. "And a hopeless one."

Olivia stabbed a hiking pole into the ground. "Yeah, well, a lot of good hope does you. Hope doesn't save people. Hope didn't save—"

She didn't finish her sentence. She didn't have to. They both knew what she was talking about.

They were quiet for a while as they struggled on. Olivia scanned the trees for moss now, as well as blue blazes. She checked her watch again. They had eaten at Lily Pond at 11:00. It was now nearing 1:30. The sun would set in six hours, and it would start to get dark earlier than that, especially if this cloud cover didn't break.

Just as Olivia was beginning to let her fears get the best of her again, she felt the ground change. The balls of her feet started stinging a little, and her toes pressed up against the insides of her shoes. Her knees felt achy, and the muscles on the front of her thighs were sore. They were finally going downhill. Thirty minutes later, she could hear water. She stopped and motioned to Melanie to listen.

"The river," she said.

Olivia picked up the pace, crashing through bushes and tripping on rocks and roots, ignoring the pain in her hip. A moment later she could see it. She wanted to cry, but she just kept stomping through the ferns and fungus to the water's edge. Melanie caught up with her a few seconds later. Olivia gripped Melanie's upper arms and pulled her in for a hug made awkward by the packs.

"We did it!" Melanie said. "We found the river!"

Olivia threw her pack to the ground and felt her legs buckling as she came down from her heightened state of anxiety. She sat down hard on the ground and felt the tears of relief that she couldn't stop anymore slide down her face. Melanie plopped down beside her and put an arm around her shaking shoulders.

"Are you okay?"

The voice didn't belong to Melanie.

Twelve

MELANIE LOOKED UP to see a man coming up out of the water. He wasn't particularly tall or particularly fat or particularly handsome or particularly anything at all—except wet. Water dripped from his olive-green waders and a beige canvas bag slung across his body, and trickled down his bare forearms beneath the rolled-up sleeves of an orange-and-green-plaid button-up flannel. His hands were empty.

Melanie was about to stand up when he knelt down to their level.

"You're a bit off the path, aren't you?" he said.

He had a kind face that somehow looked both concerned and unsurprised, as though he had expected them to tumble out of the forest miles from any trail but was nonetheless troubled by the state they were in. They must look quite a sight after hours pushing through the undergrowth.

"We lost the trail for a while, trying to avoid the muddy parts," Melanie said.

Olivia seemed at last to be able to pull herself together. "Is this the Little Carp River?"

"Yes," the man said. "But if you're looking for the trail, you're about a mile away from it at the moment. Maybe more."

Melanie pulled out a water bottle for her sister and unscrewed the top, but Olivia was focused on the map she'd retrieved from her back pocket.

"Can you tell me where we are on this?"

The man edged closer, took a moment to orient himself to the map, and pointed. "Right about here."

Melanie pushed the water bottle into Olivia's hand. "What are you doing way out here?"

He looked down at his waders and smiled. "Fishing. Downstream it's a bit overfished, so when I come out here I like to visit these upstream areas off the beaten path."

"We're supposed to be on the Little Carp River Trail," Olivia said, getting to her feet and brushing the dirt off her rear end. "I'm assuming we can just follow the river downstream and we'll get there?"

"Might take a while, but yes."

Olivia sighed. "I don't know what to do about our campsite tonight. There's no way we'll make it before dark now."

"Which one are you staying at?"

Olivia quickly folded the map up and tucked it into her pocket. "We'll figure it out." She yanked up her pack and slipped her arms through the straps. Melanie saw her tuck the knife into her pants pocket.

She understood why Olivia didn't want to tell a man they'd just met where they were sleeping that night, but she didn't have to be so brusque about it. "Thank you for your help . . ."

"Josh," the man supplied.

"Thanks, Josh. We appreciate it. Best of luck on your fishing." Melanie struggled to stand with the heavy pack still on her back. The man—Josh—held out a hand. She took it and he helped her to her feet.

"You're welcome to use my campsite tonight," he said. "I'm right on the river, just past the Greenstone Falls cabin where the Little Carp Trail meets the Cross Trail. It's not too far. And if I have that site, I imagine yours is quite a ways further since the backcountry sites are so spread out in this section." He looked up at the sky. "You're right that you'll be hard-pressed to get where you're going before dark."

"Thanks, but—" Olivia began, but Melanie cut her off.

"Just a minute." She pulled Olivia aside and turned her to face away from Josh, who politely took a few steps away to give them some privacy.

"What?" Olivia whispered harshly. "We are not staying with some strange man out in the middle of nowhere."

"He seems very nice, and he's willing to help us."

"We don't need any help. We found the river on our own and we'll find the trail on our own and we'll camp on our own."

"How far is our site?"

Olivia said nothing.

"Let me see the map."

Olivia sighed. "If he's right about where we are on the river, it's at least six miles away."

"Are you crazy? We can't hike six miles in"—she checked her watch—"five hours. And eat. And rest. And set up the tent. And—"

"Okay, I get it," Olivia said. "But we can't just trust this guy.

We know nothing about him. We can't go to sleep with him just outside the tent."

"You slept with a *bear* outside the tent."

"That's different."

"Yeah, this is a person, not a large carnivore. Someone who is polite and doesn't look like a serial killer and who seems genuinely concerned about us."

"We're as close to the road as we are to his campsite. Maybe we should call this trip what it is—a bit of a disaster—and just see if someone can take us to our car."

"You mean hitchhike? How is hitchhiking with a stranger— who then has us in his car and can take us anywhere he wants— better than pitching a tent at this guy's spot? And no, I don't want to call it quits. This trip is not a disaster. And we haven't even seen the best spots yet. You said there would be waterfalls—"

"We saw a waterfall."

"One waterfall! You promised me eight. And Lake Superior. And the Lake of the Clouds. And the overlooks. All the best stuff is yet to come. I am not giving up halfway through just because it got hard."

The look on Olivia's face told Melanie the barb had hit a tender spot. Maybe Olivia's only tender spot.

Her sister narrowed her eyes. "What's that supposed to mean?"

"I think you know."

"You're such a child."

"I'd rather be a child than whatever it is you've become." Even as she said it, Melanie regretted it. She didn't even mean it. But she was in it now. "You go ahead and hitchhike to the car if you want. I'll take my chances with Josh."

Olivia gaped. "That's not fair."

"Oh, you want to talk about fair?"

Olivia planted her hands on her hips. "Sure. Hit me with your best shot."

"Was it fair that you just left and went back to school when Mom and Dad died, leaving me to sort everything out on my own?" Melanie started, holding up one finger. "Was it fair that you never called Grandma Jean and Grandpa Lou or Grandma Ann or Aunt Susan and Uncle Craig or even sent them a card for ten years?" Two fingers. "Is it fair that you've never come to see me in Petoskey? Or that you didn't invite me to your graduation?" Three, four. "You can't just quit when things get hard. You can't just quit your family. That's not how it works."

Melanie hadn't exactly meant to say those things. They were things she'd thought—for years—but she never imagined she'd just blurt them all out like that. She waited for Olivia to say something. She could see her sister gathering up the words in her mouth, like the pulling back of an arrow in a bow.

"Maybe I did leave. Maybe I did quit my family—what remained of my family. But at least I didn't betray Mom and Dad by getting all chummy with the guy who killed them."

Melanie could feel her face beginning to crumple. She'd known that Olivia wasn't happy that she'd forgiven Justin for the crash. But she'd tried to keep her relationship with him a secret. It was why they met in Grand Rapids rather than Rockford, which was too small a town with too big a gossip network. It was why the move to Petoskey had worked out so well. No one there knew them, knew their history, knew their secret.

There their odd friendship could grow, unscrutinized. There they could both try to move on with their lives.

Melanie took a slow, cleansing breath. She would not let Olivia drag her into defending herself. "I'm finishing this trip, with or without you." She turned to tell Josh that they would camp at his site, but he'd disappeared. "Nice going," she said to Olivia.

"Me? You're the one who's freaking out here."

Melanie walked down to the water and looked first downstream and then up. Josh was standing in the middle of the river in water up to his knees, casting a fly into a still spot downstream. Melanie waved to him, but he was focused on the water. A moment later the line caught and tightened. Josh alternated between reeling it back in and letting it run out until suddenly a huge fish leaped out of the water. Another dance between drawing in and letting go until finally the fish could not resist the pull any longer. Josh held it firmly in his hand and removed the hook. Melanie assumed he would put it back into the water, but instead, he slipped it into the canvas bag at his side.

She waved again, but now it seemed superfluous. He was already walking toward her through the water with a smile on his face, like he knew what she was about to say.

"Decided to take me up on the offer?" he said when he reached the shore.

"How'd you know?"

"If the answer was no, you'd already be gone."

Melanie smiled and held out her hand. "I'm—"

"Melanie." He took her hand and gave it one firm shake.

"Yes." Had she told him her name? He must have heard Olivia say it. He must have heard a lot of things. "Please forgive us if we didn't seem grateful for your offer. We've had a rough day. Actually, between you and me, we've had a rough decade. My sister's not so keen on the idea, but I believe in fate and there's no such thing as coincidence, and for us to come out of the woods right here, where you were randomly fishing way off the trail? Well, that's fate."

Josh smiled. "That's not quite what I'd call it, but you certainly are right where you need to be, and right on time." He indicated the bag at his side. "A fish this size is really too much for just me."

"Oh, thank you, but I'm vegan."

He raised his eyebrows and gave her a little nod as Olivia walked up. He held out his hand to her. "Olivia."

Had Melanie told him *her* name? They must have been arguing a lot louder than she thought. How embarrassing.

Olivia gave his hand a cursory shake and pointed to the map. "Is this the spot?"

"Yes," Josh said. "I'm already set up there, but there's plenty of room for your tent."

"We won't be imposing on you?" Olivia said.

"Of course not. Meeting people along the way is one of the best parts of any journey. And I had a feeling I'd have company tonight."

"Oh, I get feelings like that too," Melanie said. "Once I found a dog wandering around and I had a feeling its name was Sadie, and then when I found the owners and they came to pick her up and told me her name, it *was* Sadie."

"So when do we start?" Olivia said.

Josh shrugged. "I'm ready if you are."

"Lead the way."

Thirteen

OLIVIA COULDN'T BELIEVE she was doing this. Following some strange man deeper into the woods. If Josh had been a woman or a young couple or even those three loud people from the parking lot, it would be totally different. But no. The one person out in the woods they run into is a bearded man in a plaid flannel shirt with an unsettlingly calm demeanor. If she saw this in a film, she'd walk out, disgusted with how stupid the heroine was. Likely their story would be made into a movie someday—one of those poorly acted TV movies about tragic unsolved mysteries. It would be called *Who Killed the Greene Girls?*, and she and Melanie would be painted as simpletons lured to their brutal deaths by a man played by a C-list actor with one expression, and the expression would say *I lure simpletons to their brutal deaths.*

The one saving grace in all of this was that Josh's campsite was not nearly as remote as many of the backcountry sites. If anything happened, anyone staying in the two nearby cabins would hear their screams, and they were close enough to the road that they could run there if needed to find someone who would pick them up and take them to their car.

They walked along the river, Josh in the lead, Melanie in the middle, Olivia bringing up the rear. Every so often, Josh would look back to make sure they were keeping up with his brisk pace, and if they were lagging he would stop to let them catch up. He even offered to carry a pack. Olivia would have liked nothing more than to be relieved of her heavy burden, but allowing Josh to carry it would have made him more of a hero than he already was. She did not want to be dependent on the kindness of this stranger, and to let him carry her pack would be admitting that she needed his help. But she didn't. She could take care of herself.

Despite the less-than-ideal situation, Olivia tried to enjoy the walk. The river's gurgling flow was a constant pleasant drone. The breeze whispered through the browning trees. It was beautiful out here. But it was hard to focus on these good things. Because once she stopped obsessing about how dumb it was to follow Josh, she started obsessing about how awful the fight with Melanie had been. Olivia had had no idea that Melanie felt so . . . abandoned. She had always figured that they were both coping in their own unique way and that Melanie was happy with her choice to stay behind, just as she had been happy with her choice to move on. Yet all these long years Melanie had been quietly building up a pile of grievances and accusations.

Was that what this trip was about? Getting her alone in the woods, where she'd have to listen to her sister berate her for her conduct for the past ten years? Did Melanie actually think anything she said could not be trumped by the fact that she'd befriended Justin Navarro? If Melanie thought Olivia was just going to hand her a free pass for that, she had another thing coming.

It was already late afternoon when they saw the first sign of the trail—a straight wooden bridge crossing the river in the distance.

"There it is!" Melanie said, turning back toward Olivia with a huge grin across her face.

"That's the spur trail," Josh said. "It connects the main trail with the parking area off the road."

Despite her fatigue, Olivia quickened her pace. "How far is the parking lot?"

"Another mile," Josh said.

"Is there a ranger stationed there or anything?"

"No. Just a gravel lot and a pit toilet," he said. "By the way, whenever either of you needs to stop, just let me know."

Olivia frowned. She hadn't thought of peeing out in the open anywhere near this guy. "Are you parked in that lot?"

"No, I'm way down at Pinkerton Creek."

They reached the bridge, and Olivia took a moment to appreciate the feel of a man-made structure beneath her feet. Strange how a level surface was so foreign to the natural world. Just another reason to doubt that the world had been made specifically for humans, who had to do so much to alter the environment to make it more to their liking. If God had created everything for them, wouldn't he have created it to suit them more?

"We're coming up on Overlooked Falls," Josh said. "It's just a few hundred feet down this way. Why don't you drop your packs here and we'll take a quick break."

He started walking before they could answer. Melanie leaned back against a tree and unbuckled her straps, then let the pack slide down to the ground. She waited for Olivia to do the same.

"I'll keep mine on," she said.

Mel shook her head and practically skipped after Josh. Olivia struggled on behind. They had been walking so long through wild terrain that the path here felt wide and luxurious. Dead pine needles beneath her feet cushioned her steps and softened the sound of her footfalls. In a moment, she couldn't see Melanie or Josh ahead, but when she came over a small rise, she caught sight of them down by the water. Josh, in his waders, was standing in the river, and Melanie, a couple feet away on land, phone in hand, was taking pictures of the falls. Then she turned the lens on their new companion and took a picture of him. Olivia could imagine what Melanie would put on her blog about their benefactor. Then her heart sank at the thought of what she might write about her cantankerous sister.

Olivia stepped off the path and over large boulders down toward the river. The falls were nowhere to be seen, though she could hear them.

"Aren't they sweet?" Melanie said when Olivia reached her.

Olivia turned to look upriver, and there they were. A series of small waterfalls tumbling over resistant rock. At the topmost level, the river split in two around a large outcropping of rock, and the water leapt down in two falls, joining back up for a distance of perhaps fifteen or twenty feet, only to split again around an immovable stone. The bedrock was brown, etched with cracks and faults and peppered with moss and fallen yellow leaves. It was truly a beautiful sight. The kind of thing Olivia had been most looking forward to seeing on this trip out into the wilderness. A moving postcard.

Could Melanie have been right when she claimed that Olivia had never even sent a card or a letter to anyone in her family for the past ten years? What kind of a person did that? What would her parents have thought if they knew?

But they didn't know. Olivia made a mental note to send apologies to her neglected relatives. She'd fix it, and then she wouldn't need to feel guilty.

Beside her Melanie sighed. "I'm so glad we didn't miss this."

Josh looked back to them and smiled. "It's nice, isn't it. And it's not even the best one, in my opinion."

"Have you seen all the falls in the park?" Melanie said.

"At one time or another."

"Do you live up here?"

"I'm from Paradise."

"Oh," Melanie said, "so these falls must seem pretty puny to you after Tahquamenon Falls."

Josh sloshed through the water back to shore. "They're not better or worse. Just different. Sometimes you need the kind of powerful experience you get from the big falls like Upper Tahquamenon, and sometimes you need something quieter than that. Just like sometimes you want a nice big crackling campfire and sometimes all you need is a single candle."

"Well, I need a big crackling campfire," Melanie said. "I've been cold all day. How far is it to the campsite?"

"Just about a mile," Josh said.

"Are you ready to go, Ollie?"

Olivia didn't care for Melanie using her childhood nickname

in front of a stranger, but she nodded. Watching two people walk around unfettered by packs had her feeling truly exhausted.

They walked back up to the wooden bridge where Melanie had left her pack.

"Could you hold this a second?" Josh asked her, handing over the fly rod.

"Sure," Melanie said.

Then Josh scooped up her pack and swung it onto his back.

"Oh, no, you don't have to do that."

"It's no problem," Josh said, loosening the straps to fit around his larger frame. "I don't mind at all."

"Well, okay," Melanie said. She picked up her hiking poles in her free hand. "Do you want to use these?"

"You keep those. I'll take back the rod. It's not easy to walk through a forest with a fishing pole and not get it all hung up on branches. It would be easier for me to carry it."

With the pack on his back and the canvas bag with the trout in it hanging just below his right hip, Josh led the way across the bridge and down another trail on the opposite side of the river. This time, Melanie motioned to Olivia to go next, but Olivia declined.

"You go first," she said. "I'll be slower."

"Want me to take your pack for a while?"

"No. Let's just go. It's not far now."

They hugged the river most of the way, and Olivia watched the fallen leaves speed effortlessly by on their way to Lake Superior a little less than seven miles downstream. There were several more petite drops with unnamed falls and cascades as the river hurtled itself down the resistant bedrock.

Twenty minutes later, Josh stopped and pointed toward the water. "Greenstone Falls."

They followed him a little farther downstream and down to the river, where again they had to turn back to look in the direction they had come from in order to experience the beauty. Perhaps fifteen feet wide, Greenstone Falls was a picturesque cascade dropping a gradual six feet over rounded rocks and boulders into a swirling pool of foam and leaves. Though it was still cloudy, the yellow trees that framed the waterfall seemed to shine with a light of their own.

Beside her, Melanie was taking more pictures.

"Why don't I take a picture of the two of you?" Josh offered.

"Oh, yes! Thank you," Melanie said, handing over her phone. She sidled closer to Olivia. "Take that pack off, for goodness' sake. It'll be a better picture without it."

"But then I'll have to put it back on again."

Melanie snapped open the waistband strap. "Just take it off. I'll carry it the rest of the way." She was yanking it off before Olivia could do much to stop her.

Josh took the pack from her with one hand and leaned it against a rock.

Melanie pulled Olivia close. "You're all sweaty."

"Of course I am. You would be too."

"Turn this way," Josh commanded. He framed the shot. "Smile."

Olivia obliged, but the smile felt fake. She had utterly lost control of this trip that she had so meticulously planned. Wrong turns, lost trails, uninvited guests. And now she was being told to smile.

Josh handed the phone back to Melanie. "Not much further now."

Olivia tried to snatch her pack back up, but Melanie beat her to it. She stumbled a little under the weight. "Holy cow. This is so much heavier than mine. Olivia!"

"It's just because you've been walking without one for a while. It always feels heavier to put it back on."

"No, it's because you've taken more than your fair share of the weight. No wonder you're limping. Either you let me carry the tent tomorrow or at least break it up half and half. And what else is in here that's so heavy—besides your other can of SpaghettiOs?"

Josh laughed. "SpaghettiOs?"

Olivia rolled her eyes. "I don't need any further critique on those, thank you very much." She walked back up to the trail and took the lead position. Melanie and Josh followed.

A moment later, they passed the first cabin, followed by a wooden bridge leading across the river to the second cabin. Less than ten minutes later, Olivia came upon a cleared area right on the river's bank with a fire ring.

"Here we are," Josh said as he and Melanie came up behind. "See, plenty of room."

"But where's your tent?" Olivia said.

"I don't have one." He pointed off toward the woods. "I'm a hammock guy."

There, strung between two sturdy trees, was a lightweight green-and-black zip-up hammock. Beside it, hung on a tree and nearly blending in with it, was a compact backpack.

"You travel light," Olivia said. "Where's the bear pole?"

Josh indicated a spot in the trees. "Over there, but I don't use it."

"What do you do with your food bag?"

"I don't have one. I just fish and do a bit of foraging."

"But what if you don't catch anything?" Melanie said, dumping Olivia's pack at her feet.

"I have some flatbread in my pack. But when I go fishing, I always catch something."

"And you don't worry about bears?" Olivia said. "You know you're supposed to hang that stuff on the poles. It's super dangerous to keep it in your pack."

"Oh, I just hang the pack a ways away at night. I've never had a problem with bears." He slid Melanie's pack off his back and leaned it on a makeshift log bench by the fire ring. "Need some help setting up your tent?"

"Sure," Melanie said at the same time Olivia said, "No thanks."

"We've got it," Olivia said.

"Suit yourself. I'll get a fire going and prep this fish." He walked into the trees and down toward the river.

"That was rude," Melanie said.

"Listen, we're perfectly capable of setting up our tent—I did it on my own last night—so why would we need his help?"

"He was just being polite."

"I'm not interested in feeding his ego or his hero complex. We're not two damsels in distress."

"We kind of were," Mel broke in.

"No," Olivia said as she started to unpack the tent, "we figured out what we needed to do on our own with limited tools and resources. We found the river, just as I thought we would, and we would have been perfectly fine without this guy. Other than carrying your pack, which he didn't have to do, he's done absolutely nothing for us, which is fine because we don't need any help anyway."

"Oh? How much further is it to our reserved campsite?"

Olivia unrolled the tent in one violent motion and laid it on the most level piece of ground. "Three miles, which we could have done."

"We would have been setting up the tent in the dark," Melanie said, pulling out the poles and stakes.

"I have no doubt that we would have managed just fine."

"I don't think I would have been collecting firewood in the dark. So we would have been eating in the dark, in the cold, and then we would have just gone right to sleep. Sounds super fun."

"I don't want to argue about this anymore. You got your way. Here we are, risking our lives with some random guy, just like you wanted."

Melanie threw up her hands. "Random? Of all the places we could have reached the river, of all the possible times we could have reached it, we come out of the woods right there, right then, when a nice, helpful person is there, way off the trail. How can you think that was random?"

"Because how could it not be?" Olivia pushed a pole through a sleeve on the outside of the tent. "There's no other logical explanation than that it was a coincidence."

Melanie caught the pole from the other side and affixed it to the metal eye ring attached to the corner of the tent. "Can't you see how crazy that is? If everything is just coincidence, you know the mathematical chances of anything existing at all? Let alone a planet as full of diverse, complex, interrelated life as Earth is?"

Olivia stuffed another pole through another sleeve, jabbing it toward her sister but saying nothing. She clipped and tied and pulled and adjusted.

"It's just strange," Melanie continued, "that someone as smart as you are, with all those expensive degrees, wouldn't see how unlikely it is that all this came from nothing on its own with absolutely no guiding force."

Olivia snapped open the fly and fixed Melanie with a look. "So, you don't think anything at all is just a coincidence?"

Melanie shrugged. "No."

"You believe *everything* that happens is something God or the Universe or whatever has orchestrated?"

"Yes."

Olivia gave the fly another snap and picked up the last pole. "You realize that if that were true, it would mean that this same God or force or whatever orchestrated the accident, right? That it *wanted* our parents to die."

Melanie caught the pole on the other side of the sleeve and stared at Olivia.

"You can't just believe in the good stuff without dealing with the bad, Mel," Olivia continued. "If fate sent you to meet a guy in the woods because he uses a hammock and therefore has plenty of room for your tent at his campsite, then fate also sends one car on a collision course with another. It's not exactly an accident if it was planned out from time immemorial. And I can't believe in any kind of God who would do that."

They finished setting up the tent in silence. Olivia was sure that Melanie must be running through arguments in her mind, but so much time passed that it was clear she couldn't think of any retort. Because there wasn't one. Believing in nothing was better than believing in something that brought comfort when it was convenient but left you out in the cold when it came to the hard stuff in life. Her parents had died because of the unfortunate fact that they were in the wrong place at the wrong time. Nothing more.

When she had pounded the last stake into the ground, Olivia stood up. Josh had gotten the fire going. Melanie was nowhere to be seen.

Fourteen

MELANIE LEANED AGAINST the rough trunk of an enormous pine tree and shut her eyes. Why did every conversation with her sister have to be like that? It hadn't always been that way, had it? They had once had so much fun together. They used to tell each other secrets and laugh until their stomachs hurt and conspire with each other against babysitters. Olivia used to stand up for her. Now it just felt like she was stomping all over her.

The worst of it was, Melanie had never actually thought through the full implications of her belief that there were no coincidences, and now, without all the online friends and followers who stood at the ready to buoy her spirits, she didn't know what to do. Anytime she ran into something hard in life, she'd just post about it on Twitter or Facebook and her community would pounce on her with encouragement and positive vibes, even quoting her own words from her coaching videos back to her. Justin too had largely been supportive—even if he'd seemed less apt to agree with her on the finer points and more likely to stay silent on spiritual matters since he started attending a church. No one ever just came right out and told her she was dumb for believing what she did as Olivia had.

As she had to Olivia.

Why had she done that? It was breaking her one rule—never go negative. Negative statements hurt, no matter how well reasoned or carefully delivered. She never told her clients they were wrong. How was that helpful? And here she'd told her sister—the lawyer—that she hadn't thought something out. When the truth was it was Melanie who hadn't thought something out.

Had the Universe chosen her parents for destruction? Her kind, civic-minded parents who never hurt anyone? Could some things be coincidence and other things not? That didn't seem very consistent. Though consistency had never concerned her before. She believed a bit of everything because a bit of everything felt true and right.

"There you are."

Melanie jumped and put her hand over her heart.

"I think your sister's worried about you." Josh stood a few feet away to the right. He had removed his waders and his hands were in his pockets. "We're about ready for dinner. Just waiting on the flames to die down a bit. Are you hungry?"

"Oh, sure." Melanie stood straight and brushed off the back of her pants. "Though you're wrong about Olivia. We're kind of in a thing right now. She's probably happy for a few minutes without me."

Josh stepped aside to let Melanie pass. "If you don't mind my asking, what's the problem?"

"Oh, nothing," she said as she picked her way back toward the tent. "Just sister stuff."

"I know we just met," he said, "but can I make a suggestion?"

"Fire away. I will always take a bit of advice."

"Assume the best about her."

Melanie stopped walking. "I always assume the best about people. And anyway, I don't think she's a bad person. We just don't see eye to eye on something and we're arguing about it."

"I'm not talking about whether she's a good person or a bad person. I'm talking about how she's feeling inside."

"I don't really get what you mean."

"Whatever you're fighting about, where is she coming from? Is she coming from a place of pride, where she feels she has to be right?"

"Definitely."

"Or," Josh continued, "is she coming from a place of fear, where she's afraid to be wrong?"

Melanie thought for a moment. She couldn't imagine Olivia being afraid of anything.

"Because in my experience, when it comes down to it, most people are ultimately operating from a place of fear, not a place of assurance. It makes them defensive, makes it hard to listen to other points of view. Just food for thought. And speaking of food . . ." Josh swept his hand toward the fire, inviting Melanie to continue the walk back to camp.

As they came out to where Olivia could see them, Melanie examined her. Her hands were planted firmly on her hips and her mouth was set in a line. When they got closer Melanie could see the two deepening wrinkles between Olivia's eyebrows that had been there since college. She didn't look afraid. She looked irate.

"Where were you?"

"I was just over there," Melanie said, pointing, then she continued on to her pack and got out her food bag and a water bottle.

"I don't have plates," Josh said as he poked at the fire and positioned a small folding grill rack over the glowing coals, "but I do have pita bread that works just as well." He laid the two fillets of the fish he had caught and dressed on the grill and then pulled out a compact travel salt-and-pepper shaker.

"Melanie doesn't eat meat," Olivia said.

"I'm fine with what I've got in my pack, thanks," Melanie said.

"What about you, Olivia?" Josh said.

"Oh, she eats meat," Melanie offered.

"Great. Have you ever had fish that was caught just a couple hours ago?"

"I can't say that I have," Olivia said.

"You'll love it," he said.

Josh tended the fish, then got out the pita bread and passed it around. Melanie took some to be polite, though she normally tried to be gluten free in solidarity with those who had celiac disease. Their host parceled out some fish between Olivia and himself and looked in Melanie's direction once more to offer it to her. She shook her head and smiled.

"Tell him why you're a vegan," Olivia said.

"She doesn't have to explain herself to me," Josh said.

"It's because she believes in reincarnation and she doesn't want to accidentally eat our—anyone she knew."

"That's not—" Melanie started.

"Oh, and also just in case animals have souls. She's covering her bases."

Melanie stared hard at Olivia until her sister met her eyes.

Olivia stared right back and raised her eyebrows as if to say, *Am I wrong?*

"What do you believe about that, Olivia?" Josh said.

Olivia broke away from Melanie's stare. "I don't believe in reincarnation. And I don't believe animals have souls. Or people, for that matter."

Josh nodded, but not in agreement. Melanie knew that nod. It was a noncommittal nod, one that said "I hear you but I don't agree with you, and I don't want to get into it right now." She got that nod from people a lot.

They ate in silence for a minute. Melanie waited for Josh to add his opinion to the discussion, but he remained quiet.

The light was beginning to dim a little. Night was approaching. Their second night on the trail. Not where they were supposed to be. Not sharing their deepest thoughts and longings like she'd hoped. Just sitting on a log, a foot away from one another. A foot that might as well be a mile.

"Why do you come out here all alone?" she heard herself asking.

Josh put another chunk of fish into his mouth and chewed thoughtfully for a moment before swallowing. "I like to spend time out in God's country."

"But why don't you come out with friends or family?"

"That's a rude question," Olivia said.

"No it isn't," Josh countered. "I enjoy spending some time alone now and then. And like I said, I always meet new people out here."

Melanie tore a small piece of pita off the whole. "What do you do? Like, your job."

"I do a bit of everything. I build things, I fix things, make things beautiful."

"Like houses? Do you build houses?"

"Sometimes. I build tables and mantelpieces. Cabinets. I fix plumbing and engines."

"You do all that in Paradise?" Olivia said. "Seems like too small of a town to sustain that kind of business."

"Most of my work is outside of Paradise. I travel all over."

Melanie spoke around the pita in her mouth. "Do you have a website? I could look you up when we get back to civilization."

"No website."

"How do you run a business without a website?" Olivia said.

"It's mostly a word-of-mouth thing. People just tell other people about me."

Melanie laughed lightly. "It's like you're from another era. My whole business is online."

He waited for her to continue.

"I'm a life coach. I do it mostly through my blog and videos on YouTube and social media and stuff. Just sending out encouragement to people, you know?"

"And what do you do, Olivia?"

"I'm a prosecuting attorney."

"She's very good," Melanie piped in. "You know that story a while back about the guy who had swindled a bunch of old ladies out of their life savings, pretending to be investing for them? She sent that guy to prison. And a bunch of others. She hasn't lost very many cases."

Olivia looked at her. "How do you know?"

Melanie shrugged. "Just because you don't know what's going

on in my life doesn't mean I don't know what's going on in yours." Even as she said it, she hoped it was true. If Olivia really knew what was going on in her life, it would get real ugly real fast.

Soon the last bites of dinner were eaten and night was closing in. Josh put some more wood on the fire and blew on the embers. It flared up, and Melanie basked in the heat. Olivia went off to hang up the food bags, brush her teeth, and use the facilities, such as they were, before it got pitch-black, then she disappeared into the tent. Melanie stayed close to the fire. She didn't want to go into the tent with her sister. She didn't want to start fighting again. Being near Josh was better. He seemed like the calm center in their sisterly hurricane. Across the fire his face glowed a warm orange in the darkened woods. She couldn't decide if he was handsome or not.

"How long are you out here for?" Melanie asked.

"This time, I think at least two more nights."

"Where are you going tomorrow? Or will you stay at this camp the entire time?"

"Tomorrow I'm heading down the Cross Trail to Superior for one night, then I'll be heading up the Big Carp River for the salmon run."

Melanie frowned. "So you're not going the same way we are?"

"No. The Cross Trail takes me directly to where I need to be. But you're in for some nice hiking tomorrow. It's one of the best hikes in the park. Besides being up on the escarpment."

"It'd be nicer if you were with us," she said, then immediately regretted it. She didn't want him to think she was flirting with him. She just really liked his company.

Josh smiled at her across the fire. "I'm sure we'll meet up again sometime."

"I hope so." Then it felt like it was time to call it a night. Melanie always tried to follow those gut feelings. And to stay one moment longer would make it awkward. She stood up and waved. "I better get to bed before Olivia wonders what's happened to me again. I'll see you tomorrow."

Josh returned the wave. "Good night."

Melanie dispensed with the evening rituals and climbed into the tent and over Olivia, who was lying in the dark, still but obviously not sleeping. She changed into her pj's as quietly as possible, trying not to kick her sister, then slipped into the sleeping bag Olivia had prepared for her without her asking or knowing or even really thinking about the fact that a sleeping bag needed to be prepared. Olivia, ever the older sister. Melanie lay there in the blackness and wondered if she could fall asleep with her eyes open since it was just like having them shut.

Olivia's voice rose out of the dark somewhere near Melanie's feet. "Hey, Mel?"

"Yeah?"

"I'm sorry." It was quiet for a beat. "I was kind of a jerk today."

Melanie waited for her to continue. But it was apparently all she had to say.

"Miss Crabapple! The papers, if you please!"

Olivia sat at one end of the dining room table, wearing her father's old glasses and ringing a small gold bell. At the other end of the table, Melanie tore a sheet of paper from an electric typewriter found at a neighbor's garage sale the day before and rushed it over to her sister.

"Your speech, Mr. President!"

"Madame President," Olivia corrected out of the side of her mouth. Then loudly, "Miss Crabapple, how do you ever hope to be secretary of state when you can hardly manage being secretary of this office?"

"Yes, Mr.—Madame President. Yes, of course."

Olivia strode to the window, gripped her nonexistent lapel, and stared into the middle distance, which was really just the lilac bush in the backyard. Then she ran her eyes over the speech she had just been handed. "Miss Crabapple, the fate of the country is at stake and you hand me this gibberish?"

"You didn't give me enough time," Melanie said in her own voice.

"Shh," Olivia hissed. "Go get the hat and sit in the living room. You're a reporter now."

Melanie took off the elbow-length gloves and shawl she had donned as Miss Crabapple and put on a fedora from the dress-up trunk.

"Pad and pen," Olivia directed.

Melanie slid the legal pad and a black fountain pen from the table and sat in the wingback chair.

"No, you're on the couch," Olivia said.

Melanie sighed and changed places. "Come on, just give the speech."

Olivia walked to the center of the room and pretended to rest her arms upon an invisible lectern.

"Friends, countrymen"—she nodded at Melanie—"reporters from all the most important papers in the world."

Melanie nodded back, her invisible mustache twitching.

"I come to you today not just as your president but as your friend. We stand on the brink of war. The aliens that—" She looked at Melanie. "Does it have to be aliens?"

"Yes. You said they could be from anywhere."

"Fine." Olivia addressed the rest of the living room. "The aliens that have invaded Earth can only be stopped if we put aside our differences and join forces. The very human race is at stake! But we must also be aware that these aliens can take on human form, masquerade as one of us."

"Hey, I didn't write that," Melanie said.

"I'm improvising."

"But—"

"They may look like someone you've known for years. Like your own parents." She pointed a finger at Melanie. "Like your own sister!"

Melanie shot up from the couch. "I'm not an alien!"

"That's exactly what an alien would say!"

Melanie threw down the legal pad and the pen. "I'm not playing anymore."

"Wait!" Olivia said, grabbing her arm to keep her from leaving the room. "Okay, you're not an alien. You're not an alien."

Melanie allowed Olivia to turn her toward the kitchen, where *her parents were washing and drying the dinner dishes to the sounds of eighties pop music.*

"But maybe they are," Olivia whispered.

Melanie stifled a giggle. "Okay."

Olivia removed the glasses and Melanie took off the hat. They dug around in the trunk for the two thick sticks that served as swords, magic wands, and conductors' batons, depending on the need. Now they were laser guns. They crept slowly, quietly, toward the kitchen's swinging door. The song ended. They stood stock-still, like statues, until the next one on the CD began. They flanked the door. Olivia pushed it slightly open with her gun.

There they were. Aliens. At the sink. Not washing dishes. No. They were developing a toxic chemical soup that they would unleash upon an unsuspecting planet within minutes. They must be stopped.

Olivia charged into the room, Melanie at her heels, both screaming and waving their laser guns in the air.

The alien that looked like their dad dropped a wet dish, and it shattered on the floor.

The girls stopped shouting. Looked from the shards on the floor to the faces of their stunned parents.

"Out!" their mother said.

They scurried out of the room. Melanie began to cry. Olivia quickly disposed of the sticks and closed the trunk while Melanie stood in the dining room, tears streaming down her face.

"Shhhh," Olivia soothed. "Shhhh."

She could hear the pieces of the broken plate being collected. Then she thought she heard another sound.

"Shhhh," she said again, this time to quiet her blubbering sister.

Melanie swallowed hard and wiped her nose on her sleeve.

Was that . . . laughter?

Olivia peeked through the swinging door again. Her parents were sitting on the kitchen floor, faces red, mouths stretched in mirth, practically crying as they tried to suppress the laughter. She opened the door the rest of the way, and her mother schooled her features, but her dad couldn't stop.

"Sorry," Olivia offered. She felt Melanie come up behind her.

Their mother motioned them into the room with one arm and elbowed their father with the other. "Would you stop?" she said to him. Then to the girls, "Come here."

They shuffled forward into the room, the door swinging closed behind them.

"I don't think I have to tell you that was not a good idea, right?"

The girls shook their heads.

"You shouldn't sneak up on people, and you shouldn't shoot at them, and you really shouldn't do those things when they have wet dishes in their hands, right?"

The girls nodded.

Having recovered for the moment, their father added, "You're lucky that wasn't one of the good dishes."

They nodded again.

"Okay, come here," he said.

Olivia and Melanie walked into their parents' open arms. They sat there in a giggly pile on the wet kitchen floor. And all was forgiven.

148

Fifteen

OLIVIA OPENED HER EYES. She could make out the tent around her in the gray light of almost dawn. How long had she slept? She felt the reassuring hardness of the gas station knife in her hand, ready to be flipped open and used to defend herself and her sister should the need arise. Her sister. She struggled to unzip the mummy bag from the inside and sat up. Melanie was there. On her side. Still asleep.

Olivia lay back down. But then she needed to pee. This was the worst part of backpacking. Having to get up off the ground after a day of hiking and go out into the cold and drop your pants. Guys had it so easy.

Every joint creaked and every muscle screamed in protest as she slid out of the tent and into her shoes. Blisters on her heels and the tops of her two littlest toes felt like lightning rubbing against the inside of each shoe. With some effort, she pulled herself into a standing position and zipped up the tent door, then stumbled out from under the extended roof of the fly and into the murky morning. Her breath came in clouds as she searched her pack for the toilet paper and shovel.

She walked a few dozen feet into the woods and then looked around to make sure Josh couldn't see her, but she couldn't even see his hammock from where she was. She quickly dug her hole, did what she'd set out to do, and covered everything up. Back at her pack she used the hand sanitizer and ran her eyes over the surrounding trees. Where Josh's hammock should have been, there was nothing. No pack hanging up, no foldable grill rack standing over the ashes in the fire ring. Had he already left? Had she imagined him?

Olivia quickly took stock of their things and found nothing missing. She retrieved the food bags and filtered the water, and then she realized that she was incredibly cold. She climbed back into the tent and snuggled back down into her sleeping bag just as Melanie was waking up.

"It's freezing out there," she said.

Melanie groaned. "I told you we should have done this in the summer."

"I'd rather be cold than sweating and swarmed by mosquitos."

"I guess."

They lay in the gray light, Olivia trying to warm up, Melanie moving and flexing inside her sleeping bag.

"My back is killing me," Melanie said.

"It'll be fun putting those packs back on."

"Wrong."

"We should get going as soon as possible. Get a jump on things. We have a lot of ground to make up."

Melanie groaned again.

"Hey, I gave us an out yesterday. We could have hitched back to the car and slept in the little cabins again last night. You wanted to keep hiking."

"And I still do," Melanie said. "I just need to get moving and I'm sure I'll be fine. Maybe Josh can make another fire this morning."

"He's gone."

Melanie sat upright in her bag. "Gone?"

"Gone. I find it a little strange that he didn't say goodbye when he seemed so friendly yesterday. But then, there you go. He was a weirdo after all."

Melanie slumped over.

"You look like you're a larva about to pupate in that thing," Olivia said.

Melanie unzipped the bag and let it fall away. "Holy mackerel, it's cold out there!"

"I told you it was."

"Crap. I have to pee."

"You just gotta do it. Get up."

Melanie crawled over her. "I'm borrowing your shoes. Mine are too far away from the door."

"Whatever."

Olivia helped push Melanie out the door and into a semi-standing position, then zipped up the tent and started changing into her clothes. Two days in and she was feeling grimy and smelling ripe despite using deodorant and wet wipes. She ran a hand through her hair. "Ew," she said out loud to no one. "I'm never going hiking again."

She pulled it into a ponytail, put on a ball cap she'd had since college, and started rolling the bags and deflating the pads. She'd gotten hers done and had started on Melanie's by the time she came back.

"Give me my shoes, would you?" Olivia said. "I need to stand up. I'll finish the bags in a minute once I can stretch my legs."

"I can do my stuff," Melanie said.

"You have to do it really tight to fit it in the stuff sack."

"I know."

"Okay, be my guest."

She left Melanie in the tent and rummaged through her food bag for the second can of SpaghettiOs. She sat on the log and ate the nearly frozen pasta while staring out across the river, completely spaced out and mind blank, only coming to when the plastic spoon came back out of the can empty. She stood and rinsed the can in the river, then added it to her trash bag. She had some pears and drank some water. Then finally Melanie was unzipping the tent to come out. Olivia pushed her shoes toward her with her foot.

"What the—there's something in my shoe," Melanie said.

Olivia leaned over to see under the fly. "What?"

Melanie held out a round black object. Olivia took it from her and opened it. "It's a compass."

"There's a note," Melanie said. "'So you can find your way in the wilderness. Josh.'" She looked up at Olivia. "What a sweetheart. I hope he doesn't need that."

"He seemed like he knew where he was going," Olivia said. "Did he leave his phone number or anything? I'd like to return it at some point or at least pay for it."

"No, and anyway, I think he meant it as a gift, free and clear."

"Are you about done in there? I want to pack up the tent, and you need to eat something."

Melanie held out her hands, and Olivia pulled her to her feet. "Pack away. I'm starving."

Twenty minutes later, they were ready to leave. Melanie rubbed her arms while Olivia consulted first her watch and then the map.

"How many miles?" Melanie said.

"Let's just start walking and not think too much about it. It should be easy, anyway. All we have to do is stick to the river. It's all downhill from here to Lake Superior."

"And we get to see some more waterfalls, right?"

"Right."

They headed west out of the campsite, following the blue blazes of the North Country Trail, a 4,600-mile footpath stretching from the eastern border of New York to the middle of North Dakota. Altogether their trip would take them on just nine miles of the NCT, and most of it they'd hike that day. One hundred and seventy-five miles to the east lay the only other stretch of the NCT Olivia had ever hiked—the trail she'd been hiking when the ranger had found her to tell her of her parents' accident. So even though this was one of the nicest hikes in the Porkies, according to both Josh and the always authoritative word of the internet, there was a part of Olivia that wanted to get it over with. She felt a strange buzzing in the soles of her feet with every step, as if the memory ran through the trail like electricity through a power line.

They made good time despite the cold and their aching muscles, which did loosen up a bit as they walked. Other than a quick stop for water, they didn't slow down—and didn't speak—until they reached the first ford of the day, which would bring them to the spot where they had meant to camp the night before. They wordlessly removed their hiking boots. Olivia's feet were hot and red and one of her blisters had burst, but she forced her water shoes on and waded across the shallow but quick-running river. On the other side, shoes and boots were exchanged once more, and Melanie wandered over to the campsite fire ring, presumably in search of residual warmth.

"There's not going to be any fire left," Olivia said. "This was supposed to be our spot, so no one slept here last night."

"Oh yeah?" Melanie said. "Come see."

Olivia strode over, skeptical. But Melanie was right. It did feel warm. Olivia poked the ash with a stick, releasing the banked embers, which sent up a little flame.

"Ooh! Get some sticks," Melanie said.

"We're not making a fire. We're leaving in a minute. You can't make a fire and leave it. These people should have completely extinguished their fire before they left. And," she added more indignantly, "they shouldn't have even been here!"

"Don't you see though?" Melanie said. "Someone else needed this site. Maybe they got lost too. Or maybe someone turned an ankle and needed to stop for the night. But we got lost and ended up with Josh so that these people could use our open site. So it all worked out."

"Or," Olivia said, "there were just some people hiking who didn't make reservations ahead of time and thought they could do whatever they darn well pleased and take any site they wanted. I bet it was those three we saw at the trailhead where we parked the car." She started looking around the campsite for evidence to support her theory.

Melanie threw up a hand. "Why do you always think the worst of people?"

"Because, in my experience, people are pretty much the worst. You don't know because you live in a happy little echo chamber full of rainbows and unicorns, but I deal with the worst humanity has to offer on an almost daily basis. My whole job is about making people who break the law pay for their crimes. Sometimes it's heinous, like rape and murder, and sometimes it's just people being selfish jerks and not caring about anybody else because all they can think about is themselves and what they want. I have no respect for people who have no respect for the rules. The rules are for the good of everyone."

Olivia realized she was ranting and stopped, though she had much more to say on the topic. She bunched all the embers together with the stick and poured some of her water on them, sending up a plume of smoke, then she spread the whole mess out. "You want to eat lunch at a waterfall?"

Melanie said nothing.

"What?" Olivia prompted.

"My life isn't all rainbows and unicorns."

"Fine. But my point stands." She shifted her weight off her sore hip. "Ready?"

Melanie lifted her hands and her eyebrows in the universal sign for *duh*. Olivia bit back a sigh and started walking.

Just a minute away from the campsite flowed Trappers Falls, which looked more like a waterslide than a waterfall. Olivia and Melanie silently dumped their packs and pulled out their food bags, which were lighter now after two days of hiking. Positioning herself on a stone ledge littered with yellow leaves, Olivia pounded some string cheese and jerky, then started shoving handfuls of nuts into her mouth. She was ravenous, and she wasn't sure why.

"I never really thought about the fact that your job was so negative," Melanie finally said.

"It is what it is."

"It must wear you down though. Day after day dealing with the worst people can do to one another."

"It's definitely a drag sometimes," Olivia said. "But it is satisfying when you know you've gotten a dangerous person off the streets. You feel like you're doing some good. Of course, it doesn't always work that way. There are guilty people that go free. And there are people who get lighter sentences than you wish they would. You see some of the same people come through the court system again and again." She stopped talking for a moment and stared at the water. "It's frustrating, really. What do we have if we don't have a society of people that can function? I mean, it's hard to say if our prison system even works at all except to keep some dangerous people out of the general population. But there are so few who come out of it and seem to be able to make something of their lives. It's not always their fault—society doesn't make it easy for them to reintegrate. It's like, once you've been branded this way, you can never escape it. There's no forgiveness. You're just . . . out."

Melanie nodded. "It sounds like you're under a lot of stress with your job."

"Don't tell me I should meditate or drink special teas or anything."

Melanie laughed. "I wasn't going to."

"Okay, see that you don't." Olivia tied up her trash bag and shoved it back into her food bag. "I'll say this—it's not always fun, but it is necessary. And it seems to be something I'm good at, so there you go."

"You are good at it. You're good at everything. You always have been."

Olivia shook her head. "No, I'm not."

"Yes, you are. You played every sport, you got all A's, you were always getting some leadership award or going on some special trip to somewhere or other because you were one of the smart kids."

Olivia put a hand on Melanie's knee. "You want to know the truth? I wasn't good at everything. I just immediately quit the things I wasn't good at. You don't remember them because I didn't do them long enough."

Now Melanie was shaking her head. "No, I don't believe that."

"It's true. You know I tried out for the fall play my freshman year of high school when you were still in junior high?"

"You did?"

"Yes, and when I didn't get the lead role, I quit. I wasn't going to play some background character with no lines."

"That's crazy. Why would they give you the lead as a freshman? That's not how it works."

"It's how I thought it should work!" Olivia laughed. "And did you know I took piano lessons for a week, and then I quit because I thought playing 'Mary Had a Little Lamb' was infantile and the teacher wouldn't let me jump ahead into better songs because she said I wasn't ready for them?"

Olivia was enjoying the incredulous look Melanie was giving her, so she kept going.

"I quit doing anything artsy when nothing I painted looked like it did in my head. And I never sewed anything after I sewed a little pillow top I was embroidering onto the pants I was wearing. And I never helped Mom cook because I once burned a pan of snickerdoodle cookies and was so angry at myself I cried." Olivia was really laughing now.

Melanie smiled. "I loved cooking with Mom."

Olivia pulled up short. She hadn't meant to mention her mother. And now the memory of that ill-fated attempt at baking became the memory of her mother handing her a freshly laundered softball uniform, which became the memory of her father's ecstatic face the first time she hit a home run, which became the memory of the four of them at a Detroit Tigers game, where she caught a foul ball with her bare hands, chipping a bone in her finger. She didn't know she was crying until Melanie wiped at her cheek.

"It's okay to talk about it," Melanie said. "And it's okay to cry about it."

Olivia looked at her sister, whose eyes were red and shining, whose smile was a little shaky at the corners. Then she stood up and wiped at her own eyes and nose. "We should get going again."

She picked up her pack and her hiking poles and took a few steps up from the river and back onto the trail. In her peripheral vision, she saw Melanie put her face in her hands for a moment before standing up and brushing the dirt off her pants.

"We're three miles from Lake Superior," Olivia said.

Wordlessly, Melanie put her pack back on and walked up to her. Olivia silently implored her not to say anything. To just drop the whole thing, forever and always.

Melanie touched her arm. "I'll lead for a while." She held out her hand for the map. Then she headed into the yellow glow of the trees.

Sixteen

MELANIE HAD BEEN SO CLOSE. So close to breaking through to the other side of grief. After ten years. As close to a breakthrough as Explorers Falls was to being an actual waterfall. To Melanie it just looked like someone was draining their pool down the driveway for the cold months. They didn't even stop walking to look at it.

Her spirit felt just as drained. Olivia knew what was good for everyone else, but she couldn't see what was good for herself. It was hard for Melanie to do all the grieving for the both of them, all alone with no one in her life who really understood. Aunt Susan was a support, but she lived so far away. And losing a sister wasn't quite the same as losing both your parents so young. Just when you feel so utterly lost in the world and in need of guidance. And anyway, Melanie knew what it was like to lose a sister too. Olivia wasn't dead, but she may as well have been.

Though, there was Justin. He understood something of what she was going through. His grief wasn't the same as hers, but it was grief nonetheless.

Propelled by her frustration and aided by the lay of the land along the river, Melanie walked faster than she had the previous two days, and especially faster than earlier that morning when the unannounced departure of Josh had her feeling deflated. She knew she should slow down a little and intentionally enjoy the old-growth hemlocks and the maples that glowed yellow and orange all around her. But her feet were following her racing mind.

Now that Olivia had been on the cusp of crying, it would be that much harder to get her back to that vulnerable place. The conversation on the banks of the river had no doubt inoculated her to further discussion about all they had lost, like getting a flu vaccine. But there was still hope. Melanie just had to find a different strain, a different way in, something that Olivia could not stay silent about.

She needed an argument.

The only question was, about what? Melanie had to choose carefully. Not every subject would lead them to their shared loss. And there was a plethora of subjects about which Olivia was more knowledgeable than her. Melanie had to be able to hold her own and keep things going. And it couldn't seem like she was baiting her. As a lawyer, no doubt Olivia knew how to spot leading questions.

She was still contemplating the best way forward when she felt Olivia's hand on the back of her arm. She was about to ask what was up when she saw that her sister's finger was over her lips. Melanie looked at her hard. Olivia turned Melanie's shoulders around a little further, stepping back so that she could see what was behind them.

Melanie felt her breath catch. Perhaps thirty or forty yards away, a black bear was casually ambling toward them. Melanie tried to ask Olivia what they should do, but no sounds could get past the jagged lump of ice in her throat.

"Don't move," Olivia whispered between labored breaths. "Don't move and don't run. It's been walking behind us for a few minutes. Or at least, I noticed it a few minutes ago. It looks young. Maybe it's the one that slept by our tent."

Melanie found her voice. "What do we do?"

"Nothing. For now."

"But shouldn't we scare it away? Aren't you supposed to make loud noises and stuff?"

Olivia shrugged and breathed deeply, which became a yawn. "Yes. I thought you'd want to see it first though. You were walking so fast it was hard to catch up to you without running, which you don't want to do in a situation like this."

Melanie was equal parts touched that Olivia had thought of her and confused by her own reaction to the bear. She'd always thought she had a psychic connection with wild animals. But this was real. This was terrifying. And here Olivia was yawning at it, as though being followed by a bear out in the woods where no one would hear your screams as it ripped you to pieces was as normal as walking out to get the mail.

The bear seemed to notice that they had stopped walking, and it too stopped. Melanie silently prayed that it would turn around and go in the other direction. Instead, it stood up on its hind legs and bobbed its head, sniffing the air. Young or not, on its hind feet it was as tall as a man. Melanie's heart rate ticked up another notch.

"What is it doing?" she whispered.

"It's just smelling us."

"Us? Or our food?"

The bear dropped to all fours again and took a couple steps toward them.

"Should we leave something for it?" Melanie said.

"That's pretty much the worst thing we could do. Then it will see us as a source of food. Us and every other hiker who comes by. That's the kind of thing that makes bears dangerous."

"This one already seems dangerous."

Olivia laughed lightly. "Whatever happened to Dr. Melanie Dolittle? I thought you'd be thrilled. You seemed so disappointed about missing it the other morning."

"Being visited by a bear and being followed by a bear are two very different things."

"That or you're just a lot of talk." Olivia whacked her hiking poles together and yelled, "Hey!"

"Don't do that!" Melanie ground out. "You're going to make it mad."

"You want to get rid of it or not?" Olivia said at a normal volume. "You were the one who brought up making loud noises. And you're right. You're supposed to make noise the whole time you're hiking. It's our fault for being so silent for the last mile. And the needles have softened our footsteps. Really, we should have a bell on one of our packs, but I didn't want to have to listen to a bell ringing incessantly. Just be ready, okay?"

"For what?" Melanie said incredulously.

"Not running. Don't run. Just be ready with your poles to jab at it if it comes too close."

Before Melanie could stop her, Olivia took several long, quick strides toward the bear, smacking the poles together and shouting, "Get out of here! Go on! Get out!"

The bear took a few quick steps backward and then looked at them as if it was all some big misunderstanding.

Olivia stomped toward the bear and then stopped short and let out three sharp barks like a dog. The bear skittered away, looking back twice more, and then disappeared over a ridge.

Olivia turned back to face Melanie with a grin. "How about that?"

Melanie's legs quivered. She wanted to dump her pack on the ground, lie down on her back for a few minutes, and take some big, slow, calming breaths. But more than that, she wanted to get as far away from that bear as humanly possible.

"You all right?" Olivia said.

"I'm fine."

"Gosh, I did not expect that kind of reaction from you. I thought I'd have to keep you from going up and hugging it."

"Well," Melanie started. But she didn't know how to finish. She hadn't expected that reaction either. She started walking again, looking back over her shoulder every minute or so. But all she saw was her sister.

Within ten minutes they reached another backcountry camping site.

"No wonder that bear was headed this way," Olivia said, pointing to a little pile of garbage in the fire ring. "Someone has apparently never heard of 'leave no trace.' And I bet I know who." She picked up a beer can with her fingertips.

"Why would they leave their trash here?"

"Probably thought the next people would just burn it in their campfire. Stupid, stupid, stupid." Olivia dropped her pack and fished out her garbage bag.

"You can't take that with us if that's what the bear was after," Melanie said.

"I have to. It's what they should have done. You think we should leave it so that the next people at this site have a bear to contend with?"

Melanie tried to cross her arms, but the pack straps made it difficult. She settled for clenching her fists at her side. "Well, I don't want a bear to contend with."

Olivia stuffed the trash into her bag. "This is the right thing to do. You should never be afraid to do the right thing."

"That's rich," Melanie mumbled. Olivia looked up, but Melanie turned away and pretended she hadn't said anything. Then she remembered that she had wanted to get into an argument with Olivia before they were interrupted by the bear. "I think it's perfectly rational to be afraid of a bear."

"Of course it is," Olivia said. "I just didn't think you would be."

"You think I'm not rational?"

Olivia made a face. "You really want me to answer that?"

Melanie's hands went to her hips.

"Anyway, that's not what I meant," Olivia said. "I mean you love animals. Like, *love* them. You used to pet everything you laid eyes on—stray dogs, injured squirrels, that disgusting pet millipede in Mr. Fletcher's classroom. You once had a funeral for a dead toad."

"I remember that," Melanie said. She started down the trail and Olivia followed.

"Something had pulled out its entrails," Olivia said. "It was so gross. And you picked it up with your bare hands. And *kissed* it."

Melanie smiled at the memory. "I felt bad for it."

"That's what I'm saying though. You have such deep feelings for animals. It was just odd to see you scared by a bear. Totally rational, don't get me wrong. Just surprising."

And just like that, Melanie had her in. "You know, now that I have a moment to think about it, it surprises me too. A lot. But I guess we can't choose our reaction to things sometimes. Our fight-or-flight instinct kicks in, and that's all we can do."

"What I saw back there was not fight or flight. That was fright. That was freeze. Freeze into a solid block of ice."

"Yeah, I guess it was," Melanie said. "It felt a little like my first dance recital. I don't know if you remember that."

"Oh yes, I remember. You came out on stage and then just stood there, completely still, while all the other little girls danced around you."

"Yeah, well, this felt like that." She chose her next words carefully. "What sends you into fight-or-flight mode?"

It was quiet for a moment. All Melanie could hear was the constant whoosh of the river, the soft squeak of her pack, and the sound of her own feet.

"I suppose I fear the unexpected. That's why I wanted to be the one to plan a trip that was your idea."

"And why you're glued to this map," Melanie said, waving it at her.

"Exactly," Olivia said. "In the courtroom, I never want to be taken unaware by a surprise witness or a new piece of evidence.

It's all about knowing ahead of time what people will say and having a ready answer."

"I guess that makes sense," Melanie said. "But the bear was unexpected—twice—and you didn't seem like you were afraid of that."

"It wasn't unexpected. I knew from researching the park that black bears were a factor. And I knew from reading up on bear behavior what to expect should we encounter one. So the one we saw today didn't feel unexpected at all. Even the one that slept by the tent—I was only really afraid when I thought it might be a person out there. Because a bear will generally behave according to its instinct, so you know what to expect. But a person might do anything, especially if they were intoxicated or on drugs."

Melanie considered this. It was obvious to her where this fear came from—from their parents' very unexpected deaths. If Olivia were one of her life coaching clients, she would just go ahead and say that to her. And if Olivia were one of her clients, she would nod thoughtfully and say, "You know, you're right, Melanie. You're absolutely right. All of my problems can be traced to that one event." Melanie heard stuff like that all the time. She was good at her job.

And Olivia was good at hers. Some of that surely could be traced back to what had happened to their parents. Melanie wondered not for the first time what their lives would be like had the accident never occurred. She would have finished school, earned a degree in art history, and been working at a museum in London or Paris or New York. Olivia would still be a lawyer, but maybe she and Eric would have gotten married. Maybe she'd have a baby.

And what about their parents? They'd be deciding what to do in their retirement. They'd stay close to home to see their grandchildren, of course, but with frequent trips out to see Melanie in her glamorous big-city life.

"What about you?" Olivia said, breaking into Melanie's thoughts. "Besides bears, I mean. I know you got over your stage fright."

Melanie didn't say anything for a while as she tried to pin down what exactly it was that she was afraid of.

"Do you want my help?" Olivia said. "Because I think I know the answer."

"Okay, what?" Melanie said.

"You're afraid of being wrong."

Melanie stopped walking and turned around. "What?"

"Why else would you believe in every religion and fad spiritual system out there except that you're afraid to commit to one? And why would you be afraid to commit to just one? Because what if you're wrong? What if you choose one, just one, forsaking all others, and you choose the wrong one?"

Melanie shook her head and resumed walking. "That's silly. No matter what I chose, there would be millions of other people who believed the same thing. I wouldn't be alone in that belief, so why should I be worried about what other people think of my choice?"

"No, that's different. I didn't say you were afraid of *looking* wrong. I said you were afraid of *being* wrong. If you pick the wrong one, well, there are consequences, right? There's hell or being reincarnated as a lower life form, or even just missing out on having a fun life because you were part of some religion that was all about renouncing the pleasures of this world and taking vows of silence and eating just bread and water and wearing only scratchy clothes."

Melanie said nothing.

"Anyway, that's just my educated guess," Olivia said, and Melanie could hear the smirk in her voice.

A moment later, the trail led straight to the riverbank. Across the shallow water Melanie could see another blue blaze. The second crossing of the day. As she removed her hiking boots, she argued with Olivia in her head. She wasn't afraid of being wrong. Why, she only barely believed in the concept of wrong. She didn't like to tell people they were wrong about anything because everything was about perception and the lens you saw the world through. Who was she to say something was wrong? Unless it was, well, murder or cheating or stealing or stuff like that. Some things you *did* were right and wrong, but a person's private beliefs? Melanie didn't believe in imposing on that with a value judgment.

She didn't fear being wrong. Her fear went deeper than that. She had felt it when she saw the bear on the trail. She had felt it three years ago when she had such terrible food poisoning that she couldn't get up off the bathroom floor to reach the phone and call Justin to come take her to the hospital. She had felt it as a small child when she'd jumped into a neighbor's pool without a life jacket after seeing Olivia do just that, only Melanie couldn't actually swim and had to be saved from drowning by her mother.

Melanie wasn't afraid of being wrong.

She was afraid of dying.

Seventeen

OLIVIA SHOULD HAVE KEPT her mouth shut. Even if she did believe it. And even if she wasn't the one who'd started them down this uncomfortable conversational path to begin with. She leaned against a tree, pulled off her hiking boots and socks, and tried to think of something funny and self-deprecating to say that might break the tension that expanded within Melanie's silence. But nothing came.

Melanie pulled her pack back on, picked up her boots and her poles, and stepped into the steady stream of water.

"Seems kind of strange that they would have us cross the river back there just to recross it downstream, doesn't it?" Olivia said. "I mean, how hard would it have been to cut the trail along just the one side?" She was about to put her pack back on when she heard a scream, then a splash. "Mel!"

Olivia ran into the water after her sister, who lay on her side, water piling up against her pack and flowing over her legs. Olivia grabbed her hand, but the pack was taking on water, making it impossible to right her from that angle. Olivia stepped over Mel's legs so she was upstream and yanked up on her pack. Melanie struggled to get her bare feet back under her. Then she was standing in the river, water dripping from everywhere except for one dry shoulder and half of her hair. Her hiking poles hung from her wrists and tapped against Olivia's side as she helped her to the far shore.

"Are you okay? Did you twist an ankle?"

What would they do if one of them couldn't walk out? They were more than three miles from the nearest trailhead. Melanie's cheeks were pink, her teeth were chattering, and her lips had an unsettling purplish cast. It was still only around forty degrees.

"We have to get you out of these clothes." Olivia snapped open the waist strap of Melanie's pack and helped her out of it. "Take them off, right now," she said as she unzipped the pack and began pawing through it. But the contents of Melanie's pack were wet as well. Olivia wanted to scream at her for not packing everything in Ziploc bags as she'd instructed her.

What's done is done and can't be undone.

Without a word, Olivia left the pack there in the dirt and rushed as quickly as she dared back over the slippery river rocks to her own pack. She pulled it on, grabbed her boots and poles, and crossed the stream once more, then dumped everything onto the ground and found her hand towel.

Melanie was still fully clothed. Olivia started stripping her down from top to bottom. She wrung out her hair, pulled off her coat and her shirts, and dried her as best she could with the small towel. She gave Melanie one of her own T-shirts and the jacket off her back. Then she got to work on the lower half. Her pants were too big around Melanie's slim waist, but she pulled the drawstring tight. She dried Melanie's boots as best she could and checked the size. Despite being a bit taller than Olivia, Melanie wore a size nine to Olivia's nine and a half. Olivia thought but a moment before putting another pair of socks on Melanie's feet, followed by her own completely dry boots. Melanie was still in such shock from the cold, she didn't seem to notice.

Olivia looked intently into her eyes. "Are you okay?"

Melanie managed to nod.

"Are you still cold?"

She nodded again.

"But nothing is broken or twisted?"

Melanie took a few small steps.

"Okay, here's the deal. We need to get you moving. I'm going to pack this stuff up so we can keep going. In the meantime, I need you to just walk around in a little circle to get the blood flowing. I think we're close to the lakeshore. Maybe someone will have a fire going where we can warm you up some more, okay?"

Melanie nodded again but did not move.

"So start walking," Olivia said.

There wasn't a lot of room, but Melanie dutifully obeyed, making a tight oval around the spot where Olivia knelt in the fallen leaves squeezing as much water as possible out of everything in Melanie's pack before refolding, rerolling, and repacking it.

"Okay, we're ready," Olivia finally said. She handed her dry pack to Melanie, then pulled Melanie's wet pack onto her own back.

"Wh-what are you doing?" Melanie said through her shaking.

"You said you wanted to carry the tent," Olivia said.

"B-but—"

"No buts, let's go." She held her hand out for Melanie to go first, which she did without further argument.

For a few minutes they walked between the Little Carp River to their left and a steep wooded hill to their right before the trail opened up and the land beneath their feet spread out to the northeast. It wasn't more than twenty or thirty minutes before they could hear the sound of another waterfall. Traders Falls was about halfway between the river crossing and the shore of Lake Superior. The falls were small and picturesque, but neither Melanie nor Olivia slowed their determined pace to admire them.

"Are you warming up?" Olivia called up to Melanie.

"A bit, yeah," Melanie said.

Her voice was no longer shaking, and Olivia took that as a good sign. Now she turned her worrying over to the next problem. Everything in Melanie's pack was wet. Her clothes, her underwear and socks, her towel, and quite possibly her sleeping bag, though Olivia hadn't had time to check it out. They still had two nights and two days left on the trail before they got to their car, unless they could find someone who would give them a ride from the Lake of the Clouds to the Government Peak trailhead where they had started. If it stayed cool and cloudy, there was no way the stuff would dry out enough to use. Olivia had one more set of clothes left, which meant they'd both be wearing the same clothes for a couple of days. That in and of itself was not a big deal. They'd just be extra gross and grimy when they got out of the woods.

What worried her was what they would do during the cold

nights on the cold ground. One person could barely fit into a mummy bag, let alone two. If Melanie's sleeping bag was wet, of course Olivia would give Melanie her bag. But then what would she do? She wouldn't even have much for extra clothing to put on.

The farther they walked, the more she ran over this problem in her mind. And the more she ran over it, the more the hard truth came to the surface—they couldn't spend another night out on the trail. In her obsessive poring over the map earlier, Olivia had located the spot where Josh had said he parked, the trailhead at Pinkerton Creek. That was their last chance to cut the trip short before they were locked into at least eleven more miles of hiking—and more than fifteen if they couldn't find a ride at the Lake of the Clouds. Surely at this point Melanie would agree that it would be better to take their chances hitch-hiking than walk into certain hypothermia for at least one of them.

When they came to a small wooden bridge leading off to the left, they finally paused. A sign indicated that the North Country Trail continued over the bridge, as did the Pinkerton Trail, which would lead them to the parking lot and South Boundary Road. If they continued going straight, they would be on the shore of Lake Superior. Already the wind was picking up, reminding Olivia that of course the lakeshore would be even colder than the woods.

Melanie pulled one of her water bottles from her pack on Olivia's back. "We should have done it this way the whole time."

"Me with your pack?"

"No, just carrying each other's water bottles. Then they

wouldn't be changing hands so many times because we can't reach our own when our packs are on."

Olivia pulled one of her bottles from the pack Melanie was carrying. "I hadn't even thought of that."

They both took a few long swigs. This close to the lake, there was no reason to scrimp. They had three quadrillion gallons of fresh water at their disposal—enough to cover the entire land surface of both North and South America with a foot of water.

"So where are we?" Melanie asked.

"Well, that's what I wanted to talk to you about. I've been doing some thinking, and considering the present state of things, I want to propose a change in plans."

Melanie got a little wrinkle between her eyebrows and waited for Olivia to continue.

Olivia pointed down the trail. "That way is Lake Superior, where we might find someone with a fire where you can warm up some more and maybe, if we could find some way to hang things up near it without catching anything on fire, dry a few things out." She pointed at the bridge. "That way is the road. And the lot where Josh said he was parked."

"Okay," Melanie said slowly.

"Here's the thing. Everything in your pack is wet. Luckily I was carrying the tent, so that's dry. But all your stuff is wet. And it's going to be cold again tonight. And that's dangerous. When people die out in the woods, it's not usually because of a bear attack or starvation, it's because of hypothermia. Well, the leading causes are falling, drowning, and heart attack, but in our case those aren't really an issue, because we're not rock climbing or canoeing down dangerous rapids and we're youngish and at least passably fit. So if something gets us, it's probably going to be hypothermia."

"Where did you get that list?"

"Backpacker.com. I think the article was called 'A Dozen Ways to Die.'"

"Oh."

"Anyway"—Olivia patted her pockets—"I think we need to admit that this is the point at which we should throw in the towel and call this trip finished." She twirled her finger at Melanie. "Turn around, would you?" She started digging through the pockets of her pack. "I know you're going to want to keep pushing forward, but sometimes . . . huh . . ."

"What?"

"I can't find the map." She spun Melanie around again. "Did you see what I did with it?"

Melanie twirled her finger now. "I think I had it last."

Olivia turned her back to Melanie. "I just emptied out your entire bag and repacked everything. It wasn't in there."

"Did you look in every pocket?"

"Yes." Olivia spun back around to face her sister. "Oh no."

"What?"

"You had it."

"That's what I said."

"No, you had it. In your hand."

Melanie shook her head and mouthed *no*, but she didn't look at all like she believed herself.

"You dropped it," Olivia said.

Melanie nodded slowly.

"In the river."

Melanie nodded again. "Olivia, I am so, so sorry. I had it under my arm because I couldn't hold it and my poles at the same time."

It must have fallen when Melanie did and been washed downstream when Olivia was preoccupied with getting her sister out of her wet clothes. It was gone. The map was gone.

"Well, that settles it," Olivia said. "We have to stop. We have to cross this bridge and take that trail out to the road and hope that someone comes by before dark. What day is it?"

"Now, hold on," Melanie said. "Let's just think a minute."

"That's all I've been doing for the last half hour, Mel. Trying to think our way out of this mess. And this is it. This is the plan."

"Just hang on a second."

"No, it's over. What is it, Saturday? Sunday? Is it still the weekend?"

Melanie looked at her watch, but it had been in the water too long. No matter how she shook her wrist, it would not wake up.

Olivia looked at hers, noting the low battery symbol in the corner. "Monday. Crap. No one's going to be here on a Monday in October. Tourist season is over, and people coming up to see the fall colors would come on a weekend, not a Monday. Everyone's back at work."

"Not Josh," Melanie said.

"Right, and he said he was parked at this trailhead. We should get down there as fast as we can so we don't miss him."

"Wrong. I mean, yes, that's where he said he parked, but he won't be there. Last night he said he was going to the salmon run on the Big Carp River."

"He left so early in the morning though. He probably already finished fishing and headed back to the car."

Melanie was shaking her head again. "I don't know. I got the feeling he'd be around for a little while. He didn't seem like he was in any hurry. And he did say something about running into each other again on the trail, didn't he?"

"Melanie! We have no map! All of your stuff is soaking wet! This is ridiculous! We can't go wandering around in the woods with no map and no idea where Josh is. Even if we found him, how is he going to help us? All the guy had was a hammock. He's not going to suddenly have an extra dry sleeping bag."

"He gave us a compass."

"A compass can't keep us warm!"

"Stop!" Melanie held up her hands. "Just stop. You're freaking out because this has all been really unexpected. This wasn't in your plans. But I'm the one who fell in the river. I'm the one who's cold. I'm the one who made a blunder. And I will be the one to figure out my situation. You think you have to fix this, but you don't. You think you have to run everything because no one could run it as well as you can, but you don't. I am an adult. I have been running my own life for ten years without your input. I think I can manage to make my own decision about how to handle this."

Olivia pressed her lips together and planted her hands on her hips. "Well?"

"Just give me a second!"

Olivia looked down at her feet, which were aching in Melanie's damp, too-small hiking boots.

"Okay, how far is it to Lake Superior?" Melanie finally said.

"I could tell you—if I had a map."

"Oh, please. How do you not know that map by heart now? Ballpark?"

Olivia sighed. "I don't know. We're probably less than ten minutes away."

"What time is it?"

"It's already past three."

"Here's what I want to do. I want to keep going to the lake and just see if there's anyone there who might be able to help us or who might have an extra map or something. If there's anyone there, we can ask if they've seen Josh, and then that might help us decide what to do. If it seems like we're alone out there, then maybe we think about taking that other trail to the road."

Olivia raised her palms to the sky. "Don't you see that the later it gets, the less likely it is that anyone will happen by in a car? That hitchhiking in daylight and hitchhiking at night are two very different activities? Every minute we spend out here makes it less likely that we'll get picked up at all."

"Thirty minutes isn't going to make much of a difference. We've already wasted ten minutes just standing here doing nothing."

Melanie had her there.

"Fine. Thirty minutes and no more. If we haven't found anyone who can help us in that amount of time, we bail."

"Fine."

"Here." Olivia shrugged out of Melanie's soggy pack. "You can take this back." She bent to untie the boots. "And these torturous things."

"Why are you wearing my boots?" Melanie said, looking down at her own feet.

"Because they were wet and mine were dry." Olivia stepped out of the boots and stretched her toes.

"You didn't have to do that."

"But I did, didn't I?" She motioned to Melanie to take off her boots. "But my feet can't take much more, so give me mine back."

When they were both reequipped with their own stuff, Melanie grasped Olivia's upper arms and looked into her eyes. "You're a good sister."

Olivia pulled away. "Let's get this over with." She headed for the next marked tree down the path.

Eighteen

MELANIE COULD FEEL the power of the lake even in the woods. The wind was high and cold, and the rhythmic waves crashing against the shoreline quickened her pulse and her pace. When they came out of the trees, she caught her breath. Superior was a deep gray-blue, flecked with the white of breaking waves all the way out to the horizon, where it merged seamlessly with the cloudy sky. The smooth tumbled stones that made up the beach were a darker gray, slick and wet and adorned with the occasional orange leaf that had lodged there. Large bodies of boulders hunched in the surf, and the skeletons of dead trees and driftwood lay like petrified lightning.

This was what she hadn't realized she'd been longing to see. The waterfalls were pretty and the fall colors were dazzling, but Lake Superior was something altogether different. It was power. Raw power, gathered up and gathered up and then released in a relentless onslaught as it battered the shore. People thought of fire as the most powerful of the four elements, but to Melanie it had always been water. She could see it at home in Petoskey on the shores of Lake Michigan, but Superior was in a category of its own. It was constantly cold, even at the height of summer. It was treacherous, as the many shipwrecks littering its bed attested. It seemed almost to be calculating, as though it worked a will known only to itself. On a still summer morning it might be glassy and serene, but now as the cold season began it felt delightfully malicious.

To her life coaching clients, Melanie was always advocating things that would bring them peace and serenity—fountains, gardens, meditation, therapeutic massages, walks in the forest—because of course that's what they needed. In an anxious world, her clients were the stressed-out, the burned-out, and the down-and-out. They came to her looking for balance and a sense that everything was going to be okay.

But Melanie had begun to think that she had perhaps just a bit too much serenity in her life. Her predictable, comfortable life. Her days that started with green tea and ended with chamomile-peppermint. Her wardrobe of earth tones. Her house with its tastefully minimalist, Zen-like atmosphere. Her collection of yoga-friendly music that had no hooks, no rise or fall, just a constant, insistent middleness. So on the few occasions she was met with something like Lake Superior in October, she savored it with an almost guilty sense of pleasure, like she was flirting with a dangerous man.

For a moment as she stared at the writhing lake, Melanie forgot about everything else. She forgot about Olivia and the map and her plans for her sister's spiritual awakening. She forgot how cold she was, how sore her muscles were, how dirty her hair felt. She forgot about the decision they would have to come to in twenty minutes. She stood facing the wind and the water and felt supremely thankful. Though to whom, she was not quite sure. Not the lake itself, for it seemed either indifferent to her or bent on her destruction. If not that, then to something bigger. To whatever had made the lake. Or to whatever had made the glacier that carved out the lake. To whatever force or spirit ultimately controlled all of this. For she was sure that there had to be something or someone out there. Someone she was always kind of searching for in her own haphazard way. But never quite finding.

Eventually she became aware of another sound above the waves, insistent, harsh. Olivia was saying her name.

"What?" Melanie finally said.

"Your teeth are chattering. Come on. We need to check out the other campsites and see if we can get you out of the wind."

As she looked at her sister, Melanie felt another, smaller wave of gratitude overwhelm her. Maybe Olivia hadn't been there for her when their parents died. Maybe she'd shut her out when she'd forgiven Justin for his part in it. But she was here for her now. She meant well, even if her brand of love was more of a shove toward safety than a hug amid the trial.

On the way to the lake, they had passed three empty campsites near the mouth of the Little Carp River. Olivia thought there might be half a dozen more scattered along the mile or so of shore between there and the mouth of the Big Carp River. All they needed was for one of them to be occupied by someone and Melanie knew she could convince Olivia to stay on the trail. She didn't have answers to all of Olivia's practical objections—the possibility of a wet sleeping bag was the greatest obstacle—but she never really spent a lot of time worrying about practicalities. Things would work themselves out. They always did.

"You know, we could go a lot faster without the packs," Melanie said. "We can come back for them if we need to, or if we don't find anyone they'll be waiting for us on the way back to the bridge."

"That's a good idea," Olivia said.

They leaned the packs up against a birch tree and started walking again. Without a pack weighing Melanie down, it felt like floating. She thought that as much as she enjoyed hiking, she could enjoy it so much better without shouldering such a heavy burden of worldly goods. Josh did it right. He didn't carry around a tent or a sleeping bag or even much food. He simply went along his way and trusted that there would be enough for him.

A few minutes went by before they saw the next site, which was empty, the fire ring cold and dead. Just on the other side of a small creek there was another. Also empty. Several minutes later there was another. Same story—no people, no tent, no fire. At any moment, Olivia would say that the allotted time was up and they needed to turn around and get themselves to that trailhead parking lot.

"Let's just try one more," Melanie said to preempt her.

"Okay. Just one," Olivia said.

They crossed another creek on a wooden bridge and resumed walking. Melanie couldn't get the time from her malfunctioning watch—and she sure wasn't going to ask Olivia and therefore remind her that they were running out of it—but it felt like they had walked nearly twice as long as the distance between the last two sites when they finally came upon the next one. Melanie's heart sank. It too was empty, the only sign of previous human habitation one of those plastic on-the-go flossers she felt like she had seen dropped in every parking lot for the past five years.

"Gross," she said.

"That's it. We tried. Now we have to face facts. Let's go get our packs. I only hope we haven't missed our ride."

A flash of blue between the golden trees caught Melanie's eye. "I think I see someone. Come on."

She didn't wait to see if Olivia would follow her. In a moment she was back on the rocky shoreline, where thirty or forty feet away, a man stood looking out at the water just as she had been not half an hour ago. She said hello, but the wind blew the sound back down her throat. She tried again, but he did not hear. Finally, she was near enough to tap his shoulder, but before she had a chance to, he looked her way with a smile.

"Melanie."

When he said her name, she recognized that it was Josh.

"I thought we'd see each other again." He looked past her and called out, "Olivia," and waved at her to join them. "Have you set up camp nearby?"

"No," Melanie said.

"Where are your packs?"

"We left them back down at the Little Carp River," Olivia supplied.

"Oh?"

Melanie shared a glance with her sister. "Are you camping around here?"

He pointed farther down the shore. "I'm the last site before the cabins. It's maybe five minutes from here."

"Do you have a fire going?" Olivia said. "Mel's had a chill today and she could use some warming up."

"I hadn't started it yet, but I've got all the wood gathered. You're welcome to join me."

"It's not too windy for a fire out here?" Olivia said.

"Not at that site. It's off the shore a bit, back in the cedar trees. They block the wind." He started walking. "Follow me."

"So, you're not going to leave the park tonight?" Olivia said as they followed behind.

"I hadn't planned on it," Josh said. "I was upstream earlier today and the salmon are running thick. Not too many other fishermen out right now. It's a great time to fish and just enjoy the quiet."

They stepped back onto the trail. Josh strolled along with his hands in his pockets. "Where are you two camping tonight?"

"Our site is quite a bit further up the trail that runs along the Big Carp River," Olivia said. "Near a crossing, I think. Before you climb the escarpment."

"I know the spot," Josh said. "That's around where the few other fishermen I've talked to are staying. Most of the spots on the lakeshore here are pretty cold and windy in the fall. Your site is about four and a half miles away. Though, if you have to go back and get your packs, that's going to add almost three more miles. No way you'll get there tonight."

"Right," Olivia said. "We know that."

"Once you get off track it's hard to get back on," Josh said.

"This whole trip has been harder than I expected," Olivia said.

Josh looked back and smiled, but it wasn't a smug smile like

Melanie thought they might see from such an obviously accomplished outdoorsman. He wasn't laughing at how unprepared they were. He wasn't pitying them either. His smile reminded her of her father smiling at her when she fell off her bike and skinned her knee. Caring, concerned, but also showing her that he was proud of her for trying, for doing something she hadn't been sure she could do. It was the kind of smile that helped you get back up.

"You're welcome to stay with me," he said.

Just then they reached his spot back a bit in the woods. There was indeed significantly less wind. Josh's hammock hung between two trees, barely swaying every so often. Wood and sticks were piled up next to the fire ring. He immediately started making a little tepee of dry leaves and pine needles and the smallest sticks, over which he made another of slightly larger sticks. Blocking what breeze there was with his body, Josh leaned over the fire ring and scraped a couple pieces of metal together. A moment later a flame was shivering in the midst of the kindling. He moved a stick here and there, and the fire caught, stronger, licking up to the second layer of fuel.

Melanie held her hands over the flames. To someone who had been so cold, the feel of actual heat was nearly miraculous. "What was that?"

Josh held out the device. "Flint fire starter. Never hike without it." He carefully added a few larger pieces of wood to the fire. "So, what happened today? Why are you so cold?"

Melanie looked to Olivia, expecting her to relay the story of her klutzy sister who fell into a river. But Olivia raised her eyebrows and dipped her head, indicating that it was Melanie's blunder so it was Melanie's story.

"Well, most of the day went pretty well. The morning anyway. We crossed the river and had lunch at Trappers Falls."

"Where we were supposed to camp last night," Olivia interjected.

"We saw—was that Explorers Falls?"

Olivia nodded.

"Right, Explorers Falls. And then just a bunch of hiking. Everything was going really well until we got to the second crossing. I slipped somehow, I don't know how, I guess the rocks were slimy or something. Anyway, I fell, and even though the water was pretty shallow, of course everything got soaked. Like, completely soaked. I had to change my clothes, but everything in my bag was wet because I didn't put my clothes in Ziploc bags"—she nodded at Olivia—"even though she told me to, so she gave me some of her clothes and even switched shoes with me. I've been cold ever since, and we were hoping to find someone with a fire so I could warm up."

Josh had been listening and nodding as Melanie relayed her story. Or, most of her story. She couldn't bring herself to say that she had also lost their map. Olivia could add that detail if she wanted.

"So it's good that we happened upon you," Melanie said, by way of wrapping things up.

"That's a rough day for sure," Josh said. He looked like he was deliberating what to say next. "So why did you leave your packs behind?"

"Here's the thing," Olivia jumped in. "Back at the junction with the Pinkerton Trail, I suggested that we needed to just call this trip a disaster and hike out so we could find a ride back to the car and stay in a motel tonight. Somewhere she could get a hot shower and sleep in a warm, dry bed. Because, sorry, but I think we're flirting with something really dangerous if we stay out here in the cold, and I think you'd agree with me because you obviously know what you're doing out here."

She paused, ostensibly for Josh to acknowledge the correctness of her opinion, but he merely waited for her to continue.

"But Melanie didn't want to do that and thought that if we could find someone to help us out—I don't know how, beyond having a fire to warm up at—then we could keep going. And it was quicker to check that out without packs on than with, so we left them and were going to just go back for them on the way out of the woods."

"Or," Melanie interjected, "we would just grab them and bring them back to wherever we ended up. So I guess that's what we'll do since we found you."

"But," Olivia said, her voice a little louder, a little more insistent, "Melanie is forgetting that we have a bigger problem to address. All her stuff is wet, so she's not prepared to go any further on this hike, and she can't even sleep out here tonight because her sleeping bag is wet. And while I'll give myself a few extra blisters wearing her shoes so that she has dry feet, I will not knowingly subject myself to death via hypothermia just so she can stubbornly continue a trip I didn't even want to go on in the first place."

Melanie clenched her jaw. She had no response to Olivia's practical arguments, but she wanted to lash out at her for being . . . well, her. No one had ever had the ability to make her feel small and stupid like Olivia did. Melanie took a few deep breaths and then turned her back on the fire to warm the other side of her. And also so she didn't have to look at Olivia.

"You obviously know your way around the woods," Olivia continued behind her. "What would you do in this situation?"

Melanie braced herself for Josh's assessment, which would surely fall in line with Olivia's.

"I guess that depends," he said.

Melanie turned around again so she could see him. He was already looking at her.

"Why are you on this trip?" he said.

"What?" Olivia said. "What kind of question is that? It's a hiking trip. We're here to hike."

"Okay, but there are much easier places to hike. You're not avid hikers, right?"

Melanie laughed. "That's pretty obvious, isn't it?"

He smiled. "Right. So why here? Why now? Why a hiking trip and not some other kind of trip, like a visit to a city with museums and restaurants and shops? It's a lot more trouble to plan and execute a wilderness hike than it is to spend a weekend in Chicago. So why here?"

"Why are you here?" Olivia snapped.

"I'm fishing," Josh answered calmly.

"Okay, why are you fishing here instead of somewhere else?" she pressed.

"Stop it, Olivia," Melanie said.

"What? I'm just asking what he was asking."

"This is where the fishing is good at the moment," Josh said, "so this is where I am. But my mission out here is not what's in question. Why are *you* here?"

"Why does it matter?" Olivia said. "Why we're here makes no difference in whether it's smart to continue or not."

"It makes a difference in whether you're willing to face hardship to see it through. For instance, if you're out here because you thought it would be fun and neither of you is having any fun, then there's no real reason to persevere, is there? If the point is to have fun and you're miserable, then the decision is easy. Abandon ship."

Olivia crossed her arms and looked about to say something, but Josh continued.

"But if the point of the trip is something else altogether, then you need to weigh that purpose against the trouble you're running into and decide if it's worth it to push forward anyway. Trouble, in and of itself, isn't a reason to quit something."

Melanie found herself nodding.

"So, my original question stands. Why are you on this trip?"

Melanie took a stab. "To reconnect. With each other."

"Which you could do a lot of places, I suppose," he said.

"Okay, true. But it's easier to reconnect in a place like this where there are no distractions than in a city where there are shows and exhibitions and stuff."

"So it was your idea." Josh poked at the fire with a piece of driftwood, then dug the smoking end into the ground to put it out.

"We've barely spoken for ten years," Melanie said quietly. "It felt like we had some catching up to do."

"What happened? If you don't mind my asking."

"Hmm?"

"Sisters not talking for ten years? Something must have happened."

Melanie looked at her sister, whose face was set like stone. "Our parents died ten years ago in a car accident. We were on a hiking trip when it happened."

"That's horrible," Josh said, his brow knit with what seemed like real concern.

Melanie nodded and stared at the fire. "It was really hard. We were both in college. After that we kind of went our separate ways. I quit school to take care of stuff at home, and Olivia . . . left."

"This is a waste of time," Olivia said. "This whole trip has been a waste of time. We need to go, Mel. We can't stay out here and you know it. Whether or not you've gotten what you wanted from me, it's time to leave. We can talk in the car on the way home, if that's what you want."

"That's not what I want," Melanie said. "I mean, it's not the only thing I want. And anyway, you'd find it just as easy to change the subject in the car as you have here. You're right that this has been a waste of time. You've made sure of it."

Olivia scowled. "Excuse me? Who got us lost in the woods? Who got herself completely soaked in cold water because she didn't want to buy water shoes, and whose clothes got wet because she didn't want to buy plastic bags, making it fundamentally dangerous to keep going? If anyone's trying to sabotage this trip, it's you. You've made everything harder. You completely destroyed my itinerary. You even managed to lose the map! I'm just trying to get us out alive at this point. I figured out where to go when we were lost. I scared away the bear that was following us. I sacrificed my feet so yours would be dry. I've been doing everything in my power to make it so you can take this stupid hike that you think will miraculously heal our relationship and make me feel better about my parents dying and you chumming around with the guy who killed them, even though that's utterly ridiculous to the point of being insulting."

Melanie squeezed her lips together and counted to five. She would not cry. "Go on then," she said, her tone measured. "If you're having such a bad time, take one of the packs and hitch-hike to the car. You can sleep in a motel, and I'll see you in a couple days if you're not too high and mighty to come back and pick me up. Or I'll get an Uber, if they have any up here. Or maybe Josh can drop me at a bus station. Just leave the tent and the dry sleeping bag and some food. I'll do the rest of the hike myself."

Olivia came around the fire to where Melanie stood, resolute. "That's absurd."

"Why? Because it wasn't your idea? Because it's not part of your plans?"

Olivia threw up her hands. "No, because you're inexperienced, you have a terrible sense of direction, as we have established, and you have no map."

"Josh knows where he's going. I'll follow him."

Olivia stepped closer and lowered her voice. "That's the stupidest thing you've said yet. You don't even know this guy."

Melanie made no effort to talk quietly. "He was pretty helpful yesterday and nobody got raped or murdered. I'm pretty sure it'll be okay."

Olivia punched her in the arm. "You idiot," she hissed. "It's a lot harder to overpower two women than it is to overpower one. You have no idea what he's capable of."

Melanie looked to where Josh was standing, eager to draw him into the argument just to make her sister squirm. But he wasn't there. She gave Olivia her own punch in the arm. "You're the idiot." Then she stalked off to find Josh, Olivia hot on her heels.

They found him back on the rocky shore at the water's edge, standing just out of reach of the waves.

"Did you figure it out?" he said without turning around.

"I'm going on," Melanie said before Olivia could say anything.

He looked at Olivia. "What about you?"

She picked up a rock and flung it into the churning water, where it vanished. "I don't know what to do here. She won't listen."

Josh looked at each of them in turn. "How about this. Olivia, what if you and I go back to where you left the packs. Melanie, you stay by the fire and keep it going and keep warm. And if, when we get to the packs, you want to keep going to the road, you can go ahead and I'll bring the other stuff back here to Melanie. Otherwise, we each grab a pack and come back here."

Olivia shook her head. "No, Melanie needs to come too, that way we can both leave if we choose to."

"I think Melanie's already made her choice though."

Melanie nodded vigorously.

"You just need to make your choice. Quit or push on."

"This is totally none of your business, and you're not getting it anyway," Olivia said. "The choice has already been made for us. She can't sleep in a wet sleeping bag."

"Did you ever actually pull that bag out to see if it was wet?" Melanie asked.

Olivia hesitated. "No, but everything in the pack was wet. All of your clothes were wet. Of course it would be too."

"But it's in a separate stuff sack, which, for all we know, might be waterproof. I mean, I can't imagine you getting anything less than top-of-the-line equipment."

Olivia was silent, and Melanie knew she had her. She had actually out-argued the lawyer for the moment. Olivia was all about evidence-based beliefs, and now she found herself lacking evidence. She'd have to go get the sleeping bag in order to prove her point.

"Fine," Olivia finally said. "Josh and I will go back to the packs. If the sleeping bag is dry, I'll come back and we'll finish this hike together. If it's not . . . you're on your own."

Nineteen

STU-PID, STU-PID, STU-PID. With each stride, the word ran through Olivia's brain. Left, right. *Stu-pid.* Sometimes it was directed toward Melanie. Sometimes it was directed toward herself. Either way, it was an accurate description of both of them. Melanie was being reckless. She was being belligerent. Both of them were being stupid. And a bit selfish. Now that word took the place of *stupid* in her interior monologue, one syllable per step. *Sel-fish.*

"What do you get out of this?" she asked Josh, her tone almost accusatory.

"Pardon?" He slowed his pace and moved over as much as he could to allow her to come up almost beside him.

"Why are you walking nearly three miles you don't have to, to carry a load for someone you've only barely met, after watching her and her sister fight like children about whether or not they should cut a pointless trip short?"

"The trip doesn't seem pointless to me. Your sister said it was to reconnect."

"That's her reason, not mine."

"Then what's yours?"

"Ugh, stop changing the subject. I ask a question and you ask a question. Just answer. Why are you helping her?"

"I thought I was helping both of you."

"You're not. You're helping with her plans and hindering mine."

"See, but there's the reason for my question: I thought you shared those plans."

Olivia gave him a puzzled look.

"To reconnect."

She rolled her eyes. "Oh. No. That's not what this trip is about for me."

"Why not?"

She picked up the pace a bit. "I don't feel some gaping hole in my life that needs to be filled. She might, but I don't."

This was not entirely true. Olivia felt an enormous hole where her parents had been. But Melanie couldn't fill that. Nothing could.

Josh matched his stride to hers. "Why did you agree to the trip?"

"For two reasons. First, because Melanie is like glitter." Olivia wiggled her fingers in the air. "You know how you can never really get rid of glitter once it enters your house? That's what Mel is like. She's that one annoying Christmas card you pull out of the envelope that's just covered with glitter, and it gets all over the place and you're picking it off yourself until Easter. She just keeps calling and texting and emailing. I had to say yes to stop her."

Josh was smiling. Olivia wanted to be irritated by this, but he had a pleasant smile.

"And what's the second reason?" he said.

"Because I knew I'd have to plan it. I mean, I could have been nicer about it, but everything I said back there was true. She'd fall off a cliff if I wasn't watching her. She's too distracted for hiking in the wilderness. She doesn't pay attention to details. She thinks everything will just work itself out." She shook her head. "Probably just the natural result of her being the baby in the family."

"And you being the oldest."

Olivia shrugged. "I guess. She's always had someone watching out for her, and a lot of the time when we were young, that was me. If something happened to her, I was the one in trouble."

Josh grinned again. "Gee, I wonder how she has survived without you for nigh on a decade."

He was right. Melanie had survived. She'd made a lot of big decisions on her own: distributed an estate, sold a house, moved to a different city, created a career out of nothing but a lot of mumbo jumbo. Maybe Olivia wasn't giving her enough credit.

"What are your religious beliefs?" Josh asked.

"That's a super-weird-bordering-on-rude question to ask someone you just met."

"I only ask because of what you've been through with your parents. And it's pretty clear your sister believes in something."

"She believes in everything. Questions nothing. Just sucks it all in like a cosmic vacuum cleaner picking up all the junk out there."

"And you? What's your motto? Question everything, believe in nothing?"

"I definitely don't believe in God."

Josh glanced over. "Sure you do."

Olivia stopped walking. "Excuse me, but I think I know my own mind. I haven't believed for a long time."

He stopped and looked at her, a thoughtful turn to his mouth. "Let me ask you this: to what in your life do you devote the most time, effort, and passion?"

She didn't even have to think about the answer. "My job."

"And in what do you find your sense of self-worth? Where's that rooted?"

Olivia shrugged. "In my job, I guess."

"So if you do your job well and guilty people are convicted and serve their time, you've done a good job and you feel good about yourself."

"Right."

"What if they aren't convicted? What if you know without a doubt in your mind that someone is guilty, and they get off on some technicality, some procedural thing that went wrong? Then what?"

"I feel angry," she said.

"At what? The system? The jury?"

"Well, partly, I guess. But I'm upset with myself too because I always feel like there could have been something I missed or something I could have hit harder during questioning or cross-examination."

"So, your job is where you spend your time, energy, and passion, and when something goes wrong you feel like you're at fault and your sense of self-worth suffers?"

"Yes, I suppose that's accurate."

"Easy. Your job is your god. Or one of them. Let's try another."

Olivia started walking again. "I don't like this game."

Josh followed. "Who is the final arbiter of truth in your life?"

"What?" she threw over her shoulder.

"How do you decide if something is true?"

"I look at the evidence and use reason to deduce the truth."

"There's another one then. Reason. The human mind. Your own human mind. So, you. You are your god."

"I see what you're trying to do. Let's just say I don't believe in a higher power, some divine being out there puppet-mastering all of this. I believe in science. Observable fact. Nothing more. Nothing less."

"And yet you didn't trust me when you first met me. You hadn't observed anything about me, yet you made a judgment."

"That's not true. I observed that you were a man, and I deduced from what I know of men as a sex that you might be dangerous. That's completely reasonable. And, I'll add, I trust you more now than I did at first because I gathered more firsthand information about you as an individual—namely that you didn't steal anything from us or attack us when we were sleeping, and also you shared food with us. And gave us a compass—thanks for that, by the way."

Despite herself, Olivia was enjoying this conversation. She loved to argue. But arguing with Melanie was like trying to play tennis with a golden retriever. She could never get a good volley going. Josh, on the other hand, was a skilled partner. He had a lot to say and wasn't afraid to hit hard. It wasn't mansplaining—she'd had plenty of experience with that in both law school and the courtroom. It was more like talking to an expert witness who was confident that what he was saying was true and accurate to

200

the best of his knowledge, that it was true whether or not anyone else believed it.

This was also what was beginning to bother her about the whole thing. He was just as confident as she was. And they couldn't both be right.

"However, despite beginning to trust you, I don't entirely like you."

Josh laughed. "And why is that?"

"You have the irritating habit of not answering my questions even though I've answered a ton of yours."

He tipped his head to the side. "Or is it just that you don't like my answers?"

Olivia laughed then. "Nice try. You still have not answered my only real question, which is, what are you getting out of helping us? Besides, perhaps, not having our deaths on your conscience when you get back to civilization and read about two inept lady hikers gone missing in the wilds of the Porcupine Mountains."

He smiled. "I think maybe you've answered your own question." He pulled a hand out of his pocket and pointed at the two packs still leaning against the birch tree. "And don't be so conceited as to think you two are the first people I've put on the right path. I'm always looking for opportunities to do what my father would have me do."

"What does that mean?" Olivia knelt down by Melanie's pack and started pulling at the straps that held the sleeping bag in the stuff sack to the frame.

"My dad was a ranger in this park. His job was to prepare people for what they'd face, to give them the rules and enforce them. But he was also called upon to rescue them. To track down those who had strayed from the trail. Sometimes he had to physically carry people out to safety."

Olivia unsnapped the compression straps on the sack and pushed the tightly packed mummy bag out. "I guess that's why you're so comfortable out in the woods."

"And it's why I'm helping you. I do what he would want me to do."

Olivia unfurled the mummy bag and ran her hands over every inch of it, front and back. Then she shoved her arms inside and searched for wet spots. After a minute she groaned out loud. "Dang it."

Josh smiled down at her like he knew what she was going to say next.

"It's dry."

"I called the top bunk before we even got in the car this morning."

Olivia stood in the doorway, hands on hips, frowning up at Melanie, who was sitting cross-legged on the top bunk and hugging her once-white stuffed bear, Bruno.

"You had it last year," Melanie said, squeezing Bruno tighter.

"But I called it. You have to call it."

"Nuh-uh. It's my turn."

Olivia expelled a lungful of air and spun around. "Mom!"

Melanie lay down on her side and buried her nose in Bruno's matted fur. He smelled kind of bad, but in a good way. A way that reminded her of all their picnics outside, when she'd take him and a snack in the wagon up the sidewalk until she reached Mr. Barkley's house and lay a blanket out right by the chain-link fence that kept his rottweilers in. Mr. Barkley wasn't his real name—at least she didn't think so—but it was what she called him because of the dogs. She would sit there most summer afternoons with Bruno, passing bits of cheese and crackers through the fence and wiping the dog slobber off her fingers with the blanket.

Right now she had to pee. Bad. But she couldn't leave the top bunk if she hoped to keep it. They didn't have bunk beds at home, so their week renting the cabin on Lake Michigan each year was her only chance to sleep in one.

Olivia stomped back into the room. "Come on, Melanie."

Melanie smiled. Olivia hadn't quoted Mom saying anything. Which meant Mom either didn't care and wanted them to work it out themselves or that she was on Melanie's side.

"No, it's my turn," she said sweetly.

Olivia reached up and grabbed Bruno by a leg.

"Hey!" Melanie pulled him back.

Olivia yanked again and Bruno almost slipped out of Melanie's hands. She wrapped her arms around his squishy middle.

"I called it!" Olivia said, pulling harder.

Melanie felt herself being pulled to the edge of the bed. But she would not let go, she would not give in. She locked her teeth onto Bruno's ear like one of Mr. Barkley's rottweilers with a bone.

"Melanie!"

Olivia yanked once more, and Melanie felt herself going over the side. She was falling face-first to the cabin floor below. Then the room spun and she was looking at the ceiling. Her tailbone connected with the hardwood, then her back, but not her head. Olivia was standing next to her, one arm extended, rigid, eyes as wide as Melanie had ever seen them.

Bruno's ear still clenched between her teeth, Melanie took big breaths of air through her nose. Olivia pulled her arm back and knelt at Melanie's side.

"I'm sorry, I'm sorry, I'm sorry, I'm sorry," she kept saying.

Melanie sat up, dazed. She opened her mouth and scraped a few strands of Bruno's fur off her dry tongue.

"Are you okay?" Olivia said.

Her mother appeared in the door. "What happened?" Then she saw Melanie on the floor. "What happened?" she said again.

Olivia opened her mouth, but Melanie spoke up first. "I fell off the top bunk. Olivia was just helping me up." She stood and rubbed her backside.

"Oh my goodness, are you okay?" her mother asked, turning her around to inspect the damage.

"I'm fine," Melanie said.

"I think maybe you're not ready for the top bunk, sweetie," Mom said.

Melanie nodded. After a little more fussing, their mother left to finish unpacking. Melanie went to use the bathroom. When she came back in, Olivia was sitting on the bottom bunk with Bruno in her lap.

"Thanks," she said, holding the bear out to her sister.

Melanie nodded and took Bruno by the paw.

A few minutes later they were in their swimsuits. The afternoon flew by in a flurry of sandcastles and rock collecting and diving into the waves on the big lake. Then dinner and showers and a game of Sorry! Then it was bedtime. Melanie slipped under the covers of the bottom bunk and listened to Olivia trying to get comfortable on the top. Their parents came in for kisses and good nights. When they left, all was quiet except the sound of crickets through the open window.

Melanie tried to fall asleep, but Olivia kept moving around, making the bed shake and creak. Finally, Melanie saw her sister's legs silhouetted by the night-light, and Olivia dropped to the floor.

"Want to switch?" Olivia said.

"No, it's fine."

Olivia stood there for a moment. Melanie scooched back toward the wall and pulled back the covers. Olivia slipped in beside her and pulled the covers up over her shoulders. Their faces were inches apart, Bruno shoved into the space between them.

"Thanks for saving me," Melanie said.

"Huh?"

"Your arm. You flipped me on my way to the floor."

"Oh. Yeah. I didn't even think about it. It just happened."

"Well, thanks."

Olivia let out a little laugh. "I guess it's the least I could do. I did pull you off in the first place."

"Mom told you it was my turn, didn't she?"

Olivia sighed. "This bear smells terrible."

Melanie giggled and turned the other way, bringing Bruno with her.

"Next year," Olivia said from behind her. "Next year, it's yours."

Twenty

MELANIE PLACED ANOTHER broken branch on the fire and shifted it around with the stick Josh had been using. The tip flickered and smoked, and she dug it into the dirt as he had. She eyed the dwindling pile of sticks and logs with some measure of anxiety. She didn't want to use up all of the fuel, and she was afraid of leaving the fire untended to find some more. The thought of getting lost—again—kept her by the sputtering flames, giving them just enough of a nudge to keep going.

She kept checking her watch and then remembering for the twentieth, the thirtieth time that it wasn't working. How long had Olivia and Josh been gone? And when Josh finally returned, as she kept reassuring herself he would, would Olivia be with him? Or had she finally had it up to here with her little sister as she so often had when they were kids, when Melanie wasn't playing by the rules and Olivia would stomp off and leave her in the basement with a board game or on the lawn with their Barbies and model horses?

If she didn't come back, would it be weird to be here alone

with Josh, a strange man she'd only met the day before? If Olivia did come back, would that mean suffering through two more days of her bad attitude?

Melanie tried to reconcile the woman who had rushed to help her at the river with the one who had so thoroughly belittled her in front of a third party. But if she thought about it, of course that's how it had always been. Olivia the protective older sister had to take care of Melanie the flaky baby sister. Olivia the judgmental critic had to point out all the ways Melanie fell short of her expectations.

Why had Melanie wanted to see her so badly? She had been doing just fine on her own for years. She felt good about herself, mostly. She had plenty of friends and followers to connect with. She had Justin. Why had she invited Olivia back in—no, insisted, dragged her kicking and screaming—when Olivia had so clearly wanted nothing to do with her? When she would have been better off without her?

Right at that moment, Melanie decided that she hoped Josh would come back alone. She didn't want to see Olivia again— not on this trip and maybe not ever. Possibly when they were old ladies. But maybe not even then. Olivia could walk right out of the woods and catch a ride with some lunatic out on the road. She could pick up the car and . . .

Oh. It was her car though. Olivia wouldn't drive Melanie's car back home. She'd wait for her, probably at those little cabins they'd stayed in, and meet her at the trailhead a couple days later, all clean and snug and well rested, while Melanie would probably have to be practically carried out by Josh. And then Melanie would have to listen to her I-told-you-so's all the way back to the carpool lot in Indian River. Melanie would be rid of her for two days and then be stuck with her for at least eight hours with stops—more if they stayed somewhere overnight to break up the trip.

Melanie put another stick on the fire and poked at it. Why was having a sister so hard?

She checked her dead watch again. Then, voices. She strained her eyes toward the sound. Movement. A laugh. Olivia's. She saw them through the trees, Josh and Olivia, packs on, grinning and looking like an Eddie Bauer catalog. All they were missing was the wire hair fox terrier leaping after a stick. Melanie was simultaneously relieved and irritated. Relieved to see them—yes, even Olivia—but irritated that they seemed to be having such a good time together without her. That Olivia was having a good time at all.

Josh caught sight of her and waved. Then Olivia quieted down, as though she was what they had been talking and laughing about and now they had better hush up.

"Looks like you kept the fire going nicely," Josh said as they drew near. He removed Melanie's pack from his back and leaned it against a cedar tree. "Also looks like we're going to run out of wood before long, so I better scare up some more." He shared a look with Olivia, who nodded and took off her own pack, then he strode off into the trees.

"What was all that about?" Melanie said.

"What?" Olivia said.

"That little knowing glance."

Olivia made a face. "There was no glance."

"Mmm."

Olivia held out her hands in a "what gives?" gesture. "You're not happy to see me?"

"I didn't really think you'd bail."

"Well, anyway, it turns out the sleeping bag is fine. I kind of wish I'd taken the time to check it earlier. It would have saved a lot of stress. And walking." She busied herself removing the tent from her pack and beginning the ritual of unrolling and setting it up. "Want to give me a hand?"

Not especially, Melanie wanted to say, but she strove not to be a petty person. Pettiness was so often a factor in her clients' unhappiness. Not being able to let go of little snubs or unintended insults. She routinely gave out a mantra for people struggling with this smallness of spirit: *What I cannot free rules over me.* She'd read it years ago on the inside of a Dove dark chocolate wrapper. She needed to let go of the tiny seed of bitterness she'd allowed to burrow into the soil of her heart and instead embrace her sister's change of mind without suspicion or resentment.

She leaned over to take two corners of the tent and shook it out with Olivia, like shaking out the blanket onto the hide-a-bed for their long-ago sisters' sleepovers.

"I'm glad you're back," Melanie said. She was fairly certain she meant it. Because the Olivia who returned was not quite the Olivia who had walked away a little while ago. "So, what were you and Josh talking about when you got back? You actually looked like you were enjoying yourself."

Olivia smiled. "You know, I was. It's interesting. He must be our age or pretty near to it, and yet there's something about him that seems older. I don't know if it's the way he talks or what he talks about, or if it's just a result of him growing up out in the middle of nowhere up here—his father was a park ranger—but I don't know. That can't be it. He sounds too educated."

"That's kind of judgy—implying that it's surprising that someone raised up here wouldn't be educated."

"That's not what I mean, exactly. It's just . . . well, you'd know if you talked to him much."

"I guess I'll have plenty of time the next couple days."

Olivia pushed a tent peg into the ground. "Oh, I don't think it's really necessary to make him walk with us the rest of the way. He was just offering that as a favor if I didn't come back. We shouldn't hold him to that. He was just being a good guy."

"So let him be a good guy. I think it would be better with him. You looked like you were having a nice time when you walked up. What did you say you were talking about?"

"We were . . . well, I guess we were arguing more than talking."

"It didn't sound like an argument."

"It was. It was just . . . it was philosophical. It wasn't personal. He didn't flip out when I disagreed with him."

"Oh, I get it," Melanie said. "He wasn't *sensitive*."

"Exactly."

Melanie shoved a tent pole through a sleeve toward her sister. "Hey! Careful!"

"Don't take it personally."

Olivia rubbed her arm where the pole had hit her and bent down to guide it into place. "What is with you? I thought you'd be happy I came back and that I was getting along better with Josh, and here you're jabbing me with sticks."

"It was an accident."

"Sure it was."

Before Melanie could respond, Josh walked up with an arm-ful of wood. They put up the rest of the tent in silence. When it was done, Olivia reached into her pack, retrieved the skein of nylon rope, and tossed it at Melanie. Harder, Melanie thought, than she really needed to.

"What is this for?" she asked.

"Clothesline."

Melanie stomped around the campsite for a moment looking for a suitable spot, then began tying one end to a tree branch.

"Not there," Olivia said. "Closer to the lake."

Melanie glared at her and walked to the side of the site that was closest to Lake Superior, then started to wrap the rope around the trunk of a sapling.

"No, I mean way closer," Olivia said. "Like as close as you can get to the edge of the woods. Where there's lots of wind."

Melanie spun around. "Perhaps you would like to do it?"

Olivia approached with her hand held out. "Sure."

Melanie shoved the rope into her hand.

"And I'll just take your pack too so I can hang up all your clothes for you," Olivia said as she lifted the pack onto her back. "Maybe by the time I get back, you can have the beds made in the tent. Can you handle that?"

Melanie's face burned as she realized that off in the periphery, Josh had seen this whole childish exchange. "Fine," she said.

When Olivia was out of sight, she threw the pads and bags through the open tent door. Then she followed them in and zipped the door shut behind her. Sitting cross-legged on the cold, hard ground, Melanie whisper-screamed into her hands and then punched a sleeping bag. She felt just like she had when she was twelve and Olivia had embarrassed her in front of the neighbor boys when they were playing Truth or Dare. Olivia had dared her to French-kiss one of them, and Melanie thought that a French kiss was licking another person's mouth because Olivia had told her it was kissing with your tongue. She couldn't look Kyle Wilson in the eye for years.

"Knock knock," came Josh's voice from outside the tent. "You okay?"

"Yeah."

A pause. "You sure?"

"Yeah, I'm fine, Josh." She started unrolling the sleeping pads as if to prove that she was indeed okay. Would someone who was not okay be able to inflate two long blue rectangles? She took a deep breath and began to blow into one of the valve stems.

"Listen," Josh continued, "Olivia and I talked a bit about your parents' accident on the way back."

What? She had talked to Josh, a complete stranger, rather than her sister?

"I think maybe she's ready to talk to you about it. She just doesn't really want to argue about the afterlife stuff at this point."

Melanie stopped blowing. "Is that so? Is that what she was talking to you about? 'The afterlife stuff'?"

"A bit."

"And I suppose you don't believe in anything either? Is that why you're telling me this?"

Josh unzipped the tent door partway. "No. I'm telling you this because she was ready to talk to you when we got back, but then you started picking at each other like children. I thought you said you wanted to reconnect. It's just, this doesn't seem like reconnecting, is all," he said. Then he zipped the door shut.

Melanie could hear his footsteps head off toward the lake. She finished blowing up the sleeping pads and unrolled the bags. He was right, and it annoyed her. Why was she suddenly shooting herself in the foot just when it seemed Olivia might be taking a few steps to meet her in the middle? She needed her journal so she could try to make sense of her jumbled thoughts.

Her journal! Had it gotten wet when she fell in the river? And where was her phone? It had been in her pants pocket.

She stumbled out of the tent to find that she was alone again. How long did it take to hang up some wet clothes? Was Olivia out there reading her journal? Going through her texts to Justin?

As much as she didn't want to leave the warmth of the fire, she could not stand idly by while Olivia pried into her personal life. Melanie would have to tell her what was going on eventually. But in her own way, at the right time.

And this was not the right time.

Twenty-One

OLIVIA SNAPPED A PAIR of Melanie's leggings in the air and laid them over the makeshift clothesline she'd strung between a quaking aspen and a dying white birch tree. The wind off the lake blew them back toward the forest like a flag. It was the last of the clothes in the pack, but not the last of the casualties of Melanie's fall. Olivia had found her phone in a pocket. She took the battery out and arranged the pieces of the phone on a wide, flat stone to dry. It might power on later, or it might not. But even if Melanie had to get a new phone, she'd likely still have all her pictures on the card or in the cloud somewhere.

The thing that she knew Melanie's heart would break over was the journal. If she'd used a pencil it would have been fine. The pages would have dried wrinkled, but they'd still be readable. But she'd used pen, and all along the outside margins her loopy cursive letters bled together into an illegible mass. It was like their relationship. Like someone had been writing their story, and some dumb accident, a momentary shift in balance, had wrecked it. No amount of wishing could undo it.

"How's it going out here?" Josh's voice hit her ear like a soft breeze.

Olivia lifted her head from where she crouched over the journal. "Okay, I guess." She held up the journal. "This will never be the same."

Josh took the book from her as she stood. He riffled the damp pages and shook his head. "That's a shame."

"She's going to be really upset about it."

Josh handed the journal back to Olivia. She turned a few pages.

"There are some in the middle that didn't get it too bad. She might be able to read some of it and figure out what she was saying." Opening to a page, Olivia caught sight of her own name. She shut the book before she could read any more—not because she wasn't curious about what Melanie was saying about her but because she was. She deliberately placed the book on the rock next to the pieces of Melanie's phone.

She felt the corner of a T-shirt flapping on the clothesline. "Do you think this will be enough?"

Josh felt the leggings. "Should be. It's good she brought pants other than jeans. Denim takes forever to dry."

"Probably we should have gotten hiking-specific clothing that dries super fast. I could have done that. I don't know why I wasn't prepared for something like this."

"You can't be prepared for everything."

"You can try," Olivia said.

Josh regarded her with a thoughtful twist to his mouth. "And that's what you normally do, isn't it? You want to be ready for anything."

216

"Doesn't everyone? No one likes being caught off guard."

"Always being on guard against what *might* happen to you seems like kind of an exhausting way to live. When you block out the possibility of bad surprises, don't you lose the possibility of good surprises too?"

"You sound like Melanie."

Josh laughed. "She may be onto something there. Let me ask you this: when's the last time you were pleasantly surprised by something or someone?"

Olivia bit the inside of her lip a moment. "When we found you. Both times, I guess."

"Okay. And you wouldn't have had those pleasant surprises if you hadn't had a couple things go wrong, right?"

"If we hadn't had those accidents, we wouldn't have needed your help at all. You would have been just another person on the trail. Actually, we wouldn't have even crossed paths because we would have made our campsite that night while you were still out on the river fishing. You would have been inconsequential."

Josh sat on the rock next to Melanie's journal. "But you did have those accidents. You did get lost and we did cross paths."

"So? If we hadn't lost the trail, it would have made no difference if we never met at all."

"How do you know that? Can you see every contingency into the infinite future? How do you know you weren't meant to meet me all along?"

Olivia put her hands on her hips. "Because nothing is *meant*. Not in the sense you're using the word. I thought we'd been over this already."

"All right. Let's look at this from a different angle. Cause and effect. Do you think you and Melanie would have had all the same conversations you've had in the past couple days if you hadn't gotten off the trail? Would you have even had the same thoughts in your own mind if everything had gone according to your plan?"

"Of course not. I will allow that my thoughts and our conversations were affected by what happened."

"You might say they were *effected* by it. Caused, not just influenced."

Olivia tipped her head in concession. "Perhaps. But the fact that there is a cause and an effect doesn't mean there is a mind behind the cause. Every part of the planet might be said to eventually affect every other part of it, but that doesn't require a mind or a will. There are laws of nature that behave in predictable ways that are interacting with one another." Josh opened his mouth, and Olivia rushed on. "And don't give me that crap about an ultimate cause or an unmoved mover. I've heard that argument before."

He closed his mouth and smiled. "And you avoid talking about it because you've already decided it doesn't fit into your worldview."

Olivia shook her head. "Don't pretend like you know my inner thoughts. Don't think that because I told you a little bit about my life, you somehow have any authority to say anything about it."

Josh didn't respond. Just kept smiling that knowing smile. Who did he think he was? Pretending to know what she was thinking. She was trying to think of what else to say to get that look off his face, to jab him like she jabbed unreliable witnesses on the stand, when he stood and brushed off the back of his pants.

"I've got wood to carry and fish to fry," he said. "I'll see you back at the campsite."

Olivia watched him disappear into the trees, then squatted down to rummage through Melanie's pack again even though she knew there was nothing else in there. A moment later she heard footsteps coming up the path.

"Look, I don't want to talk about it anymore, all right?" she said without looking up.

"Well, excuse me," came Melanie's voice. "I was just coming to see if you needed any help."

Olivia stood. "Sorry, I didn't mean you. I thought you were Josh."

"Oh." Melanie glanced at the full clothesline. "Do you need any help?"

"No. All done."

"Okay."

They stared awkwardly at each other for a moment.

"Hey, did you see my phone anywhere?" Melanie said.

Olivia pointed to the rock. "I didn't try to power it on. It needs to dry out first."

"My journal!" Melanie snatched up the book and cast Olivia a suspicious glance.

"I didn't read it. It's unreadable anyway."

Melanie opened it and frantically flipped through the pages. "No! No, no, no!"

"I'm sorry, Mel."

"I had something really important recorded in this one." She sat down hard on the rock. "Now it's gone. All of what happened, all I felt about it."

Olivia said nothing, and she especially did not say that this wouldn't have happened if Melanie had put the journal in a plastic bag as directed.

Melanie dropped the journal on the ground and put her face in her hands.

Olivia sat down and put an arm around her shoulders. "You still know it happened though, right?" she tried. "You still know how you felt."

"Right now, maybe. But what about twenty years from now? I'm not going to remember it as clearly."

"Gosh. Twenty years? What's so important you want to remember it perfectly twenty years from now?"

Melanie's teary eyes met hers for just a moment, then she looked at the journal on the ground. "Nothing." She straightened her back and stared out at the lake, her limp curls blown back from her blotchy face by the wind. "This trip sucks."

Olivia laughed. "Yes. Yes it does." She rubbed Melanie's back. "But we're going to finish it anyway. Who knows? Maybe it'll get better."

"It's gotta be all uphill from here, right?"

"Sure. I mean, yes, literally it's basically all uphill from here because Lake Superior is the lowest elevation in the park."

"Oh, Ollie," Melanie said, giving her a half-playful shove. "You're the worst sometimes."

Olivia smiled. "I know. It's an art, really—exasperating people." She stood up. "Speaking of which, did you see Josh when you came out here?"

"No. You exasperated him?"

"Other way around. He's apparently imperturbable."

"What were you two talking about?"

"This and that. How I'm too concerned about being prepared for every contingency and how I'm suppressing evidence of a god to fit my own agenda. Your standard light conversational fare for someone you've just met."

Melanie laughed. "I swear I didn't put him up to that."

"Right."

"Honestly. I'm just glad you weren't out here talking about me."

"Oh, Melanie. You're not as interesting a topic of conversation as you think you are." She pulled Melanie to her feet and handed her the food bag from her pack. "Come on. Let's go eat dinner. We can come back for this stuff later."

They started up the path.

"First thing I'm going to eat when we get out of these woods is a giant burrito smothered in cheese and sour cream," Olivia said.

"That actually does sound kind of good," Melanie admitted.

"Well, get your own. I'm not sharing."

Twenty-Two

MELANIE PICKED THROUGH the contents of her food bag. When she'd chosen this stuff at the grocery store, she'd been excited to eat it. Now it was just a random jumble of disparate items that had no business being in the same bag. Like the weird off-brand Halloween candy left, sad and unloved, in a plastic pumpkin come December. Not one thing looked like it could satisfy her hunger. These were snacks, not meals. She'd just been snacking all this time. She needed something substantial.

Next to her the firelight flickered across the pale pink flesh of the trout on Olivia's makeshift pita-bread plate. Josh had caught and grilled up two small fish: one for Olivia and one for himself. When he'd extracted the pita bread from the bag in his pack, Melanie noted there were only five pieces. That would leave only three after tonight, and Josh had said he was staying in the woods at least one more night, with a long hike back to the car after that. She couldn't very well ask him for a piece. So she sat silently by the fire, muscling down another protein bar and wishing she was in her kitchen at home.

Nothing was going right. She'd been a fool to think a ten-year rift could be solved in just a few days. To think that Olivia's heart of stone would soften if she could just say the right words and pull on the right heartstrings. Nothing short of a divine act could make that happen.

Now her journal, her backup plan, was destroyed. If she was going to tell Olivia about what was going on in her life, she'd have to say it out loud. And even though she'd practiced saying it in the bathroom mirror in the days leading up to this trip, she was never confident she'd be able to get the words out of her throat when the time came.

Melanie felt herself slipping into a pit, like she'd slipped on those rocks in the river. She was going down, not into cold, rushing water but into a still, dank darkness she knew all too well. She closed her eyes and tried to focus on something else. The cool air at her back. The heat from the fire on her face. The feel of the ground beneath her feet. The sound of leaves dropping from the trees. The physical world. But the most physical thing she felt at that moment was still the gnawing hunger in her gut.

All at once she became aware of Josh standing beside her, extending a pita that cradled several large chunks of cooked fish.

"What? No," she said by reflex. "I'm—"

"You're hungry," Josh said.

"I have plenty."

"So do I."

"No," she said, shaking her head. "Then you won't have enough."

"I always have enough, and then some," he said, offering it again to her.

This time Melanie took it. She knew these fish were not her

parents. She'd always known it, she realized. They had not come back as animals of some kind, or even other people. She knew it as plainly as she knew that it would never be the right time to tell Olivia about Justin. That she just needed to get it over with. She lifted the fish to her mouth and took a bite, savoring the taste, remembering the big family meals they'd had with their parents. Then she swallowed it down and stared hard at the fire.

"Justin asked me to marry him."

She winced as she said it, as though expecting a blow. But nothing happened. Nothing was said. She risked a glance at her sister. Olivia was staring at her. Glaring at her. Lips slightly parted, fire dancing in her eyes.

"I haven't told him anything yet."

Melanie didn't want to hear the kinds of things Olivia was undoubtedly lining up in her brain to shout out at any moment. All of the anger that was building up inside of her. Even so, she wished she'd get it over with. The silence was somehow worse.

"I said I needed to talk to you first."

At that, Olivia stood up and threw the pita bread with the fish to the ground. "You're sick," she spit out. "You're seriously sick. How have you let him gaslight you like this? Are you out of your mind? Or are you just stupid?"

Olivia's words fell like hailstones on Melanie's battered spirit, and she felt herself shrinking beneath them.

"What am I supposed to say to you right now?" Olivia continued. "What did you think I would say? 'Oh, hey, that's great, sis, congratulations, when's the big day'? 'If only Dad was alive so he could walk you down the aisle'?" Her voice rose another register. "He's the reason Dad will never walk you down the aisle! He's the reason Mom will never cry joyful tears on your wedding day! He's the reason I couldn't stand to talk to you or even look at you for the past ten years! And now you're going to marry him?"

"I didn't say I was going to—"

"The fact that you're close enough to him that he would even dream of asking you that question—it's just unbelievable! I knew you moved up there to be near him. I knew it! I knew where he went when he left Rockford. And then a couple months later you move up there too and you think I'm not going to figure it out?"

Olivia took a few sharp steps away from the fire, then turned around and came back, stopping at Melanie's feet, looming over her like a vulture over a deer carcass on the side of the road.

"If you thought I was done with you before, you have no idea what you're in for now. When I get into my car in Indian River, that will be the last time you see me. Ever. Understand? I don't want to have anything to do with you ever again."

Olivia stalked off to the tent and zipped herself up into it. Melanie crumpled. Hot tears stung her chapped cheeks. Her breath came in choking gasps. She felt the pita bread with the fish on it being removed from her hand. Josh settled down next to her on the log and put an arm around her shoulders. It felt like her heart was imploding, like it was being sucked in on itself until it was a single small, hard piece of gravel stuck in the wall of her chest.

How was it that this was both exactly what she'd expected and yet simultaneously so much worse? How could she have imagined for one moment that Olivia would give her a chance to explain herself? To explain that no one in the world understood her as well as Justin did. That no one knew her sorrow like he did. That he was so, so sorry for the pain he had caused in both their lives. That he'd agonized over it. That he'd considered suicide, even going so far as to plan it out and write a note. That he credited her forgiveness with stopping him from taking his own life. That he'd finally found his peace with God and realized that his life was still worth something. That while he could never undo what he had done, he could move forward.

But Olivia would never listen to all of that. She didn't want to forgive. She'd wanted him to stand trial all those years ago for manslaughter, but no one else in the family agreed. No charges were filed, and she'd never forgiven them for it.

Slowly, Melanie ran out of tears. She wiped her eyes and nose on the sleeve of Olivia's jacket, only realizing then that she was wearing it. She looked up at Josh, embarrassed by how long she had been in his arms, embarrassed by the spectacle he'd just witnessed, feeling she owed him some sort of explanation but knowing she didn't have the energy to offer one.

He rubbed her upper arm and let out a breath. "You want to borrow my hammock tonight?"

In spite of herself, Melanie managed a laugh. "Yes." She sniffed. "But no. Of course not."

"Why 'of course not'?"

"Then you'd have nowhere to sleep."

"I'd sleep in the tent."

"With Olivia?"

"Presumably, yes." Josh stood and tossed the remains of Olivia's discarded food into the fire. "I think at this point, between the two of us, she'd rather have me in there, right?"

Melanie stood. "I guess." She brushed off the back of her pants.

Josh reached for her food bag. "I'll take care of all of this. Why don't you head down to the beach and see if your stuff is dry?" He fished a compact flashlight out of his pocket and tossed it to her. "It'll be getting dark soon."

Wrong, Melanie thought. Things were clearly already as dark as they could get.

She started down the path that led to the lake, still trying to regulate her breathing after her sob session. It had been six months or more since she'd cried that big for that long, and at the moment she was having trouble recalling what the last one was all about. With her journal destroyed, she wasn't sure if she'd ever remember.

Why hadn't she listened and put everything in plastic bags as instructed? Why was Olivia always right? Was she right about Justin too? She certainly knew him better than Melanie did. All of the personal revelations over the years — about his family issues, his problems in school, his years of dabbling in drugs — Olivia had already known all of it and never divulged any of it to Melanie. She'd kept Justin's secrets for him. It was what best friends did, after all.

When they'd found out that it had been Justin driving the other car, Melanie expected Olivia to show at least some concern for him. Instead, she'd burned him out of her life for good, just as it seemed she was now ready to do to her own sister. How could Melanie ever hope to have a relationship with someone who allowed no room for mistakes, no room for repentance?

The rocky shoreline of Lake Superior was littered with blobs of black and gray and blue. Her clothes, blown off the line and now strewn along the beach. She crisscrossed the stones, snatching up pants and shirts and sports bras, hoping she'd manage to get it all, hoping that a hiker would not stumble upon a pair of her underwear at some later date. The task took her far enough afield that she lost track of the clothesline and the large flat rock that held her journal and the pieces of her cell phone.

She scanned the trees for the line of rope. When would she ever stop getting herself lost?

Her arms full of clothes, she stumbled over the wave-rounded stones, willing herself in the right direction. Or what she thought might be the right direction. It did cross her mind that if she were out here long enough, Josh would eventually come looking and find her. But she didn't want to be found. She wanted to find her own way.

What she needed was to start thinking like Olivia. She stopped walking. The wind blew her limp hair across her face, and she noted the direction. If her clothes had been blown off the line, that was the direction they would have gone, and she'd already gathered them all up, so she started walking the other way down the beach, sticking near the trees, scanning up and down. Twenty or so yards ahead a flash of white caught her eye. The ink-stained pages of her journal flapping in the wind.

She quickened her pace. There was her phone in pieces on the rock, the clothesline hanging rather limp between two trees, and her pack, blending in with the general brownish-green of a nearly denuded shrub. She folded her clothes haphazardly with no regard for what was clean and what was dirty. At this point in the hike, did it really matter? The second a clean article of

228

clothing touched her body, it would be dirty. She zipped up the pack and put her cell phone back together but resisted the urge to try powering it up. Maybe tomorrow.

Lastly, she picked up her journal. The pages were mostly dry but so wrinkled she couldn't close the book all the way. Was it even worth taking? Melanie almost left it on the rock before remembering Olivia's reaction to the trash in the fire ring and her "leave no trace" rule. She'd bring it with her and find some appropriate way to dispose of it later.

She sat down on the rock and stared out at the lake. The wind was dying down and the sky was dimming. Melanie hugged herself tightly against the cold. What would it be like to see Olivia the next morning? Would she even talk to her? Look at her? Would Josh have to be their go-between and mediator for the rest of the hike? That at least might make things tolerable. Then there'd be the long, agonizing drive back to Olivia's car.

And after that? Nothing? If she told Justin yes, certainly. But what if she told him no? Could Olivia get over the fact that she'd even considered marrying him? She'd have to choose: Justin or her sister. Or had she already lost her sister for good?

Melanie stood up. It was time to get back to the campsite.

She was buckling the straps of her pack when she noticed something being pushed up onto the shore by the waves. More trash. She picked it out of the water, turned it over, and laughed out loud. The Universe certainly had a sense of humor.

Twenty-Three

OLIVIA HAD ENTERED a nightmare and couldn't wake up.

Justin? Justin Navarro? Did the man have some sort of sick fascination with destroying her? If he'd followed Melanie to Petoskey, she'd have to say the answer was a definite yes. But it was Melanie who had followed him. He must have manipulated her somehow. Starting with the day of the funeral when he'd shown up at the cemetery in a new car that had to be driven by someone else because his license had been suspended. A day he knew she would be vulnerable to emotional exploitation. But marriage? That was too far. That was sick and twisted and spiteful. It was clearly designed to hurt her.

Olivia knew the accident had been just that—an accident. Unplanned. Unfortunate. But Justin knew her well enough to know she'd have no sympathy for him. Who could?

Melanie.

Simple, trusting Melanie. If he couldn't have Olivia, he'd have Melanie.

"He's your oldest friend," Melanie had said that horrible day when she'd called to tell Olivia she'd forgiven Justin. "Don't you think he's sorry?"

"Sorry? Sorry is something you say when you miss someone's birthday or shut a door in their face! Sorry is for breaches of etiquette, not manslaughter!" she'd screamed at the phone as her college roommate looked on, eyes wide and jaw slack. "You can't be friends with someone after they kill your parents!"

And now ten years later she was forced to have the same basic conversation. Marriage? How could Melanie do this to her? To the memory of their parents, which she so obviously tried to honor in the most ridiculous ways. Or was that all a ruse? Just a way for her to get sympathy and attention from other people? How often had she trotted out her personal grief in front of her followers and subscribers so she could get their thumbs-ups and their trite little messages of fake encouragement?

Olivia felt like she was going to throw up, though there was nothing in her stomach to come out. She hadn't had a chance to take one bite of Josh's fish before Melanie sprang this insanity on her. Now they were out there together. Melanie undoubtedly crying, Josh undoubtedly offering a shoulder to cry on. And what did she have? Why should Melanie get comfort while she got nothing?

"Hello?" came Josh's voice from just outside the tent. "Olivia?"

"Go away." She listened. No footsteps. "I said go away."

"How do you know I haven't?"

"I mean it."

"Yeah, here's the thing though," Josh said, undaunted. "Melanie is going to sleep in my hammock tonight."

"So?"

A slight pause, then, "So I'm wondering if it's okay to bunk with you."

"No."

"I don't snore. Much."

"I said no."

Olivia could hear Josh shifting positions, and when he next spoke, the sound was closer to her ear, as close as that bear's breath had been.

"Would you rather have Melanie in there with you tonight?"

"I'd rather have no one in here with me tonight."

Josh sighed. "I know. But here we are."

Olivia sat up and rubbed her burning eyes. "Fine. But no talking."

"Thanks."

"Wait. What do you sleep in?"

"I thought I'd try a sleeping bag."

She unzipped the inside of the tent door so she could look at him through the screen. "I mean on your person."

"T-shirt and shorts?"

"That'll do." Olivia zipped the window shut again. "Just stay out there until I say, all right?"

"Right."

Olivia unzipped the door enough to reach into her pack and get her pj's. She peeked through the small opening for Melanie, but she was nowhere to be seen. She thought of her sister's clothes and cell phone and wrecked journal on the beach and almost told Josh to remind her to get them. Then she didn't. Let her remember her own stuff. If she didn't, that was her problem.

Ten minutes later the light was dimming outside, and Olivia zipped herself into her mummy bag.

"You can come in now."

Silence. Hushed voices. The sound of a long zipper twenty feet away where the hammock hung. Then footsteps. Josh unzipped the tent and carefully climbed over her in the twilight. He leaned over her to zip the door up again, then took a moment to slide into Melanie's mummy bag and zip himself up into it. Olivia could hear his soft, regular breathing. As directed, he didn't speak.

Olivia tried to settle into the silence. Tried not to think of the fact that she was now sharing her tent with a strange man she'd stumbled upon in the woods. Tried not to think of her sister out in Josh's hammock, exposed to whatever dangers might lurk outside the tent. What if the bear came back? What if there really was a cougar?

She twisted in the mummy bag, but no position was comfortable. Her back hurt, her feet hurt, her hip hurt. The silence was so loud. She had to get her arms out or she was going to lose it. She contorted and pulled at the zipper, but it didn't budge. She sighed and pulled harder, but the stupid slidey thing would not move along the teeth. She grunted and sighed again and waited for Josh to ask her what was wrong.

"Hey," she finally said.

He shifted but said nothing.

"Can you unzip this thing? It's stuck, and I feel like I'm in a straightjacket."

She heard his own zipper and felt him moving in the almost black next to her. His hands found the zipper, manipulated it a moment, and pulled it down from the spot near her left cheek to just above her elbow. She stuck an arm out and let out her breath.

"Thank you."

Josh zipped himself back up.

"You can talk, you know," she said. "I mean, not a lot. But you can say things like 'sure' and 'you're welcome.'"

"Just trying to follow the rules," he said. "I know this is an imposition, and a good houseguest knows how to make himself invisible."

They were both quiet a moment. Olivia tried to fall asleep. But she wasn't tired.

"I'm sorry you had to witness that," she said. "You'd understand if you knew the history here. But it was bad manners anyway, to fight like that in front of you."

"Not that it's any of my business, but—"

"Oh, I know you won't let that stop you."

Josh laughed. "But I kind of got the idea that your sister was talking about the guy who caused your parents' accident?"

"Bingo."

"Hmm."

Olivia waited for more, but Josh said nothing else.

"Am I out of line here?" she challenged. "Thinking maybe my sister shouldn't marry the guy who killed our parents?"

"Well, no, maybe not. It's certainly not the normal way people might get together."

"Don't joke about this, okay? If you want to sleep in this tent and not outside on the ground with the wild animals, you will not joke about this."

"Loud and clear," he said.

Olivia took a deep breath. "It's worse than that. The guy was my best friend all through elementary, junior high, and high school. And then I went to college and he didn't. I was going to be a lawyer and he was going to be a mechanic. And whatever, that's fine. I have no problem with that. But he kept telling me I'd changed and I was too serious, and he was all jealous that I was meeting new friends and new guys at school. We had a big fight when I was home one summer. Then I went back to school. A week later I'm on a Labor Day weekend hiking trip with my college friends, and he takes a blind corner too fast and hits my parents' car. Flipped it over down an embankment."

She paused to tamp down the emotion that was starting to manifest itself in her voice.

"Then Melanie calls me to say they've been having dinner together and hanging out, and oh, by the way, she's forgiven him? And she acts like I'm supposed to be okay with that and like I'm supposed to forgive him too."

She paused so that Josh could interject some appropriate word, like "Wow" or "Seriously?" or "That's ridiculous!" But still he said nothing.

"Then she forces me on this trip so she can corner me with the fact that Justin asked her to marry him? And she somehow expects me to give her permission or my blessing or some such nonsense. So you can see, she's the one who's out of line here, not me."

Silence.

"Right?"

Silence.

"Say something, man. Anything."

Josh's voice emerged from the darkness on the other side of the tent. "That's tough."

Olivia waited for more.

"That's it?" she said. "'That's tough'?"

"It is. What do you want me to say?"

She sat up. "That it's ridiculous. That it's insane. That clearly this guy just gets off on manipulating women's emotions and that he couldn't have a more willing victim than my supremely naïve sister, who believes everything that's ever said to her so long as she can put a positive spin on it."

"I'm not going to say any of that."

Olivia expelled a little puff of exasperation. "Why not? It's true."

Josh unzipped his bag again and sat up. "You don't really want to hear what I think."

"Yes, I do," Olivia said, though she wasn't sure she meant it.

"Look, clearly there is a complicated history here. There's a lot of hurt. Real hurt. It's totally valid that you're angry. But have you ever looked at it from his point of view?"

Olivia bit her tongue to keep from shouting at Josh to get out of the tent.

"If you were friends that long, he must have known your family, known your parents. Right?"

"Yeah."

"Spent a lot of time at your house? Maybe even at your table?"

"Yes," she conceded. Indeed, their house had been a second home to him, especially when his parents were going through a nasty divorce.

"So—and I'm not saying this to diminish your pain in any way—he lost your parents too. And he had the double burden of being the cause of that loss."

This was irritatingly similar to what Melanie had said to her on the phone all those years ago. And what her friend-but-maybe-someday-hopefully-more Eric had said later that year which drove a wedge between them, leading to the end of their relationship before it even had a chance to begin. What her roommate had said, propelling her to find her own apartment.

Four witnesses, all with the same story.

But she couldn't be wrong about this. This was easy, wasn't it? This was a crime that had never been paid for. This was the scales of justice all out of balance. Did people just expect her to forgive him?

"It's hard, I know," Josh said. "Don't think I haven't had to forgive plenty of people who didn't actually deserve forgiveness. I mean, at the end of the day, who does? Everyone falls short. Everyone crosses lines. Everyone makes mistakes. Sometimes restitution can be made and sometimes it can't. Justin can't bring your parents back, so you'll never be satisfied with any length or intensity of punishment for him. There's no such thing as justice in a case like that. Unless you think he should be executed. Life for a life. That would be a certain kind of justice."

"I didn't say that," Olivia said. "Obviously I don't think he should be executed. It was an accident. I know that. But is it so wrong for me to want him to stay out of my life? Out of my sister's life?"

"Probably not. But you can't live your sister's life for her. You've got one life to live. Yours."

Olivia sighed and lay back down. Her arm was cold. Her chest was cold. Her heart was cold. And sad. And lonely. "I can't do this. I just can't do this anymore."

She felt Josh's warm hand on her shoulder. "You don't have to."

She shrugged it off. "What is that supposed to mean? Just let it go? Pretend it's not happening? Live in some delusion like my sister? A problem doesn't just solve itself if you ignore it."

"Did I say you should ignore it?"

"Well, no. But . . . I don't even know what you said. 'You don't have to.' Don't have to what?"

Josh took a deep breath and let it out. "Let me ask you this: have you been carrying your pack around in the woods for three days?"

"Obviously, yes."

"Have you been carrying your sister's pack?"

"I carried it some of the way."

"The same time you were carrying your own pack?"

"No, that would be practically impossible."

"Why?"

"Because it would be too heavy." She almost added "duh" but refrained. "What's your point?"

"I think you just made it."

Olivia sat with that for a moment. "Has anyone ever told you you're super annoying?"

"I have my detractors, yes." Josh chuckled. "But when people take the time to get to know me, they generally come around to see that I only have their best interest at heart."

Olivia sighed. "I don't know why you care at all. You just met us. You've been stuck sharing your food and watching us act like jerks to one another. And after a day or two that will be it—you'll never see or hear from us again."

"I hope that's not true," Josh said as he settled back down into his sleeping bag. "I'm kind of fond of you two."

She scoffed. "We've certainly done nothing to endear ourselves to you."

"It's nothing you've done, that's for sure," he quipped. "It's just who you are."

Olivia thought for a moment. Who was she, anyway? Apart from what she did. And if she met herself somewhere along the way, would she want to be her friend? Would she even give herself a second glance? She couldn't avoid the fact that the answer was a resounding no.

"Josh?"

"Hmm?"

"Why are you so nice?"

Josh yawned. "Just my nature, I guess."

"I wish I was nicer," she admitted.

"Well, practice makes perfect, as they say."

"Yeah."

"Good night, Olivia."

"Good night."

A moment later, Olivia heard Josh's breathing deepen and slow in sleep. She lay in the dark, trying to unravel a decade of sadness and anger and resentment, trying to discover what she was without that tangle of bitterness squeezing in on all sides. She couldn't carry both her pack and Melanie's. Carrying just her own load was exhausting enough.

As she drifted off to sleep, the thought occurred to her that it would be nice if there was a God after all. Someone who could deal with the justice that needed meting out so she didn't have to. Someone who would carry the load once in a while. Someone who would calm her spirit and challenge her intellect and just be there alongside her in the dark.

Maybe someone like Josh.

Twenty-Four

MELANIE HAD LAIN AWAKE half the night. Though she was warm enough and far more comfortable in the hammock than she had been on the hard ground, she couldn't get her brain to turn off after Josh went into the tent. For a while she could hear voices murmuring in the dark, though she could not make out any words. She could imagine what Olivia was saying. Melanie only hoped her sister hadn't won Josh to her side.

As they went about their morning tasks, she tried to read his face and his mannerisms. Had anything changed? Did she detect a bit more brusqueness? A little less eye contact? Or were those her own doing as she looked down at the ground and answered questions or responded to comments with as few syllables as possible?

They ate breakfast in shifts as sleeping bags, tents, and hammocks were packed, water was filtered, and teeth were brushed. Olivia never looked at her, never handed her anything, never spoke. When they started down the trail, Olivia took the lead, with Josh next and Melanie bringing up the rear. So angry, Mel thought, that Olivia couldn't even bear to look at her back.

The wind was cold and the sky still clouded as they walked along the lakeshore. A gull hovered silently over the water in an invisible air current, body quivering, wing dipping slightly to stay balanced. Waves reached their fingers onto the shore and rattled the rocks, knocking stone on stone, wearing each other down bit by bit. Melanie squatted awkwardly under her pack, picked up two stones, and rubbed them together. They looked almost identical. But if one was comprised of harder minerals than the other, that would be the one to survive the eons of constant clashing. The softer one would succumb, grain by grain, until nothing was left of it but some sand scattered by the wind.

Melanie tossed the stones into the lake one at a time.

Their party soon hit the mouth of the Big Carp River where it drained into Lake Superior. The trail came to a bridge crossing and made a sharp right to follow the river upstream.

"That's our turn," Josh called up to Olivia. They were the first words anyone had spoken in an hour.

They crossed the bridge and picked up the Big Carp River Trail on the other side. This path would take them inland — away from the lake, away from the cold north wind, and ever closer to the end of their hike and the beginning of the drive home. Olivia had originally planned for one more night on the trail, but Melanie was sure that once they reached the parking lot at the Lake of the Clouds, they'd be hitching a ride the rest of the way to the car.

For the next half mile, the river rambled over rocks to Melanie's right, but the sound held no pleasure for her. Where just a couple days ago she had stopped and leaned in close to hear what a creek had to say to her, now she was sure she was utterly deaf to such things. After years of reading signs and messages in everything, Melanie felt like a sojourner in a foreign land where she didn't speak the language. The rustle of the leaves, the call of a bird, the whisper of the breeze—she could interpret none of it. Maybe the Universe wasn't trying to speak to her through these things. Maybe the Universe wasn't sending hawks into her skies. Maybe they were all just vultures. Maybe there was no Universe at all. Just a universe. An infinite black void made up of nothing more than chemical reactions, where life was an accident. Just as death sometimes was.

Maybe her parents weren't out there somewhere. Maybe they were just . . . gone.

Melanie was so lost in these bleak thoughts that she didn't realize Olivia and Josh had stopped until she was practically on top of them. They were looking at the river, where a series of small ledges and inviting pools created a little paradise. A nearby sign said "Bathtub Falls."

"Nice, isn't it?" Josh said.

Melanie nodded.

"You should get your phones out," he said. "The next half mile or so there are more than a dozen cascades and falls—all unnamed but worth remembering—culminating in Shining Cloud Falls. One of the best spots in the park."

Melanie took out her phone and pressed the power button. After one heart-stopping moment of nothing, the screen lit up. She waited until all the little icons appeared, then tapped the camera and held the phone out toward the falls. But where normally she'd experience immense pleasure capturing a moment—one that would never come again in exactly the same way—she felt nothing as she hit the button. She turned her phone off and waited for Olivia and Josh to start walking again. Olivia, she noted, hadn't bothered to get her phone out at all. Of course not. She wanted to forget this trip ever happened. Just like the last hiking trip they'd been on.

The scenery for the next twenty minutes or so was achingly charming. But Melanie couldn't enjoy it. She took no more pictures, nor could she do so very easily if she had wanted to. Olivia walked so fast she was soon out of sight, and Melanie's heavy steps had her lagging so far behind that she often lost sight of Josh as well.

She should have been using this time to think through what to say when they were alone again in the car. She cared about Justin. Deeply. When they spent time together, she felt understood, known, loved. In the time she had spent with Olivia the past few days, she had often felt misunderstood, occasionally felt that she was only barely tolerated, and certainly felt judged at every turn. The choice should have been easy.

But Olivia was family. Or . . . maybe not. Family was there for you. Family supported you. Family sacrificed for you. Family loved you.

Did Olivia love her? Did Olivia love anyone?

As Melanie turned this over in her head, she came upon Josh standing in the middle of the trail.

He pointed down toward the river. "Shining Cloud Falls. Better vantage point down there."

Melanie hesitated.

"Come on. We're all going down there for a break and a snack."

She reluctantly stepped off the trail down a depression that had clearly been made by many other hikers over the years hoping for a better look at the falls. She slipped out of her pack and stretched her back muscles, keeping some distance between her and her sister, who was standing near the river. She busied herself retrieving a snack from her dwindling food supply, found a flat spot on the ground, and sat. Olivia's body obscured the view, but Melanie said nothing. Eventually her sister too took off her pack and settled down to eat, and Melanie could see the falls clearly.

Shining Cloud was not one fall but two, crashing down side by side, separated by an outcropping of rock. The one on the right fell straight down off a ledge before it hit more resistant rock and bounced off of it and into the basin below. The one on the left cascaded lazily down a more gradual decline like the flowing white hair of some wise woodland wizard. Strange that so many of the park's waterfalls were actually two falls, split by hard rock. Melanie might have found the idea friendly a few days ago. Now it seemed lonely.

As though he knew what she was thinking about, Josh said, "A couple days ago right after all that rain, I bet you couldn't see that rock in the middle there."

"Really?" Melanie said.

"Sure." He took a swig of water. "A higher volume of water can change a river's behavior dramatically. During the spring thaw this river is pretty wild. At the end of summer, it's usually calmed down a bit. Except when you get a big weather event like we just had. The more pressure you put on the waterway with extra rain or snowmelt, the faster and harder it all flows down out to the lake. Makes for some nice white water and waterfalls. But of course it makes the crossings trickier."

"Are we crossing the river today?" Melanie said.

"Twice," Josh said. "In about two miles and then again in a little less than that."

"Why don't they just keep the trail on one side of it?"

"Well, when you're cutting a trail, you're probably taking a few things into account. One, the lay of the land. Some spots are just easier to tame than others. Two, the trails may have already been there in some form long before this was a state park. There was commercial copper mining going on here before the Civil War, and before that the Ojibwe were mining with hand tools. Even the wildlife makes trails. By the time park rangers were cutting and maintaining trails, some of this was already mapped out."

"There was mining way out here?" Melanie said. "It's hard enough to get around with a backpack. I can't imagine trying to get supplies in and copper out."

"They sure tried. The mines in this area weren't nearly as successful as those up near Houghton and Calumet. Most of them couldn't make the numbers work. But there are several marked mine shafts scattered around the park. And dozens more unmarked. You'll be near one today before you get up on the escarpment."

Melanie didn't care for the way he said "you" rather than "we." She knew he intended to fish the salmon run today, but naturally they would accompany him, wouldn't they?

All this time, Olivia had sat with her back to them. Surely she'd say something now, just to clarify the plans for the day.

Or did she already know? Had she and Josh talked it over in the tent while Melanie lay awake in the hammock?

Olivia said nothing. Just tucked her food bag back into her pack and strapped it on her back. Josh, Melanie now realized, had never taken his pack off, nor had he eaten anything.

"Do you want a granola bar or something?" Melanie offered.

"Nah," he said. "I'm good."

Olivia was already heading back up to the trail, and Melanie scrambled to ready herself for more walking. Trudging, really. Putting one miserable foot in front of the other until they hit pavement. Then it would be over. Mostly.

They left the picturesque river and ascended a steep hill. Over the next hour they made their way over fairly level, if often soggy, ground beneath towering hemlock trees. When they had stopped in at the visitor center before starting the hike, Melanie had read in one of the displays that the Porcupine Mountains contained the largest stand of virgin hardwood and hemlock forest left between the Rockies and the Adirondacks. Trees saved from the clutches of the country's insatiable hunger for lumber by the rugged landscape beneath her feet. Some of these trees must have been standing watch when the Ojibwe were extracting copper from the rocks.

As she passed by some of the bigger trees, Melanie laid her hands on them, trying to feel the life and the memory within, trying to reclaim her sense of oneness with the natural world. Trying to see eagles where Olivia saw vultures. Yet all she felt beneath her hands was the rough texture of the bark, a completely practical and unmagical covering that protected the tree from bugs and fungus.

They made the first crossing, which was more difficult than any of the others had been despite Josh's steadying hand. More than once Melanie might have gone down were it not for his help. On the other side they ate a quick lunch and carried on, following the river upstream until they entered a low-lying area that was quite wet and rather unpleasant because of it. This section seemed to stretch on forever, and as Melanie slogged through she tried to make up her mind what to do about Justin.

Finally, after what seemed like hours, they reached the river again for the second crossing.

"Last time you'll have to do this," Josh said brightly as Melanie and Olivia removed their boots.

Rather than cross barefoot this time, Josh pulled on his waders before helping Melanie across. As she dried her feet and pulled on her socks and boots, he gave Olivia's hand a firm shake.

"Well, this is it," he said. "This is where I leave you."

Olivia's father pulled a large blue cooler from the back of the Explorer. "You got that, Justin?"

"Yep."

Olivia watched her dad watch Justin lug the cooler down the sandy path toward the beach.

"He's fine, Dad," she said, hoisting a beach chair under each arm.

"I still think he should see a doctor."

Olivia followed Justin's footsteps down the path but couldn't help overhearing her mother say, "He probably doesn't have insurance."

And, *Olivia thought,* he doesn't want anyone poking around in his life. *He'd told her the truth, but when her parents asked her about his limp, she told them he'd come off a dirt bike. They didn't need to know that he didn't even own a dirt bike. They didn't need to know that his dad had reappeared after six months of unexplained absence and attempted to rob his own house for drug money. That Justin had fought him off with nothing but the baseball bat he'd won at a Whitecaps game her parents had invited him to last year, twisting an ankle in the process.*

Olivia gave her head a firm shake. Forget about that now. Today was just supposed to be fun.

Melanie ran past her toward the beach, carrying nothing at all. She peeled her shirt and shorts off, kicked off her flip-flops, and high-stepped it over the scalding sand into the endless blue of Lake Michigan.

With no help from Melanie, who was busy diving through waves and occasionally screeching, the rest of the family—and Justin— laid out blankets and chairs and towels. Sunscreen was applied, handing off the tube and getting each other's backs. Mom and

Dad. Olivia and Justin. As always. Only this year there was something about Justin touching her bare back that sent little chills up Olivia's neck.

"Go get your sister and tell her to get out of there and put on some sunscreen," her mom said as she settled into a chair with a book.

Olivia dutifully headed for the water, though at an unhurried pace. Justin went down the beach in search of flat stones for skipping.

"Mom says come in and get sunscreen on," Olivia said when she finally reached Melanie on the sandbar.

"When are you just going to date him already?" Melanie said.

Olivia put her hands on her hips and waited for Melanie to comply with orders.

"He's obviously in love with you."

"When are you just going to mind your own business already?" Olivia said. "Now come on. Mom said to go in."

"He can't stop looking at you, you know."

Olivia resisted looking toward the beach to see if what Melanie said was true. "Do you want me to tell Mom you refuse to come in?"

Melanie stalked off, then dropped suddenly into the water when the sandbar ended. Olivia laughed.

"Shut up!" Melanie said, and she started to the shore with a slow breaststroke.

Olivia chanced a look at the beach. Justin stood squinting out at the water, hands on his narrow hips. Olivia couldn't tell what he was looking at exactly. There was, after all, an entire beautiful vista to view. She waved. He waved back. Then he walked into the water and headed straight for her.

Twenty-Five

OLIVIA WATCHED JOSH make his way upriver and out of sight with a measure of sadness that baffled her. All told, she had spent less than forty-eight hours in his presence, and she could count on one hand the number of hours spent talking to him. He'd helped them out in a pinch, or two, and now he was going on his way and they were going on theirs—that was it. Even so, the loss of his company sent a cloud of melancholy straight to her heart.

Just knowing he was walking the path with her had set her mind at ease. Then everything wasn't on her shoulders. She didn't have to know the way because he did. She didn't have to think about every contingency because he'd probably already experienced them all and would know what to do. It felt like having her father back, his steady footsteps somehow reassuring her that everything would be okay. That she and Melanie would get through this. Not just the hike, but all the other stuff too.

Her conversation with Josh in the tent hadn't been long, but it had been enough to nudge her thinking in a new direction. It wasn't that she didn't know Justin had lost something. It was simply that she hadn't considered it relevant given the magnitude of what she had endured. There might be any number of extenuating circumstances in a court case. But they didn't negate the fact that a law had been broken, that someone had been victimized, that justice must be satisfied.

And yet, this wasn't a court case. Her family had made sure of that by refusing to press charges, given that it was an accident and that Justin had been such a big part of their lives for so long. Facts that had seemed irrelevant to Olivia until last night. But this wasn't a trial and she wasn't acting as a lawyer, so perhaps not all the rules applied. Or perhaps there were different rules altogether.

At this point she was sure of three things. First, that it had been cowardly and selfish to abandon her family after the accident. Second, that no matter how angry she was at Melanie, eliminating her from her life was not the answer. Third, that she could not forgive Justin. Not yet—maybe not ever. But perhaps she could talk to him.

Olivia looked at her watch and then turned to face the sister she had not spoken to all day. "It's five miles to the Lake of the Clouds. We better get going."

Over the next few hours they would be struggling to climb four hundred feet up from the Big Carp River valley to the rocky cliffsides.

For half a mile or more, she sorted through her thoughts as she forced her tired legs to carry her step by agonizing step up the mountainside. The trail was uneven, the left side rising up to the summit, the right dipping down toward the river. Soon Olivia's left hip was screaming, and she tried to compensate by forcing her right leg to do more of the work.

This was what had been happening all those silent years. Melanie pulling more than her fair share of the emotional weight of their loss. She'd needed someone to lean on. In Olivia's absence, she'd found Justin. Even if Olivia tried to do her part now, it wouldn't make up for past neglect. It wouldn't get Justin out of her sister's life. And Melanie was clearly still hurting. She needed attention and rest and time to heal. She needed a break.

"Want a breather?" Olivia said, suddenly unable to keep climbing.

Melanie nodded and twirled her finger to tell Olivia to turn around. Instead, Olivia reached around to get Melanie her water bottle first. They drank long and deep. No need to be too stingy even though there would be no spots to filter water from here on out. They would be spending no more nights on the trail. They could fill up at the visitor center on the way out if it was still open. Barring that, the nearest gas station would be well stocked with far more than water.

All around them, brown needles carpeted the forest floor. Giant fallen trees blanketed in soft green moss invited weary travelers to sit and rest awhile. Overhead a breeze whispered through the lofty hemlocks. It gave Olivia the feeling of being in a church. The living trees were the columns of a great cathedral, and the fallen ones were the pews. They were even situated, incredibly, in generally parallel rows. Olivia knew from her summer research that this must be a spot that had been affected by the great blowdown of 1953, when straight-line winds came ashore from Lake Superior with the force of a tornado and left a two-mile-wide swath of destruction behind. A completely logical and scientific reason for the uncanny arrangement of logs.

Olivia unbuckled the straps of her pack and let it slide off her back. "Let's sit a moment."

She sat on a log, and Melanie settled down on another. Olivia stood, walked around to where Melanie was, and sat down next to her.

How did she start this conversation? "Sorry" was not enough. "I was wrong" was the understatement of the century. "I'll do better" felt like an empty promise.

Melanie's eyes met hers. She held her gaze for a moment, then wrapped her skinny arms around her big sister's sweaty neck. "I'm sorry," Melanie said into her shoulder. "I'm so sorry."

Olivia pulled back. "No, Mel."

Melanie hugged her again. "No, I am. I don't know what I was thinking."

Olivia gently pushed her away. "Stop. Let me say something."

Melanie leaned back and rubbed her nose with her sleeve.

"Gross, Mel. Don't forget that's mine," Olivia said with a laugh. "You're just borrowing it."

"Oh." Melanie gulped. "I can wash it and mail it to you."

Olivia waved that away. "Never mind that. I have something I need you to hear." She paused. Why was it so hard to say?

Melanie looked at her, eyes guarded, apparently ready for another blow. Shame coiled around Olivia's throat like the too-tight turtleneck her mother had forced her to wear for her fourth-grade school portrait. She'd done this to her sister. The years of verbal sparring had been nothing more to her than practice for her chosen profession, honing her skills and sharpening her tongue. But to Melanie, they'd been deeply personal—and she had been on the losing end of every single one.

Olivia took a breath. "I have not treated you fairly. Not during this trip, not during the past decade. Not after the accident, not before the accident. I've always had to be right, even when it didn't really matter, which is probably most of the time. I've treated you like an opponent, not a sister. It's not fair to you and it's not good for me." She paused to brush a small, pale-colored moth off the toe of her shoe. "I don't know why I'm like this. I've often wondered how we could possibly have had the same parents."

"Is that why you used to tell me I was adopted?" Melanie said.

Olivia laughed. "No. That was just to make you mad. You see what I mean though? You would never do that to me. It would never even occur to you to say something like that, something designed to make another person feel bad."

Melanie shrugged. "Nature versus nurture, I guess."

"It would seem so. Though we basically had the exact same nurture situation, so you must be naturally good and I must be naturally . . . evil?"

"I wouldn't say *evil*."

"Okay," Olivia said. "Maybe not evil, but definitely not good."

"Contentious?"

"Perhaps." Olivia felt something tickle the back of her hand and brushed it off absentmindedly. "Anyway, what I'm trying to say is that I'm sorry for the way I've treated you, and I'm going to make a concerted effort to do better." She turned to face Melanie head-on. "I know that you and Justin are close."

"Olivia, I—"

"No, let me finish. I know you're close, and I understand why. He was there for you when I wasn't." She forced the next words out of her mouth. "I know I should have been more sympathetic, not just about your relationship but about him directly. He had a really hard life—probably you know even more about it now than I did when we were friends, and I know a lot—and the accident made it much, much harder. I could have handled his involvement better."

Something like hope lit Melanie's watery eyes.

"I'm not saying I forgive him," Olivia hastened to say. "But I want you to know that I'm going to be reaching out to him to at least have a conversation. Someday."

"That's really good to hear, Olivia."

She smiled at her sister and flicked a fluff of seed off her shoulder. "But I wouldn't expect much to come of it, okay? It's just . . . a start. Maybe. Though, I guess I am almost kind of glad you badgered me into taking this trip. *Almost.*"

"Me too." Melanie smiled as she said it, but then Olivia saw her smile melt away.

"What?"

Melanie reached up to the brim of Olivia's baseball cap. "What is all this stuff? It looks like snow." Her eyes danced.

"It's not cold enough for snow."

"It is much warmer today than it was yesterday," Melanie agreed. "I mean, I'm not soaking wet either, but still."

Olivia stood and sniffed the air. "Mel, this isn't snow." She caught a piece in her hand and smudged it across her palm with her thumb. "This is ash."

Melanie rose to her feet. "Someone with a campfire nearby?"

Olivia took in the flecks of white drifting lazily through the forest around them. "I don't think so."

They locked eyes.

"Get your pack," Olivia said, her heart beating frantically against her ribs. She hoisted her own pack up with strength she didn't know she still had after days of practically nonstop physical exertion.

Melanie was ready just as quickly. "How many more miles?"

Olivia started walking, ignoring the pain in her hip. "Three? Maybe four? We didn't pass the mine yet, right?"

Melanie followed close behind. "I didn't see a mine. But I don't know that I'd know one if I saw it."

"Probably there'd be a sign. And it wouldn't be right on the trail. Off a ways maybe. Keep your eyes open."

"We're not going to stop to admire an abandoned mine," Melanie said incredulously.

Olivia turned to her sister. "No, but it might come in handy—if we need somewhere safe to hunker down."

Melanie's eyes widened. "No. We're not stopping anywhere. We're getting out of the woods. Today. Let's go."

Twenty-Six

AS MELANIE MARCHED along the trail, synchronizing her steps with the swift swooshing of her blood in her ears, the fear of a possible forest fire was mollified somewhat by the fact that her sister had actually admitted she had been wrong about something. About a lot of somethings. It was the type of breakthrough Melanie had been hoping for. How much further could they have gotten had they not been so rudely interrupted by the prospect of a natural disaster bearing down on them? She knew Olivia would not have gone so far as to offer her blessing when it came to Justin's proposal. But maybe, just maybe, she'd get there at some point if she was willing to at least talk to him.

Ahead, Olivia stopped abruptly. "I'm sure we should have already passed the mine, and I've seen nothing. No sign, no evidence anywhere that humans were ever here, let alone blasting holes in the ground."

"Maybe it's just nothing at this point," Melanie suggested. "It doesn't take long for nature to take over once people are out of the picture."

"You're right. Even if it were still here, it's better to be out of the woods altogether than stuck in a mine shaft in the middle of a forest fire. Whatever safety we might find from actual flames wouldn't really matter if the fire sucked all of the oxygen out of our hiding spot."

"I hadn't thought of that," Melanie said. She looked at the canopy overhead. "Do you actually see any ash here? I mean, is it possible what we saw was just from one person's fire?"

"I think that's pretty unlikely, don't you?"

"Yeah," she admitted. "But—"

"There are no campsites along this part of the trail. The last ones we passed at the river were empty. There are a few up ahead on the escarpment—we were supposed to stay at one of them last night. There are also a few spots along the lakeshore. You know where we went upriver with Josh this morning? If we'd kept going on the same trail we would have stayed on Lake Superior for miles and miles. If someone started a fire out there where it's so windy—"

"And then left it unattended—"

"Exactly. Remember that one site where the people hadn't put their fire all the way out?"

Melanie felt her jaw drop. "Those same people—"

"Yeah. And I bet I know who it is."

"But I don't feel any wind today," Melanie said, looking for a reason Olivia could be wrong.

"That's because we're on the other side of a whole line of little mountains that block it. And we're going up those mountains."

"Doesn't it seem like maybe that's the worst thing we could do? Maybe we should turn around and go back to the river. And what about Josh? He's down in that valley fishing right now. Shouldn't we find him and warn him?"

"I'm not worried about Josh," Olivia said. "I'm one hundred percent sure he can take care of himself. But the fastest way for us to get out of danger is to get out of the woods. And the fastest way to do that is to keep going the way we're going. Besides, we need to get to somewhere we can report the fire."

She started walking again. Melanie followed behind as quickly as possible, all the time wishing that life had fewer complications. If someone was in charge of this whole enterprise, why didn't they just make good stuff happen? Why were there forest fires and car accidents and broken relationships? If there was an all-powerful God, that meant he had the power to do good things all the time—but chose not to. Or perhaps he was completely good and wished good things to happen, but he wasn't all-powerful. Olivia had said she couldn't believe in a God who would cause their parents' accident. But maybe God hadn't done that. Maybe he was just as powerless to stop two cars from colliding as they were to stop a forest fire.

Maybe Olivia was right. Maybe religion was just there to make people feel like there was more meaning to life than just chemical reactions. Maybe she'd been wasting her time with her constant dabbling in spiritual things. Maybe there were no spiritual things.

After what felt like more than a mile of steady upward progress, the trail leveled out. Melanie scanned the forest for falling ash but didn't see any. Could they have imagined it? Could Olivia have been mistaken? Or perhaps she had purposefully led Melanie to believe there was a reason to rush through this last leg of the trip just so she could get it over with. Had she regretted her contrite words on the log and so cut them short with an outright lie? Had Melanie really seen ash in her sister's hand?

They emerged from the dense trees onto an outcropping of resistant bedrock with unobstructed views of the Big Carp River valley below. An unending carpet of orange and yellow unfurled beneath them, bisected by the river snaking its way through the trees. There was no smoke rising from the valley. Melanie strained to see if Josh was down there in the water, but they were too far away to spot a single man.

This high up, she could feel some breeze. But it certainly wasn't what she'd call windy. She lived on Lake Michigan. She knew windy.

Olivia motioned to a wooden bench set back from the cliff. "I think we should stop here for a few minutes and eat something. I'd like to keep pushing on, but my energy is really lagging. What do you think?"

Melanie was surprised to be asked her opinion on the matter. "Sure. I'm really hungry. And tired." She pulled out her last protein bar and unwrapped it. "You know, I haven't seen any ash this whole time we've been walking. I think we're worried about nothing."

Olivia opened a pouch of tuna salad. "It would be nice if that were true."

"It must have been something else. Some kind of fungus maybe?"

"Hmm. I have heard of some kind of invasive pest that's been a problem for hemlocks. Some kind of parasite. Woolly something-or-other." She squeezed the tuna salad into her mouth. "Something that lays eggs in white sacs."

"There you go," Melanie said. "I bet it was just some of those coming loose and falling to the ground."

Olivia didn't look convinced. She took another bite of her tuna then a swig of water. "So, what are you going to tell Justin?"

Melanie nearly choked on a bite of protein bar. She chased it down her throat with some water and coughed. "I don't know."

Olivia raised her eyebrows. "Oh, come on."

"I actually always thought you two would get married," Melanie deflected. "Then you just threw him away when you went to school."

"I didn't throw him away. He was never my boyfriend or anything."

"I think maybe he thought of himself that way."

Olivia shrugged. "I can't help that."

Melanie frowned at her.

"I'm sorry, but I never thought of him that way. So if that's what has you unsure—like I'd be angry you stole my first love or some such thing—that's not my issue with it."

"That's not it."

"Well, what is it then? Look, I'm not actually going to cut you out of my life. I shouldn't have said that. I was just surprised and angry and . . . I mean, I'm still angry and I don't forgive him, but I'm not going to make you choose between us. I'm not going to be celebrating holidays with the two of you or anything, but I'm willing to work on you and me." She paused. "I mean, you love him, right? You uprooted your life in Rockford and followed him to Petoskey."

"Yeah."

"Okay, so . . ."

Melanie sighed. "I'm not—I just—" She tried again. "I need to be sure I love *him* and not just the idea of . . . making up for you."

"What?"

Melanie twisted a little on the bench, trying to find a more comfortable position. "Like, the reason I was so nice to him at first was because you were so mean. He wanted to talk to you, not me. But I was the next best option. I felt bad about how you treated him, so I was extra nice. I listened to him like I thought you should. I became his friend because you stopped being his friend. I did all the things I thought you should be doing. And we have become real friends. But . . . do I love him like that? Or is it just that I think someone *should* love him like that?"

Olivia tucked the empty tuna pouch into her trash bag. "You know, Josh said something last night. I won't say it as well as he did, but here's the gist of it: you can't live someone else's life for them. I can't live your life the way I think you should live it, you know? And you can't live mine. Or Justin's."

Melanie nodded and looked at her muddy hiking boots.

"You're carrying a lot of weight around," Olivia continued. "You're trying to make everything right for everyone else. Maybe you need to think about yourself once in a while."

Melanie felt tears building up behind her eyes. She was exhausted by all of it. Physically and emotionally depleted. Worrying about so many other people. Not just Olivia and Justin, but all of her followers and clients. Worrying that they were eating right and breathing right and living right. Worrying that if she didn't constantly think about them and anticipate their needs, their lives would spiral out of control. That if she was gone too long from their screens, she'd lose them. And she'd have no one left to worry about. Except herself.

"Thank you for saying that," Melanie said, swallowing down the lump that had lodged in her throat. "I just want everyone to be happy and live good lives."

Olivia put her hand on Melanie's shoulder. "You don't have to answer to God for anyone else. If we mess up, it's not on you. You just have to answer for yourself."

"God? Excuse me?"

Olivia dropped her hand to her lap and looked rather sheepish, as though she'd let slip that she was taking Melanie to a surprise party. "Eh, I'm trying the idea out today. We'll see." She stood up. "Come on. We're not going to figure this all out right now. And we still have a mountain to climb."

Twenty-Seven

OLIVIA LED THE WAY forward along the trail, silently chastising herself for using that word. God. It would only get Melanie's hopes up for her when the entire notion was still strange and alien and likely to wear off the minute they were safely out of these woods and on the way back to real life. People under pressure often made bad assumptions and faulty decisions.

She remembered her father telling her about her great-uncle Gordon, who had been an altogether rotten man. Beat his wife and kids, shot the family dog after it urinated on a sofa, couldn't hold a job down because of his temper and his drinking. Bedridden with bone cancer and given six weeks to live, he'd made a bargain with God. If God got him out of that bed and made him walk again, he'd be a changed man. He did get out of that bed. He did walk again. In fact, he lived six more years.

Her father had told her that story as an argument for the existence of God, but she could read between the lines. Great-Uncle Gordon hadn't actually changed, of that she was sure. If he didn't abuse his family anymore, it was because he wasn't fast enough or strong enough after the cancer had ravaged his body. And if he didn't shoot another dog, it was because they'd sold his guns while he was in the hospital. And he used his weakened condition as a new excuse not to look for a job. The doctors were just wrong about the timeline, that's all.

So no, she reasoned, she didn't really believe in God. She'd been momentarily taken in by a fisherman, like a catch on the end of his line. Now she was wriggling her way back into the water.

She checked her watch. Nearly four o'clock. They'd lingered too long on the mossy logs beneath the hemlocks, too long at the overlook. Without her map she couldn't be sure exactly where she was, but she did know that they could make no more stops if they hoped to make the parking lot before sunset. If they missed getting a ride, they were sunk.

"How does your watch still have power?" Melanie said from behind her.

"Solar charger. It was full when we started hiking, and it's still not totally depleted."

"You think of everything."

Suddenly aware of how hot she felt, Olivia took off her ball cap as she walked and wiped her forehead with her arm. Sure, it was the hottest part of the day, but in the UP in October, that shouldn't be more than fifty degrees or so. And for the past ten minutes, they had been walking on level ground. If she felt like this now, the big climb up to the escarpment was going to be brutal.

She fanned her face with her hat and turned back to her sister. "Are you hot?"

"Oh my gosh, yes! I thought it was just me."

Olivia stopped walking, looked ahead, looked behind. For what, she wasn't quite sure, but she saw nothing out of the ordinary. For the past quarter mile on the right-hand side, the land rose up from the valley to meet them and continued far above their heads on the left. Up ahead, she could see that the land tapered down toward their level. They must be coming to some kind of gap in the mountain ridge. After that, they should begin their climb.

She started walking again. Felt the breeze pick up. Then she saw it, dancing through the trees about twenty yards ahead. Ash. She picked up the pace, urged Melanie on with a silent wave. The trail curved to the left, and the ground spread out before them, level and radiating heat through the soles of Olivia's shoes.

Melanie gasped. "Look!"

Three deer, then four, then three more bounded out of the trees and across their path, crashing through the underbrush down the hill toward the valley. Chipmunks scurried in their wake. Jays cried out and zipped through the trees.

"We need to move," Olivia said.

"Wait!" Melanie whispered.

Olivia wheeled on her to argue, but Melanie was pointing and smiling like a maniac. Olivia followed the invisible trajectory of her outstretched finger to the spot the deer had just been. A cougar stood there looking at them, body taut, eyes wide, one ear turning back toward the place it had just come from. It sniffed the air once, twice, then jogged off in the same direction the deer had gone.

For a split second, Olivia considered following it. Animals knew where to go during a natural disaster, right? They had some special sense for things like this. But she would not change course now. She was getting out of this forest. And out was up, not down.

"I told you," Melanie squealed.

"Not now," Olivia warned.

She pushed forward along the trail, speed-walking only because she couldn't run with a pack on her back. Should they ditch them in the woods? The ash was getting thicker and the heat was intensifying. She felt like she was rushing into the fire rather than away from it, but the blue blazes on the trees dictated her route.

After a few minutes that felt like much longer, the trail made a sharp right and began to rise. Another switchback, and then they were climbing what felt like straight up.

Olivia's muscles burned. Her hip cried out in protest. Her blisters screamed against the insides of her boots. Behind her, Melanie was coughing.

"Just a little further," she lied. She had no idea how much further, how long it would take them to reach the top. Or what they would find when they got there.

Despite herself, Olivia began a silent chant, much as she had when she was walking behind Josh to get the packs they'd left leaning on the birch tree. It was far less critical than her earlier chant of *stu-pid* or *sel-fish*. Those were directed at herself and at her sister. Now she directed her words skyward. *Save us, save us, save us.*

The trail made another turn, and Olivia's muscles were given a short reprieve.

Melanie got her cough under control. "Can we just stop a second? I need some water."

Olivia didn't want to stop, but her throat was parched too. "Okay, but quick."

They grabbed and gulped and shoved the bottles back into the packs.

"How much further?" Melanie said.

"How should I know?" Olivia said. "I have no map."

"Yes, you do."

"What?"

Melanie spun around. "I forgot. Front zipper pocket."

Olivia unzipped the compartment. "How—?"

"It washed up on shore near where we hung the clothes out."

This was too much. She snatched the map out of Melanie's pack. The ink indicating her plans was gone, but she could still see the depressions her pen had made in the surface. It really was her map. Impossible.

"There. We must be there, where the trail winds back and forth up the mountainside. And there," she said, pointing, "is the open spot between the peaks where the heat got so intense and the animals were running through." She looked toward the shoreline on the map. "The fire could have started at one of these campsites."

"So how much further?" Melanie repeated.

"A little more than a mile and a half and we'll be at the parking lot." She looked at her sister. "We can do this."

Melanie gave a resolute nod. Olivia rolled the map up until it resembled a relay baton, then pressed forward up the hill. One more big push and they'd be on the escarpment. From that point, it was a straight shot on level ground and they could move fast.

Just a few minutes later, they reached the top. Unobscured by trees, the valley opened up below them and the sky opened up above. But they didn't stop to admire the view. They pushed on past three empty campsites. Smoke was rising in the west to join the clouds, and the air smelled like a campfire. Were there rangers out on the trails right now, looking for backcountry hikers? Would she be met on the path by a stern-faced man bearing bad news as she had so many years ago? Were all her hiking trips doomed?

Olivia checked her watch again. 4:50. She attempted to open the map without slowing down and tripped on a tree root. She went down hard, her right knee striking a rock, sending a lightning bolt of pain up her femur, like the feeling she used to get up her arms if the bat hit the softball just wrong. She struggled to stand.

Melanie was on her in a breath, helping her to her feet. "You okay?"

"Yeah," Olivia said through clenched teeth. She was not okay. She took a faltering step and let out an involuntary yell.

"Olivia!"

"I'm fine. You take the lead. I'm fine."

Melanie hesitated.

"Go!" Olivia shouted. "I'm right behind you."

Melanie started walking, looking back at Olivia every third step.

"Stop looking at me," she said. "You're going to trip too."

Olivia struggled on, chiding herself for such an avoidable mistake. She was slowing them down. Melanie kept looking back, but now it was only every sixth step. The trail curved slightly right along the top of a ridge that had so little tree cover that for the first time they could see in the other direction, all the way to Lake Superior. Olivia stopped and stared.

Smoke rose from an ever-widening swath of forest, starting at the lakeshore and reaching inland. The fire was big and the wind was strong, but Olivia was comforted by the fact that it wasn't actually upon them. Yet.

Next to her, Melanie was holding back tears.

"We should keep moving," Olivia said. "It's got to be less than a mile. Less than a mile and we can get out of here."

She took the lead, breathing through the pain radiating up and down her leg. Every step was a fight with herself to keep moving forward. She could do anything as long as she knew there was an end point she was working toward. If her great-uncle could walk off bone cancer, she could walk off a fractured kneecap or a bone bruise or whatever this was. She could walk off the pain in her hip. She would walk out of these woods on her own two feet, blisters and all.

Fifteen minutes later, they came to another overlook where they could see the Big Carp River. Unlike earlier when it was far off in the distance, here it flowed practically to the foot of the cliff they were standing on. The water churned and boiled with salmon jockeying for the best spots in which to spawn, and there, down among them, stood a man in olive-green waders flicking a fly rod.

"Josh!" Melanie shouted. She cupped her hands around her mouth. "Josh!"

"He can't hear us from up here," Olivia said.

"We have to tell him about the fire. Josh!" She walked closer to the edge. "Josh!"

Olivia grabbed her arm. "Melanie! What do you want to do, fall off a cliff to get his attention? Back up!"

Olivia placed herself between her sister and the drop-off she'd been walking toward. Melanie took a step back. Olivia turned around to see how close her little sister had gotten to the edge. But when she pivoted on her left foot to avoid putting too much weight on her right knee, something in her hip snapped, her leg buckled, and the weight of her pack threw her off balance. She heard her sister scream.

And then she was falling.

Twenty-Eight

IN THE SPACE of one strangled breath, Melanie heard her own scream echo off the hills on the far side of the valley. Then branches breaking and her sister's body connecting with the side of the steep embankment.

"Olivia!" Melanie dumped her pack to the ground in a second and scrambled up to the edge on all fours. "Olivia!"

About twenty-five feet below, she could see the maize M on her sister's navy-blue hat, the straight line of one of her hiking poles, the boot on one of her feet. She wasn't moving.

"Olivia!" she screamed through tears. "Olivia!"

Rope. She needed the rope. She scrambled back to her pack and began emptying pockets. Where was it? Where was it? Where was it? The answer came in a sickening flash. On the beach, still strung between two trees where they had dried her wet clothes in the wind. The same wind that was now sending a forest fire ever closer.

Okay. Okay. No rope. Help. She'd have to go for help. The parking lot was close. Less than a mile. Maybe less than half a mile. With no pack she could cover it fast. But how could she leave Olivia? What if the fire jumped the ridgeline and started burning the dry autumn vegetation where her sister lay?

She crawled back up to the edge and tried to gauge the distance. She would have to climb down there herself and bring her up. Olivia's pack still had rope. She could tie it to the pack on her sister's back and drag her up the cliff.

Melanie searched the edge of the escarpment for a gentler way down, but there was none. She moved about five feet to the left of where Olivia had gone over so she wouldn't land on her if she fell, then slowly rolled over on her stomach, pushing herself back until her legs hung over the edge. Her feet searched for a spot to rest. Nothing. She pushed a little farther. A little farther. Then slipped too fast, scraping her stomach and rib cage over the rock. She fell for only a foot or two before her feet hit the ground. She grabbed wildly at a prickly bush anchored in the rock and caught it, keeping herself from sliding any farther but puncturing the meat of her hand.

Melanie got her bearings and looked for another handhold, another foothold. Inch by painstaking inch—and sometimes foot by startling foot—she made her way down to where Olivia lay against the dirt-packed root structure of a fallen tree, her face and arms scraped and bleeding. Terrified of the answer she might receive, she put her cheek against her sister's open mouth and pressed two fingers against her neck. Breath. A pulse. Thank God.

Melanie unzipped one of the side pockets of Olivia's pack and found the rope. She unwound a portion of it and tied it around the metal frame of Olivia's pack. She knew nothing about knots, so she just kept making more and more of them. They couldn't all fail. Then she looked back up the cliffside. They were much farther down than she'd thought. But it didn't matter. She would get her sister up there and get her to the parking lot and get her to a doctor. She had to.

Next to her, Olivia groaned. Melanie was on her in a second.

"Olivia! You're okay. I'm going to get you out of here, and you're going to be okay."

Olivia groaned again and tried to move.

"Just stay there," Melanie said. "I'm going to pull you up. Just stay there."

Hugging the steep slope, Melanie made her way back up the escarpment, unwinding the rope as she went and praying it would be long enough to reach the top. Three times she slipped, losing precious time and distance before her hand found a grip or her feet found a rock or root. Just as she was fearing that her strength, already sorely tested by their near sprint through the woods, would fail, Melanie finally reached the top. Gripping the rope, she lay for a moment on the rocky outcropping, catching her breath. She shouted over the side, "I'm going to pull you up!"

Now came the hard part. Olivia had always weighed more than Melanie, and the most Melanie lifted in everyday life was a bag of groceries. How would she do this?

Incline, lever, pulley. Weren't those the simple machines she'd learned about at the children's science museum during their fifth-grade field trip? She looked around for a tree. A tree could act like a pulley. But there wasn't enough soil up on the escarpment to support big trees. There was nothing up here but bushes and shrubs.

Instead, Melanie positioned herself behind a low boulder, bracing her feet against the rock. She started to pull. The rope went taut. She pulled harder. But the blood from the wound on her hand made the rope slippery. She wound some around her hand and pulled as hard as she could. Her fingers started to turn purple.

Then the rope finally budged. She'd moved her. Maybe only a few inches, but she'd moved her. Melanie pulled with renewed strength, drawing in another few inches of rope and wrapping it around her forearm. Pull, wrap. Pull, wrap. Pull, wrap. She had heard of people under duress performing great feats of strength in order to save another human being. She used to think that must be due to some otherworldly power infusing a human body with extra strength. But surely it was just the power of adrenaline, a completely explainable biological process. Melanie didn't care at this point. All that mattered was that it was working.

Pull, wrap, breathe.

Pull, wrap, breathe.

Pull, wrap, breathe.

Finally, she could see the top of Olivia's pack over the edge of the escarpment.

Almost. There.

Almost. There.

Almost. There.

There was Olivia's hat. Then her tortured face, twisted in pain. Then . . . Josh's face?

In her shock, Melanie almost dropped the rope. But she managed to keep hold. In a few seconds, Josh, with Olivia on his back, was over the edge and laying her down on the ground.

Melanie hurried to disentangle herself from the rope and get much-needed blood to her fingers.

"Olivia!" she said, rushing over. Olivia coughed and moaned and held her side.

"She probably has some broken ribs," Josh said. "Maybe a concussion."

"Where did you come from?"

"From the river. I heard screaming and saw her fall. I climbed up from below."

She stood and fixed him with a glare. "You shouldn't have left us. If you'd been here, this would never have happened." She knelt by her sister. "Is she going to be okay?"

"We need to get her to a hospital." He began unbuckling the straps of Olivia's pack. "Help me get her out of this thing. Careful."

Though every movement clearly sent spasms of pain coursing through Olivia's body, Melanie and Josh managed to get the pack off. A minute later Josh was half bent over with Olivia on his back, her right arm coiled around his neck, her left pressed against her side, where a troubling blotch of red was growing.

"What about her pack?" Melanie said.

"We'll send someone back for it."

"But there's a fire—"

"Leave it, Melanie. We can't take it with us."

He started down the trail, quickly but smoothly. Spent, Melanie struggled to keep up. Down an incline, around a wide curve, past another overlook, down another incline, around another curve, up another hill. Josh never slowed. Melanie seemed to stumble with every other step. Occasionally she heard a sharp intake of breath from her sister, but otherwise Olivia was silent. Finally, they hit a boardwalk and Melanie got her first glimpse of the Lake of the Clouds. But only a glimpse. Immediately they veered off to the parking lot, where rangers were directing traffic back down the road and out of the park.

After a quick conversation with one of the harried rangers, Olivia was carefully placed on blankets in the back of a Suburban and checked over. The ranger pulled her hand away from her side. The bleeding was clearly worse. A first aid kit appeared, and the ranger quickly bathed the wound with isopropyl alcohol and pressed a wad of clean cotton gauze against it.

"You," she said to Melanie, "get in here and maintain pressure on this."

Melanie climbed into the back of the truck beside Olivia and pressed her hand where the ranger indicated. Josh reached up to close the liftgate.

"Wait—you're coming, aren't you?" Melanie said.

"No, I need to stay here. There are a few hikers unaccounted for on the Lake Superior Trail. I just volunteered to lead a search party."

"But—"

"She'll be okay, Melanie. And I'm needed here. I'll grab the backpack and have someone take it to the hospital for you."

Then he closed the back of the truck. Melanie watched through the tinted glass as he jogged off in the direction they had just come. A second later someone got into the driver's seat.

"Ready back there?" the ranger's voice called.

"Yes," Melanie managed to croak out.

"It's thirty minutes to the hospital. I'll try to get you there in twenty. Try to keep her from moving, especially her head. It's a curvy road."

Keeping one hand and then the other pressed against Olivia's side, Melanie removed her pack and leaned over her sister. She rolled up some of her dirty clothes and tucked them on either side of Olivia's head to keep it from moving back and forth with the motion of the truck.

"Olivia, it's going to be okay," Melanie said. But Olivia's eyes were squeezed shut, and Melanie wasn't sure if she was getting through to her.

"I'm Serena," the ranger shouted back. "What are your names?"

"Melanie. And this is my sister, Olivia."

"She's going to be okay."

How did she know that? How did Josh know? What if she wasn't? What if Melanie had badgered her sister into taking a fatal trip with her? What if she lost her too?

"How long have you two been on the trail?" Serena said.

"I don't know. Three days, maybe? Four?" She looked to Olivia for confirmation but got nothing. Olivia's face was scrunched in pain, her breathing slow and deliberate, as though if her concentration lapsed she would forget to breathe.

"Beautiful time of year for it. I mean, normally. This fire . . . I just can't believe it."

Melanie didn't respond. She didn't have the energy for a conversation. But that didn't stop Serena, who probably thought she was helping her keep her mind off her troubles.

"I've been working here for nine years. Love it here. Especially in the fall and winter. Beautiful country. Before this I was down cutting trails in Columbia. But I missed the seasons. Where are you from?"

Melanie wished she would stop talking. "I live in Petoskey."

"Love that town. Kind of artsy, isn't it? I'm from Chicago originally."

She needed to concentrate, to focus her mind on her sister, to channel her energy. She couldn't lose her.

"You both live in Petoskey?"

Argh. Shut up. "Olivia's a lawyer in East Lansing."

"And you? What do you do?"

Melanie sighed. She normally loved that question. Loved sharing what she did with people, even when they didn't quite get it. But she didn't want to explain her job to Serena. She didn't want to explain it to anyone anymore. It should be simpler to say what it was she did. If it was a real thing, it would be one word that wouldn't require a long explanation. Lawyer. Plumber. Writer. Nurse.

"I'm a counselor," she said.

Vague enough to be both true and false at the same time. Kind of like her beliefs, she thought wryly. According to Olivia, at least. Did it matter that she couldn't explain what she believed in one word either? Did she have to have a label for it to be real?

"That's good. You probably have some great coping strategies for what you two have been through out there."

They all had a label. Jewish. Christian. Muslim. Buddhist. Atheist. And as Olivia said, they couldn't all be right. A thing couldn't be both true and false. And one true thing couldn't contradict another true thing.

"About ten more minutes," Serena said after a short silence. "How are you doing back there? Not too bumpy?"

"Not too bad," Melanie said. Still maintaining pressure on the wound on Olivia's side, she leaned toward the front seat and lowered her voice. "Can I ask you something?"

"Of course," Serena said, matching her volume.

"Do you believe in God?"

Serena stifled a laugh. "Oh, man. That's a big one. I thought it was going to be something about the park or the fire or something. Um, yeah. I believe in God. Why?"

Melanie collected her thoughts. "Do you think the fire was part of his plan?"

"Part of God's plan? Gee, I don't know. That's above my pay grade. There are lots of ordinary reasons a fire starts. Unattended campfire, fireworks, cigarette butts."

"People," Melanie said.

"A lot of the time, yes. But one of the main sources is lightning—that's what started the Duck Lake Fire back in 2012. My first year up here. I suppose someone could make an argument for God being involved somehow, but I don't know. Some things just happen. Lightning is a natural occurrence."

"I remember hearing about that fire. That went on awhile, didn't it?"

"Weeks. It took the DNR twenty-three days to contain it. Burned more than twenty thousand acres. That'd be like losing one third of the Porkies." She was quiet a moment. "I hope they can contain this quickly. They're predicting rain tonight. That would really help. It's a godsend we had that rain a few days ago or it might be spreading even faster. It was such a dry season."

Melanie glanced back at her sister. Olivia had been so angry when they came upon that fire ring that had been left with live embers. When she'd put the fire out, was she just delaying the inevitable? If God was all-powerful, wouldn't he just find another way to get a fire started?

"So you think this one was just an accident?" Melanie said. "Just dumb luck?"

"I think it was negligence," Serena said. "And if they can determine who is to blame, they could press charges."

Those three loud hikers at the Government Peak trailhead. Olivia clearly blamed them. But was that fair? It might have been anyone. "How would they figure that out?"

"If it started at a particular campsite and they can narrow down the time, it's easy enough to figure out who stayed there and left a fire burning. As long as they registered."

"So at least justice could be served?"

"Right. But that doesn't get the trees back."

What's done is done and can't be undone.

Someone had started a fire. Olivia had fallen off a cliff. Justin had killed her parents.

None of them could be undone. All of them were accidents. If there was a God, he had allowed all of them to happen. Didn't it follow then that he must have let them happen for a reason? That, as Olivia had said, he must have wanted their parents to die? Or even if he hadn't arranged the accident specifically, that he hadn't cared enough to keep them alive?

Did he care enough about Olivia?

Melanie leaned back and looked down at Olivia's face, which was beginning to bruise beneath the abrasions. She didn't believe in God. Certainly hadn't believed in more than a decade. Yet, just a couple hours ago she had let slip that she was entertaining the notion. One day she was an atheist, the next she was questioning that. Why? What had changed?

Olivia stirred beside her, tried to speak.

"We're almost to the hospital," Melanie said.

Olivia mumbled something.

Melanie stroked her hand. "I can't quite understand you."

"Josh," Olivia managed.

"He's okay," Melanie said. "He stayed to help find some missing hikers." Hikers who might have been the ones to start the fire.

"Josh," Olivia said again.

"He's not here right now. I'm sure he'll come by the hospital though. Just relax."

From the front seat Serena said, "We're here."

The next several minutes were a blur of gurneys and nurses and doctors and questions Melanie couldn't answer. What was Olivia's blood type? Who was her primary care physician? Was she allergic to any medications? Had she had any previous serious injuries or surgeries? Melanie didn't even know her sister's current address—Olivia's license, along with her insurance card, was in her pack in the middle of a forest fire.

Melanie's hand was cleaned and bandaged, and she was checked over for injuries and smoke inhalation. Then she waited as Olivia was poked, prodded, scanned, x-rayed, and sewn up. She haunted the front entrance, looking for Josh. She ate a garden salad from the hospital cafeteria. She texted Justin to let him know they were out of the woods and in Ontonagon in case he saw news about the fire and began to worry. Then she walked out to the parking lot to get her phone charger before she remembered that, of course, her car was still back in the gravel lot at the trailhead. She wanted to consult the map to see if her car was in the path of the fire, but she'd given it back to Olivia. Who knew where it was now? Probably at the bottom of a cliff.

A couple hours later, a doctor updated her on Olivia's injuries. A concussion, three cracked ribs, a fractured kneecap, multiple scrapes and abrasions, and a puncture wound just an inch away from her left lung.

"That in itself is a miracle," the doctor said. "As is the fact that she seems to have suffered no traumatic brain or spinal injury. But there's something else you should know."

"What?"

His face was grave. "Is there any family history of osteosarcoma? Bone cancer?"

Melanie felt her stomach drop. "Our great-uncle died of bone cancer."

His frown deepened. "The nature of Olivia's injuries concerns me. Anyone might crack a rib or two in that kind of accident. But the injuries to her legs are different. The patellar fracture—that's the kneecap—is odd because she doesn't remember hitting her knee during the fall."

"That wasn't from the fall. Or, not from *that* fall. She tripped earlier and landed on her knee. But that was when we were rushing because of the fire, so maybe she didn't remember it."

"Mmm. And the damage to her hip was not a result of anything during your hiking trip. It seems to have been giving her trouble for a while now, judging by the scar tissue there."

"She was limping. Even before the hike."

The doctor nodded thoughtfully. "Osteosarcoma is an aggressive cancer. If it's caught early enough, the survival rate is around seventy percent. But if it spreads beyond that localized spot, the survival rate drops to thirty percent. I'm not certain she has it, but she needs to make an appointment with her primary care physician as soon as possible after she gets home. And that's another thing. When she is cleared to leave, she can't drive herself. I assume you can drive her?"

"Of course," Melanie said without a thought. She would drive Olivia to East Lansing even if it meant she'd have to hitchhike back home afterward.

"And she is likely to need some help at home for a while. She won't be walking right away. She'll need the dressing on her wounds changed. Won't be able to lift things, not even a gallon of milk."

Melanie nodded, letting the magnitude of the situation sink in.

"Does she have a family?" he asked.

"I'm her family."

He pursed his lips. "Could be a big job for one person."

"Whatever I need to do."

He stood up. Though she was physically and emotionally exhausted, Melanie followed suit.

"Doctor . . . what do I tell her? About the cancer?"

"Tell her she's lucky she ended up in the hospital with a bunch of broken bones. Otherwise, it might have gone undetected until it was too late. Someone must be looking out for her."

Twenty-Nine

OLIVIA OPENED HER EYES, then shut them again immediately. She had hoped she'd wake up in her bed at home. More than that, she didn't want Melanie to realize she was awake. She wasn't ready for inane questions like "How are you feeling?" and "Can I get you anything?" She wanted to be alone and quiet and just *there*. To revel in the joy of being there instead of not being anywhere. Instead of being dead, which she was sure she should have been.

"Olivia?" came Melanie's voice anyway. "Everything okay?"

No, everything was clearly not okay. This stupid trip. Why did it have to be such a nice day when Melanie had called her? This never would have happened if it had been crappy and depressing like it was supposed to be in March.

"Are you in any pain?"

Where should she start? Her head throbbed, her side hurt, her arms stung, her hip ached, her knee felt like electrodes were being applied to it. The pain must have registered on her face, because Melanie left the room and came back with a nurse, who fiddled with an IV.

"When can I leave?" Olivia asked the nurse.

"Tomorrow morning, most likely."

"It's not tomorrow yet?"

The nurse smiled. "Not quite. Anyway, we can't let you go until we're satisfied that you won't conk out on us, can we?"

Olivia scoffed. "I just survived a forest fire and a fall off a cliff. Clearly I cannot be killed."

The nurse laughed, but Olivia knew what she'd just said was a smoke screen. Between the fire and the fall it was clear that if God was real, he was after her. She didn't know what to do with that.

"Any news about the fire?" she asked.

The nurse hung in the doorway a moment. "There were some other people brought in — smoke inhalation — but I think they may already be gone." She disappeared, off to some other patient.

"I wonder if it was those three," Olivia said. "Did Josh ever show up?"

"If he did, I missed him," Melanie said. "And it wasn't because I wasn't watching for him."

"Guess they need all the help they can get out there."

"News said they've got planes dumping water from the lake on it. And the coast guard is spraying it from boats. And it did start raining."

Melanie handed Olivia her nearly dead phone so she could read an article about the efforts to contain and extinguish the fire, which had burned through a swath of secondary-growth forest on the shoreline but had so far spared the old-growth hemlocks and pines. It was cautiously optimistic in tone, anticipating containment by the following day if the weather cooperated. Thinking of that cathedral of trees that had so unexpectedly moved her, Olivia felt like maybe she should pray they'd be unharmed. But really? Pray for trees? That was something she'd laugh at Melanie for doing. And did she really think anyone was listening? Or cared?

Olivia rested the phone on her leg above the apparatus that was stabilizing her knee. "Hey, did anyone ever bring in my pack?"

"Not yet."

"I'm just now realizing that it has my wallet and my car keys in it. I'm not going to get very far without those."

"Look at yourself. You think you can drive like that?"

Olivia sighed. "How long is this thing supposed to be on?"

"I don't know. Weeks, probably. But I've figured out a way to get you home."

"How?"

"I can get someone to meet us in Indian River so they can pick up my car there. Then I'll drive you home in yours."

"And then how will you get home from there? Fly?"

Melanie scooted closer. "Let's not worry about that until the time comes."

"I think the time is coming tomorrow if that nurse is right."

Melanie took her hand in a motherly way.

Olivia tugged it away. "That's weird."

"Olivia!"

"It is! It's weird to grab my hand like I'm a six-year-old. Just say what you need to say."

Melanie crossed her arms. "Fine. The doctor told me you'd

need help when you got home, so I'm going to stay with you and help you out."

"I don't think that's such a great idea."

"Why not?"

"Are you kidding? Think of everything we've argued about in the last few days. Do you really want more of that? Do you really think I'd be a good patient? I'll be horrible and you'll drive me crazy, and you know it."

"But you need help," Melanie insisted.

"Let's let me be the judge of that, shall we?"

"But—"

"Ms. Greene?" came the nurse's voice from the door.

"Yes?" Olivia and Melanie answered in unison.

The nurse chuckled. "I meant you, Miss Melanie. Can you come out here a moment?"

Melanie stood up. "This conversation is not over."

"I can't do even one more day of this, never mind weeks," Olivia said aloud to the empty room when the door had shut.

She swiped at Melanie's phone still in her hand. The lock screen appeared. Olivia thought for half a second and then connected the dots to make an M. It didn't work. She switched the phone over to her left hand and tried again, making the M backwards. Bingo. She began swiping back through Melanie's photos. Several of various waterfalls and colorful fall leaves and mushrooms. The one from after Melanie fell in the river. The one where they were lost in the woods. One of the tent. Some of Olivia's back as she led the hike. The one from the beginning of the trip at the Government Peak trailhead.

But none of Josh.

Melanie came back into the room carrying Olivia's pack. "Special delivery."

"Who brought it?"

"Serena."

"Who's Serena?"

"She's the park ranger who brought us to the hospital earlier."

"Oh." Why hadn't Josh brought it? "Hey, did you not take any pictures with Josh in them?"

"Huh? No, I took a picture of him."

Olivia waved Melanie's phone at her. "I don't think you did."

Melanie snatched the phone and started swiping furiously. "I know I did. I took a picture of him at those Overlooked Falls or whatever." She swiped the other way. Slowly her face fell, and she sat down hard in the plastic chair next to the bed. "Where did it go?" She kept swiping, unwilling to give up.

"Maybe something got messed up when the phone got wet. Or maybe you took it with my phone?" Olivia offered, even though she knew it was absurd. "Speaking of mine, can you get it out of my bag for me?"

Melanie looked at first like she hadn't heard her. Then she came to. "What?"

"My phone. Can you get it for me? It's in the right-hand pocket there."

Melanie did as directed, then settled back in the chair to swipe through her pictures once again. Olivia powered on her phone and blanched at all the notifications. Emails, appointments, task reminders. She had to be in court on Monday. She thought of the kinds of notifications Melanie would have after so long off the grid. Were people still sending positive thoughts to the man

290

in the motorcycle accident? Were they still sharing the video of Melanie rescuing the turtle?

She tried to imagine how Melanie would put a positive spin on their hiking trip for her blog. Wrong turns, lost trails, bear encounters, forest fire. A fall in a river and one off a cliff. Near-constant bickering. There was not one part of this ill-fated trip that was redeemable. Not one reason for it to have happened at all. A total waste of time, energy, and resources. It hadn't really fixed anything fundamental in her relationship with her sister, despite Melanie's best intentions and their conversation among the hemlock trees. It was a start, but not much more than that. It had not gotten Melanie to leave her alone as she'd hoped it would. Indeed, Melanie now seemed determined to move in with her for an indeterminate amount of time.

"So," Olivia said, "I'm happy to pay for your flight back if someone can pick you up at the Traverse City Airport and drive you back to Petoskey."

Melanie put down her phone. "Olivia, we need to talk."

"We are talking."

"This is serious."

"I know. I'm seriously offering to pay for a plane to take you home so I don't end up killing you." Olivia smiled to take the sting out of what she said, but when she saw Melanie's eyes tearing up, the smile faded from her lips. "What is it? What's wrong?"

Melanie took a deep breath. "The doctor thinks you might have cancer."

She paused as if to give Olivia a chance to talk, but Olivia found that speech was quite beyond her at the moment. Even putting one coherent thought together felt like a skill she'd never mastered, like playing the cello or speaking Portuguese.

"He's not sure," Melanie went on, "but you need to get tested when you get home."

"Cancer?" Olivia managed finally.

"Osteosarcoma. Bone cancer."

"Why?" The word sounded like nothing more than a wisp of air coming out of her mouth. "Why would he think that?" she said, stronger now.

"Your hip."

"Oh." Olivia relaxed. "It was just sore from hiking."

"No, you were complaining about it in the car on the way up."

She was? Olivia thought back. How long had her hip been hurting?

"He said they saw scar tissue built up in the X-ray. And your knee fracture bothered him."

"I fell off a cliff!"

"That's not what happened to your knee though. That was just you tripping and landing on it. That shouldn't fracture the knee of a woman your age."

Olivia's mind raced for another explanation. Not enough calcium or vitamin D or something. Didn't everyone in Michigan suffer from vitamin D deficiency because of the cloud cover?

"He said you were lucky," Melanie said. "That if you hadn't had to come in for X-rays from that fall, it could have gone undetected until it was too late to do anything."

Olivia felt like she was going to throw up, but she also couldn't remember the last meal she'd eaten. "How old was Great-Uncle Gordon when he died?"

Melanie's face turned ashen. "Forty. I think. Maybe forty-one." She rushed on, "But he doesn't *know* you have cancer. He just thinks you should get checked out as soon as possible."

Olivia worked to regulate her breathing.

"I know you'll pooh-pooh this," Melanie said, "but clearly this is fate. If you hadn't come on this trip, you'd never have known."

"We don't even know if there's anything to know, Melanie. Maybe I injured it previously and it didn't heal correctly. Maybe I have early-onset osteoporosis. If that's a thing. And until we know if there's anything to know, we're not going to talk about fate or cancer or any of it. All we're going to do is get out of here as soon as possible so we can get me home as soon as possible, so *you* can go home as soon as possible."

"Fine," Melanie said.

"Fine," Olivia said.

Melanie stood up and dug her keys out of her pack. "First I have to figure out how to get to my car."

Thirty

OUT IN THE hall, Melanie glanced at the large clock above the nurses' station. 1:17. In the morning. She'd never find someone to take her to her car at this time of night. Still, she walked down to the lobby to see what options might be open to her. The little gift and flower shop near the entrance was closed. Other than the woman sitting behind the information desk typing away at a computer, the place was empty and quiet.

"Excuse me," she said to the woman. "Do you guys have, like, Uber up here or anything?"

A pained smile spread across the woman's face. "Not really, no. Do you need a ride somewhere?"

"My car is at a trailhead in the Porcupine Mountains. I need to get it before I can drive my sister home tomorrow. Well, today, I guess."

The woman nodded, still wearing that smile that said *I can't help you*. "There's a shift change at seven o'clock," she offered. "Perhaps it would be better to wait until morning. Maybe you could find someone to take you to your car then."

Melanie tried to remember if she knew anyone in the western

UP. Where was Josh? Maybe trying to get back to his own car at Pinkerton Creek.

"Hey, can you tell me whether or not someone came in here tonight?"

"Do you have a name?"

"Josh— Oh. I don't know his full name. He was tall, early thirties, brown hair, beard, in a plaid flannel and maybe fishing waders?"

"I haven't seen anyone like that, I don't think. But I just got here at eleven. He may have come in earlier. Apparently they had several people brought in from the Porkies because of the fire. The police were even here."

"Did they arrest anyone?"

The woman shrugged. "Don't know."

Melanie thanked her for her time and headed outside to watch the rain from beneath the portico at the patient drop-off area. The wet parking lot sparkled like Christmas lights under the tall light fixtures. It would be Christmas in just a couple months. She'd put up a small tree, decorate her house, invite Justin over to watch Christmas movies and drink hot cocoa. Another year gone. Perhaps the last one she'd spend unmarried. The Christmas after that, she could be trimming the tree and baking pies with a big pregnant belly running into tree boughs and countertops. And all the Christmases that followed could be brightened by the sound of children's laughter and storytelling and wide-eyed wonder. Then grandchildren. A family. A real family.

"Melanie, right?" came a voice to her left.

She turned to see Ranger Serena standing there in the doorway.

"Oh, hi," Melanie said. "I thought you'd gone."

"I would have, but a nurse heard me coughing and wanted to check me over."

"Are you okay?"

"They let me out, so I guess so."

Melanie thought fast. "Hey, you're not going back toward the park tonight, are you?"

"You need a lift somewhere?"

"I do. My car is at the Government Peak trailhead. I don't suppose you could drop me off there, could you?"

"Of course."

"I know it's late and you probably just want to get in bed."

"It's no problem at all. In fact, it's good I happened by. They'll let me into the park, but I'm not sure they'd let just anybody in. It's closed and the roads are blocked off. As a precaution." Serena started walking out into the rain and motioned for Melanie to follow her. "I'm just over here."

They trotted out to her truck, and Melanie settled herself into the passenger seat. "You're sure this isn't too much trouble?"

"Nonsense," Serena said as she turned the key in the ignition. "When I was a teenager I hitchhiked from Chicago to Yellowstone and back, so I always give people rides when they need them. Just paying it forward."

They pulled out onto the street.

"That's incredible," Melanie said. "Chicago to Yellowstone?"

"It was stupid, is what it was. But I didn't think about that at the time. One of the best times of my life."

"There were a couple times on our hike that my sister wanted to call it quits and hitchhike back to the car. I thought she was crazy. Now I wish we had."

Serena glanced at her. "How is she?"

"Pretty banged up, but she'll pull through. Actually, it's a really good thing we didn't quit."

"Why's that?"

Melanie filled her in on Olivia's injuries and all that the doctor had said about the possibility of cancer.

"Oh my," Serena said when she was done. "God was certainly looking out for her, wasn't he?"

"You think so?"

"Well, sure. Don't you?"

Melanie stared out at the spot of road illuminated by Serena's headlights. "I do. It's just—this may sound weird and conceited, but I don't mean for it to—I'm not quite sure why God would bother himself—or herself—about Olivia. She doesn't believe in God. She doesn't believe in anything. If God was going to arrange all these events to save someone's life, why her? Why not someone who actually believed?"

Serena moved her hand slightly on the wheel to keep the truck in line with the road's sinewy path. "Don't you think that maybe someone like your sister is the one who needs that kind of intervention the most though? It's the sick person who needs the doctor, not the healthy person. The one who doesn't believe that needs convincing. And what better way to get her thinking in the right direction than sending her that kind of a sign?"

Melanie sat with that a moment. "But that's not fair. I'm always looking for signs. And then she's the one who gets them?"

"Oh." Serena sounded surprised. "I thought from our earlier conversation that you already believed in God."

"I do. I mean, I believe in lots of stuff. I believe in way more than her. Way more. I follow all sorts of belief systems."

"Hmm," Serena intoned.

"What?" Melanie said.

Serena gave her an apologetic shrug. "Maybe quantity isn't the point."

Melanie slumped back against the passenger seat and crossed her arms. Something was off about this whole thing. She was the one who searched for signs, so she should be the one who got them. She was the one who'd given Josh a chance first, so she should have been the one having the long, intimate conversations with him, the one laughing with him along the trail. She was the one who had stepped up to the edge of the cliff, so she was the one who should have fallen down it and been saved from cancer because of it.

She strove to do everything right and was rewarded with yet more work to do. Olivia did nothing at all and good things just fell into her lap, unearned.

After several quiet minutes of driving, Serena pulled up to a roadblock, spoke to an officer, and was waved through. A few moments later, she put on her blinker. "Here we are."

She pulled into the gravel parking area. Melanie's car was the only one there.

"I'll wait to make sure it starts," Serena said.

"Thank you," Melanie said. "Thank you for everything today. For getting Olivia to the hospital so quickly, for bringing the pack to the hospital—oh, hey, do you know the guy who gave you the pack? Josh?"

"Another ranger gave it to me."

"A ranger? Not a guy with a beard and a plaid flannel shirt?"

"No, it was my friend Mike. Handed me the pack and asked me to take it along to the hospital when I was about to bring in a few more hikers after you guys."

"Oh, okay," Melanie said, disappointment lacing her voice. "I was just hoping I could figure out how to get ahold of him. He helped us out a lot on the trail." Then, more hopefully, "He was the guy who put my sister in the back of your truck."

Serena shook her head. "Sorry. My superior told me someone was in there that needed to get to the hospital fast. I didn't take the time to introduce myself to anyone standing around there."

Melanie opened her door. "No big deal. Just thought I'd ask. Thanks again!" She jumped out, shut the door, and trotted through the light rain to her car. It started up with no trouble. She gave Serena one more wave, then the truck disappeared into the night.

Rather than pull out onto the road and drive back to the hospital, Melanie plugged in her phone and then leaned back, closed her eyes, and listened to the rain pinging off the car. She was exhausted in every way a person could be exhausted, and all she wanted to do was sleep. She opened one eye and peeked at the gas gauge. Not a good idea. She sat up straight, put the car in reverse, then put it back in park. She dug around in the glove box for the paper map of the Upper Peninsula Olivia had brought along to supplement the GPS. She found the Porkies and squinted at the lines indicating roads. At the far western end of the green blob that was the park, she found it.

The Pinkerton Creek parking lot was thirty miles away. Driving there and back would mean adding more than an hour to the twenty or so minutes it would take her to get back to the hospital. It was already past two o'clock. And what was her plan, really? If Josh's car was there, would she just sit around in the parking lot until he appeared? What did she plan to say to him if she did see him? And how could she possibly know which car was his anyway?

She looked at the gas gauge once more, then pulled out onto the road.

Melanie followed Olivia out of Macy's after a fruitless search for the perfect anniversary gift for their parents. Everything Olivia liked was too expensive. Everything Melanie liked Olivia hated. They'd driven down to the mall without permission to use the car for nothing. All Melanie wanted to do was get home—fast—so they wouldn't get caught.

Out in the parking lot, Olivia unlocked the door. "Oh, wonderful! Someone hit us with their door!"

Melanie came around to the driver's side where Olivia was trying to scratch red paint off the white door with a fingernail. It wouldn't come off, and even if it did it wouldn't have mattered. The little dent was plain as day.

"Well, that's just great," Melanie said. "Now we're going to get it."

Olivia unlocked the door. "Relax. Justin can fix it."

The drive back up the Beltline was quiet. Olivia had just gotten her permit and wasn't supposed to be driving without an adult, so she insisted on no distractions. Not even the radio. And the only thing Melanie had to say was "I told you so," which she sure as heck wasn't going to say to an already angry and stressed-out Olivia.

Thirty minutes later, Olivia pulled up in front of Justin's house. "Stay here," she commanded.

Melanie watched her go up the rickety wooden steps to the front door. She'd never seen the inside of Justin's house, though he was over at their house all the time. Frankly, it looked like a house her parents wouldn't want her to go into. Bad neighborhood. Unkempt yards. Cars parked on the lawn that were never actually driven.

Movement at the door. Olivia was talking to someone. Then the door closed and Olivia got back in the car.

301

"So?"

"He said to bring it up to the garage."

Olivia pulled the car up the gravel driveway, stopping as close to the garage as possible. Difficult, because the driveway seemed to be a dumping ground for unwanted items. Car parts, a kiddie pool, a pile of old bricks. Melanie wondered if her fastidious parents had ever seen the place.

Justin came out the back door in jeans and a hoodie but no coat. Olivia got out, so Melanie got out, though she would rather have stayed in the warm car.

"What do you think?" Olivia was saying to Justin.

"Easy. Twenty minutes."

He acknowledged Melanie with a nod and disappeared into the garage. A moment later he was back with a toolbox and an extension cord. He plugged a hot glue gun into the extension cord and pulled a strange-looking tool out of the box. He popped a little black disk into the tool and covered the flat part with hot glue, then stuck it to the car where the dent was.

"Umm," Melanie said, looking to Olivia. She had expected Olivia to flip out, but her sister's face was completely calm.

Justin slowly squeezed a trigger on the tool. It braced against the car, pulling back the glued disk. Then the disk popped off, leaving a round pad of dried glue on the door, which Justin peeled off. He repeated the whole process with two smaller disks, then ran his fingers over the spot.

"All good," he proclaimed.

Olivia ran her fingers over it as well. "What about the paint?"

He pulled a couple cloths and a small tub of something out of the toolbox. After a few seconds of rubbing whatever was in the tub onto the spot on the car; the red paint was gone. He handed Olivia the other cloth. "The compound has to dry. Buff it when you get home."

"Thanks," she said, giving him a hug. "You're amazing."

Something crashed inside. Then there was yelling.

"Want to come over for dinner tonight?" Olivia said casually, as though she'd heard nothing.

"Better not," Justin said.

They shared a look that Melanie couldn't read.

"Next time," Olivia said. "Let's go, Mel."

Melanie waved at Justin. "Thank you."

He nodded and watched them pull down the driveway. Then he trudged back to the house.

"Why wouldn't he come to dinner?" Melanie said.

"None of your business."

Melanie slouched low in the seat.

"Since we can't seem to agree on anything, let's just get them a gift certificate to a restaurant or something," Olivia said. "They could use a night out."

"Okay."

After a moment, Olivia said, "Sometimes he has to stay home to help his mom."

"Oh." She didn't ask for more explanation. It was easy enough to put two and two together. And Melanie would bet green money that the next time she saw Justin, the way he'd helped his mom would be written all over his face.

Thirty-One

OLIVIA WINCED as she pulled at the seat belt.

"I told you I'd get it," Melanie chided. She reached into the car over Olivia's body and blindly searched for the spot to click it in.

Olivia pushed her away. "That's even worse. I've got it. I'm not going to be able to avoid being in some pain, so I have to just work through it."

Melanie stood in the light drizzle, waiting for Olivia to get settled, then firmly shut the car door and walked around to the driver's side. It was nine o'clock. If they kept their pit stops brief, they'd be in Indian River by midafternoon and Olivia would be back in East Lansing for dinner. She thought of how good it would feel to be showered—no matter how complicated the process—and sleeping in her own bed and managed to smile through the pain.

"What day is it, anyway?" Olivia said as Melanie pulled out of the parking lot.

"Wednesday. I think."

"Strange. The whole time we were hiking, we were falling behind, and here we are going home a day ahead of schedule."

"That is a little strange."

Olivia chuckled ruefully and let out a long, low sigh. "Not one thing went as I planned it."

Melanie laughed. "Your plans were literally wiped off the map."

"Don't think I didn't notice the irony in that. If I had known any of this was going to happen, I would never have said yes to this trip."

"I know you wouldn't have. And frankly, I don't think I would have even suggested it."

Olivia eyed her little sister. "I don't know about that."

Melanie flashed a smile. "It certainly will go down as one of the worst hiking trips anyone has ever taken. Somewhere down the list from that guy who had to cut off his own arm."

And their last hiking trip, Olivia thought but did not say.

Melanie looked back at the road, and Olivia studied her sister's face. She looked tired. When Olivia had woken up that morning at seven o'clock, Melanie was not there. When she still hadn't appeared an hour later, Olivia called her phone. She knew from the amount of time it took Melanie to answer and the low, breathy quality of her voice that she'd just woken up. But she told Olivia she was out getting gas and breakfast and she'd be back soon. She appeared with a McDonald's bag at the moment Olivia was signing discharge papers. Melanie brought all of their stuff to the car as an orderly wheeled Olivia, McDonald's bag on her lap, down the halls and out the door.

Now Olivia dug into the bag and pulled out greasy, paper-wrapped breakfast sandwiches. "Is one of these yours?" she asked incredulously.

"Yeah," Melanie said.

Olivia examined them. "Which one? They look the same."

"They are the same. Sausage, egg, and cheese McMuffins."

"Umm."

Melanie held out her hand. "I'm cheating."

Olivia plopped a decidedly non-vegan sandwich in her hand. "Don't they have oatmeal?"

"Hard to eat that while driving. Just this once won't hurt. Anyway, I've been reevaluating some of that stuff the past couple days."

"You've had time to evaluate the merits of veganism when we were trying to outrun a forest fire and you were busy saving me when I fell off a cliff?"

"I didn't save you. Josh did."

"Which, by the way, what is going on with the fire? And what ever happened to Josh?"

Melanie took a massive bite of her sandwich and commenced chewing. Olivia waited.

"From what I could glean from the hospital staff talking," she finally said after swallowing, "the fire containment is going as well as it could be. We should see if we can get anything on the radio about it." She took another bite.

"What about Josh? Did he ever even come by the hospital?"

"No. I asked Serena about him—she's the ranger."

"Right."

"And she couldn't remember ever seeing him."

Olivia frowned. "I really wish I knew he was okay. I mean, I'm sure he is, it's just, the whole thing feels kind of unfinished. Like he's this big loose end just hanging out there."

Melanie nodded. Olivia bit into her own sandwich. For the

next few minutes, there was only driving and chewing, until finally Melanie said, "I went out to where his car was supposed to be parked last night."

"Yeah?"

"No one was there."

"No cars?"

"None. So I can only assume he got out fine and either drove home or is staying in some motel somewhere around here."

"Is that why you look so tired? When did you get back into town?"

"I went and looked for Josh and then drove back until I hit a twenty-four-hour gas station," Melanie said. "Gassed up then parked the car there and slept for a few hours until the phone woke me up."

"Oh man. I wish I could drive part of the way for you."

"Me too."

Olivia spun her head around and recoiled at the sudden pain. "Oh, I should not have done that."

"What?"

"Nothing. Just my neck. But I was going to say that there's no way you can drive me all the way back to East Lansing today on just a few hours' sleep."

Melanie squeezed the wheel at ten and two. "I'm not."

Olivia sighed. "I was really looking forward to being in my own bed tonight."

"You will be."

"How?"

"Well, I know you weren't keen on the idea of me coming along with you anyway."

"Yeah . . ."

"And I'm sure you have friends and coworkers who could help you out a bit during your recovery."

"Okay . . ."

"And if you don't, you'll hire help, right?" she said severely.

"Mel, who's bringing me home?"

Melanie glanced at her. "Don't be mad."

"What? Who?" Olivia said impatiently. Then it dawned on her. "No . . ."

"You said you were planning on talking to him anyway, so I figured this would give you time to do it and it would give me time to rest and—"

Olivia buried her face in her hands and groaned. "I wish you'd asked me first. That's all. I just wish you'd asked me." She took a deep breath. "I don't know if I'm ready to do this yet."

"Well, you've got at least six hours to get ready." She reached into the back seat and produced a small box, which she set on Olivia's lap. "This might help."

It was the box Olivia had asked about at the beginning of their trip. She wiped her hands on a napkin and stuck it in her pocket, then removed the lid and stared into the past. Ticket stubs from movies. Notes folded into paper footballs. A dried corsage from homecoming. A cheap imitation silver locket. And a handful of photos.

She and Justin on a trampoline. The two of them Roller-blading on the rail trail. Being dropped off at camp. Splashing each other in Crystal Lake. Eating ice cream on a bench and squinting into the sun. Her dad had taken these photos with his camera back before they all had smartphones. Olivia was intimately familiar with each one. Small holes attested to where pushpins had held them to the bulletin board in her bedroom. Her mind filled in the time on either side of the moment that had been captured. Moments that would never come again.

When she came to a picture of her and Justin at age four or five standing in the backyard in just their underwear, his tanned bare arm slung over her tanned shoulders, Olivia stopped. Starting at age seventeen, Justin would cover his arms in tattoos. In this picture, they were peppered with bruises. It had taken years of friendship before Justin divulged the things that were going on in his house as his unhappy and often intoxicated parents took out their misery on each other and on him. Despite that, in every photo of the two of them together, Justin was smiling.

At that moment, Olivia understood that her mother's refrain of "What's done is done and can't be undone" had been wrong. Or at least, it was not universally applicable. What had been done to Justin, Olivia and her loving family had, in part, undone. For many years, they had shown him how a family could be, how it should be. They hadn't removed his bruises, but they'd helped them heal.

Then Olivia left him behind. And he drifted away. And she forgot about him. Until he came crashing back into her life.

"I wondered what had become of this stuff," she finally said.

"You had to know I wouldn't have gotten rid of it."

"You have always been rather sentimental."

"I hardly think it qualifies as terribly sentimental to keep hold of a few childhood memories."

"No, I suppose not." Olivia returned the lid to the box, shrouding the past in darkness. "Music?"

"Your pick," Melanie said.

"Nah. You choose."

"You sure?"

"Sure."

Melanie retrieved a CD from her visor and popped it in. Olivia recognized it immediately as one of their mother's favorites—the first disc of Paul Simon's 1991 concert in Central Park. She had attended it with her sister Susan while pregnant with Melanie.

Olivia sank a little lower in her seat, closed her eyes, and let her mind drift back to better days. She imagined her mother singing along to the songs she'd grown up with. Imagined her father teaching her and Justin how to throw a baseball. Imagined Melanie's face when she finally got the kitten she'd been begging for. All of the photos that had been taken. All of the beautiful days that had passed by without photographic evidence to prove they'd happened. So many more happy memories than sad ones.

It was a good life. And even if that part of it was over, life could still be good. It could be better than she had allowed it to be. She could be better than she had allowed herself to be.

As she slipped into sleep, Olivia saw one more face in her memories. Josh's. And she felt sure in that moment that she would see him again someday.

Thirty-Two

MELANIE DROVE EAST, back toward Marquette, back to
the scene of the motorcycle accident nearly a week earlier. What
had happened to that man? Had he been treated and sent home
as Olivia had? Or had his funeral been held sometime when
they were tromping through the woods?

Life was so strange. The way it could go on for one person
and end for another. If there was a life force out there, why was
it always ebbing and flowing so capriciously? Who chose who
got to live and who must die, and by what criteria? Why was
Olivia's life saved by falling off a cliff and their parents' lost while
driving down a familiar street?

Attempting to fathom one being arranging all of this for billions of people all over the planet for all of time was like trying
to untangle all of the neurons in all of the brains of all those
people. To lay them all out in such a way that you could see all
the connections simultaneously, so you could see exactly which
cause created which effect.

Impossible. She used to be comfortable with that—with

the impossibility of knowing, the inscrutability of it all. When coaching clients asked her for specifics, she deliberately fuzzied things up and encouraged them to relax into the not knowing, into the nearly knowing. Specifics didn't matter. What mattered was how you felt, and any combination of ideas that made you feel some happiness in the midst of a troubled life was what was right for you.

Melanie thought about this as the names of tiny towns ticked by—Three Lakes, Imperial Heights, Beacon, Humboldt, Greenwood. Little outposts of civilization in the vast wilderness Longfellow had made famous in his "Song of Hiawatha," a tediously long poem Melanie had been assigned to read in high school, and which she discovered her father still knew by heart from his own school days. How very western these towns all sounded, as though the people who established them were assuring themselves that they could tame the dangers they might face—the fevers from the marshes, the pestilential vapors, the poisonous exhalations of Longfellow's poem—as they cut lumber and drained wetlands and platted out farmland.

At the junction for M-28, she should have turned left to stay near the lakeshore. It would have taken her right past the site of the motorcycle accident and given her the chance to see if a roadside marker had been put up, indicating the man's fate. Indicating whether or not her plea for positive vibes had been effective. But when it came down to it, she didn't actually want to know.

Instead, she followed M-41 south through nearly fifty miles of nothing but trees. The sky cleared as she got farther away from the big lake. Beech and birch trees shone bright yellow against the pines and firs, and shocks of red sumac rose like waves along the roadside. Summer's wildflowers were brown and spent. Life was winding down like an old clock. In a few weeks, daylight saving time would end and it would be dark before Melanie sat down to dinner. On the nights Justin could come over to eat or to watch a movie, it wouldn't be so bad. On the nights she was alone . . .

But she didn't have to be alone anymore. She did love Justin. And she knew he loved her. Not just the role she'd played in the wake of Olivia's rejection. Her.

It wasn't until Melanie slowed the car to take a left on US-2 that Olivia stirred. "Where are we?" she asked.

"A little over halfway to Indian River."

Olivia stretched and groaned. "Ugh. I forgot I was all messed up for a minute there."

"Do you need to take something for the pain?"

"Maybe. And I need to get out of this car and move. I'm all stiff."

"We can stop in Manistique for lunch and bathrooms."

"You mean Munising?"

"No," Melanie said. "I took a different route."

"Oh. How far to Manistique?"

Melanie checked the GPS, which had started working again as they approached the southern shore of the peninsula. "This says thirty-eight minutes."

"I don't think I can wait that long."

Melanie tapped the GPS. "Here. There's a gas station just south of this little lake. We'll stop there."

For the next twenty-five minutes, Olivia shifted and sighed

in her seat. She fiddled with the radio, flipped through CDs, never landed on anything. When they finally arrived at the gas station, Melanie helped Olivia get out of the car—not an easy feat—and hobble to the bathroom. She stocked up on water and snacks in lieu of lunch, then helped Olivia back to her seat. She was walking around to the driver's side when two women walked out of the gas station.

"That was incredible," one said.

"It really was," said the other. "I thought it would be a huge waste of time, but I think it's my favorite part of the trip so far."

"Excuse me," Melanie broke in. "What are you talking about?"

"The big spring," the first one said.

"Kitch—Kitch-ipi—oh, I can't say it. It starts with a *K*," the second one said.

"It's just north of here."

"What is it though?" Melanie said.

"It's . . . well, it's this spring."

"It's a really still pool of blue, blue—"

"Turquoise."

"Yes, turquoise water."

Melanie waited for more.

"It's hard to explain," the women said simultaneously. Then they laughed uproariously.

"You just have to see it," the first one finally said. "It's worth the drive."

"How far away is it?" Melanie asked.

"Oh, what do you think it is?" she asked her friend. "Fifteen minutes up the road?"

"If that."

"Which road?"

They pointed.

"This one here—149. It jogs, but there are signs."

"It starts with a *K*?" Melanie confirmed.

"Yes. Kitch-something. They call it the Big Spring."

"Thanks," Melanie said. The women went on their way and Melanie got in the car.

"What was all that?" Olivia said.

"Nothing. We just need to make one little detour before we go."

The walk from the parking lot to the viewing platform at Kitch-iti-kipi was slow and, if Olivia's expression was any indication, painful. When the water first came into view through the trees, Melanie felt a twinge of disappointment. It just looked like a pond. A blue one, sure, but a pond nonetheless. They came to a large deck. Through a wooden gate set in the railing, one could step onto a large covered rectangular raft, which they did. A sign indicated that if she turned a large metal wheel, the raft would move along a cable strung across the length of the spring, bringing them out to the middle.

"Oh!" Olivia said. "You can see clear to the bottom here."

In the center of the raft behind a wooden railing was a hole, a rectangle within the rectangle of the raft, and indeed you could see through the crystal-clear water to the bottom, which was crisscrossed with the remains of fallen pine trees. Melanie pulled the wheel and the raft moved a little. Pull by pull, first with her left hand, then her right, and as she tired, with both of them, Melanie slowly moved the raft to the middle of the pond, where there was nothing on the bottom but pale sand.

"Look," Olivia said, pointing into the hole in the raft.

Swimming lazily through the water were large, dark bodies of fish. A sign by the rail said that they were mostly trout—lake, brown, or brook—much like the fish Josh had been grilling for them, the fish on Olivia's knife. Another sign explained how meltwater and rainwater filled one permeable layer of rock that sat beneath another layer of rock, which was impermeable except for a few cracks. At these cracks, the pressurized water shot up into the spring at a rate of more than ten thousand gallons a minute. Where the water came up out of the ground, the sand looked as though it was boiling, though the water was only forty-five degrees Fahrenheit year-round. All quite practical and scientific and unmagical.

Maybe that was how the world really was. One vast machine. Nothing more than a collection of predictable, measurable processes. It was bleak, but that didn't necessarily mean it was not true. And if it was true, if this was the only life she'd ever have, Melanie didn't want to spend the rest of it on her own.

She looked out across the achingly blue water to the trees, which were reflected perfectly on its glassy surface. For every tree right side up, its twin was upside down. Each had a partner. Not one of them was alone.

"I'm going to tell Justin yes," Melanie said. She glanced at Olivia's face for her reaction and was surprised to see a smile there. A small one, perhaps strained, but a smile nonetheless. Melanie gave a resolute nod and looked back out at the trees. "This is pretty."

Olivia joined her at the rail. "Yeah." She pulled Melanie's phone out of her back pocket. "One more picture?"

Melanie took the phone from her. "Sure." With their backs to the outer rail, Melanie framed their faces on the screen. "You can't see much of the spring behind our fat heads."

"That's okay," Olivia said. "We know it's there."

Melanie snapped the photo, then looked at it. "You look really happy in this one."

Olivia tipped the screen toward her. "You don't."

"I'm just tired. It's been a long day already."

"So what are you going to do with this trip on your blog?" Olivia said.

"I don't know yet. Maybe nothing."

"Nothing? That hardly sounds like you."

Melanie shrugged. "It's a lot to process. And it's a lot to keep up, you know? The blog, the videos, the social media. It's been kind of nice to have a break from that this week. The thought of diving back into it all . . . well, it's exhausting really."

"What about your following?"

"I dunno. They'd get on without me. It's kind of arrogant of me to assume I'm really necessary, right? Anyway, some of the stuff I've been saying to them all these years is ringing a little hollow to me the last couple days. Maybe I need to take some time to myself." She motioned to the bubbling sand forty feet below. "I don't have that sort of thing. I am feeding and feeding other people, but nothing's really filling me back up. I just feel a little . . . empty."

Melanie could feel Olivia looking at her.

"Do me a favor, Mel?"

"What?"

"Anytime you're feeling that way, let Justin know, okay? Or

send me a text. Or call. I'll be more responsive than I have in the past. Just don't keep it to yourself."

Melanie blinked hard and nodded.

"Hey," Olivia said, turning Melanie to face her. "I love you, Mel. And I'm going to be a better sister to you from here on out."

"Okay," Melanie whispered.

Olivia pulled her into a gentle hug, and the tears Melanie had been holding in slipped out through the cracks and cascaded down her cheeks like twin waterfalls.

"Hey, hey," Olivia said. "What's wrong?"

Melanie hiccupped a sob, then sucked in a deep, quavering breath. "I don't know. I just feel so . . . so empty all of a sudden. Which is stupid. I've gotten what I wanted. I reconnected with you and I'm going to have you in my life, and I'll have Justin too and I won't have to choose."

Olivia rubbed her back. "Well, maybe that wasn't the only thing you were hoping for. Maybe that was just the stuff you could see on the outside."

Melanie wiped her nose with the back of her hand. "I miss Mom and Dad so much."

Olivia pulled her in for another hug. "So do I."

They stood there on the platform in the middle of the turquoise water, ringed in on all sides by pines and cedars and silence. Melanie pulled away and searched Olivia's eyes.

"Do you really think we'll never see them again? Do you really think there's nothing left of them?"

Olivia frowned. "I don't know. I hope not."

Melanie slumped back against the outer railing. "I'm just so tired."

"It's been a long week."

She threw up her hands. "No, I mean my whole life. I can't do this anymore, covering my bases. There are too many things I have to do, and it's all on me to do them, and what if I mess up? And you're right. You're right that they can't all be true. That one thing has to be it, the real thing. And if that one thing is true, then the things that aren't it can't be. I don't know, maybe there's nothing. Nothing beyond this life. Maybe—"

"No," Olivia said. "Don't say that."

"But you—"

"I know what I said, but . . . I don't know. Maybe I've been wrong. Frankly, I'm not even sure how much I truly believed what I was saying or if I was just saying it because it didn't require anything of me. I did nothing, you did everything. I believed nothing, you believed everything. But maybe we're both wrong. Maybe there's just one thing. One real thing."

Melanie swallowed and wiped her eyes.

"Okay?" Olivia said.

"Okay. Yeah."

Olivia smiled. "Now we just have to figure out what it is."

Melanie laughed despite herself. "Easy, right?"

"Yeah, easy."

The sun had dropped below the trees, but it hadn't quite set. The purple-gray sky was stained with tangerine at the horizon. Almost twilight, but Olivia could still make out the ball as it swished through the bright white net. She palmed it briefly and sent it over to Justin.

"One more and you're out, P-1," she said.

"I know. I know how to spell."

She could hear the smile in his voice even if it was getting hard to see in the dark.

Swish.

She set up her next shot, took it, and missed.

"Now you're in for it," he said. He dribbled up the driveway, spun to the right, then the left, then passed the ball between his legs before going for a right hook. But the ball bounced off the rim and into Olivia's waiting hands.

"Ha!" she shouted. Her laugh echoed in the August night. "You're always trying that fancy stuff, and it never works. It never works, my friend!"

"Oh, you mean this?" He hit the ball out of her hands and proceeded to dribble it step-by-step through his legs as he danced around her. "Or this?" He spun it on his finger and popped it up with his elbow.

"Or this," Olivia said flatly, hitting the ball out of his hands.

It bounced onto the grass. After a beat, they both tore after it, jostling, pushing, shoving. Then they both had their hands on it, trying to wrench it away. Justin pulled with his entire body weight and they crashed onto the lawn, legs tangled, both still hugging the ball. Olivia gave it one more giant twist, and Justin let go.

"You win! You win!" he said.

Olivia could hardly breathe she was laughing so hard, lying flat on her back, smelling grass and dirt and summertime.

Justin lay next to her, his chest rising and falling. "You win," he said again. "I'm done."

Olivia sat up. "The game's not over. You just have P-I. You need your G or you'll never be a real pig!"

Justin put his hand on his stomach. "I'm done."

"Quitter."

He popped the ball out of her hands again, and it went rolling back onto the pavement, hit the garage, and reversed course, rolling faster and faster down the driveway and into the street.

"You're going to go get that," Olivia said.

Justin didn't move. Olivia lay back down next to him. A few of the brightest stars had appeared as the sun retreated beneath the gentle curve of the earth. The grass felt prickly beneath her bare legs and arms. Summer was coming to an end. Soon she'd be leaving for her freshman year of college. It was only a two-and-a-half-hour drive from Rockford to Ann Arbor. But she knew in her heart she would not make it often. Nights like this were running out.

"You know you can use this hoop whenever you want, right?" she said. "And you can still come over here for dinner any night of the week. You can keep an eye on Melanie for me."

Justin looked at her for a long time. Too long. Then he stood up and walked across the street to get the basketball. Olivia tamped down the tears that wanted to come, thankful it was too dark for him to see her face anymore. Then he was standing over her, offering a hand.

"Get up, O. It's your turn."

321

Thirty-Three

IN THE TWO AND A HALF HOURS it took to get from the crystal waters of Kitch-iti-kipi to the gravel ride-share lot next to the Shell station in Indian River, Olivia tried to prepare herself to see Justin Navarro for the first time since she'd spotted him at the cemetery ten years ago. She looked again through the photos Melanie had saved, pulled those good memories to the front of her mind, silently practiced what she would say to him. She deliberated between a hug, handshake, or hands-free greeting. She breathed in, breathed out. When Melanie pulled in to the station, she thought she was ready.

She spotted him immediately, leaning against the wall outside. His hair was longer, and he'd exchanged his stubble for a neatly trimmed beard. The tattoo sleeves that had made him look like a drug dealer back when he was wearing oversize basketball jerseys with baggy jeans made him look like the quintessential Millennial entrepreneur now that he was sporting slim-fitting pants, a button-down shirt with rolled-up sleeves, and brown suede loafers with no socks. But he wore the same guarded expression she'd known so well. The one that had only ever relaxed into a smile when he was with her.

Melanie stopped at the gas pump. "Are you going to be okay with this?"

Olivia nodded, though she suspected it was a lie. Melanie got out of the car, ran over to where Justin stood, and gave him a long hug but no kiss. Then she disappeared into the store. Olivia pretended to be busy with her phone to avoid eye contact with Justin as he walked up to the gas pump, slid his credit card in, and lifted the nozzle.

All at once Olivia felt tremendously childish and realized that she needed to get out of the car. To use the bathroom, yes, but also because when she did finally say hello to him, she wanted it to be at eye level rather than him standing and her sitting. She removed her seat belt and opened the car door, but the apparatus keeping her knee immobilized meant she could not get out without help. She closed the door and decided to wait for Melanie, but almost as soon as it was shut, somebody opened it.

Olivia looked up to see Justin looking down at her.

"Need a hand?"

She muscled down her pride. "Yeah."

Justin took her elbow. Leaning the weight of her upper body in his sure grip, she twisted enough to get her leg out and let him lift her gently out of the car. Much smoother than when Melanie had gotten her out earlier that day. The moment she was stable, Justin dropped his hands and hooked his thumbs on his pockets. They looked at each other for one pregnant moment.

Olivia felt her heart rate tick up, and she forced herself to breathe slowly, deliberately.

She pointed into the car. "Can you grab those crutches? I need to use the bathroom."

"Of course."

He sprang into motion, and a moment later Olivia was hobbling toward the door. Inside, the clerk gave her a long, hard look. It was the same woman who had sized her up five days earlier. Olivia turned away.

In the bathroom, she caught sight of herself in the mirror and wished she hadn't. Her hair was in a greasy ponytail beneath her sweat-stained baseball cap. Her chin was scraped. A long purple bruise stretched from her temple to her jawline. A zit was brewing at the corner of her nose. She'd have to go to work like this. To explain to everyone what had happened on her big hiking trip. She wondered if her new look would work for or against her in the courtroom.

A few minutes later, Olivia gathered up her wounded pride and her crutches and headed back out into the store. Melanie was at the counter, buying iced tea and a bag of salted cashews. Olivia grabbed a Coke and plucked a newspaper from the rack near the door. Above the fold was an aerial shot of the fire in the Porcupine Mountains, accompanied by the triumphant headline "CONTAINED!" Olivia scanned the article for names, hoping she wouldn't see hers, hoping she would see Josh's. But the only people mentioned by name were park rangers. Everyone who had been in the park was accounted for, the cause of the fire was still under investigation, and the old-growth portion of the forest remained unspoiled.

"You gonna buy that?" the woman behind the counter asked. "'Cause this ain't a library."

Olivia plunked the paper down on the counter next to the Coke.

"Crazy, isn't it," the woman said, indicating the paper. She rang up Olivia's items, then fixed her with a look. "What happened to you?"

Olivia wordlessly tucked the receipt in her pocket and reached for her items, but Melanie, standing nearby, beat her to it. The woman behind the counter turned to the next person in line as they made their way outside, where Justin was now gassing up Olivia's car.

"I gave him your keys," Melanie said. "He's already got the packs in the back—I took my stuff out of mine. So I think you should be all set." Melanie put a hand on Olivia's arm. "Listen, I haven't told him yet."

"Does he know I know?"

"No. Let's not make this about me and Justin. This is about you and Justin. You'll get a few hours in the car to talk, he'll get you settled back in at home, then he'll stay the night at a hotel and fly home tomorrow, and I'll pick him up in Traverse City. He's already bought a ticket."

Olivia started toward her own car, which was dusty and covered in maple seeds. Melanie helped her into the passenger seat, handed over the Coke and the newspaper, then stood in the open door.

"Hey," she said. "I know this didn't turn out like either of us planned. But believe it or not, I think things are going to get better from here."

Olivia nodded. "They will."

Melanie frowned. "Promise me you'll call your doctor first thing tomorrow morning."

"Promise."

"And keep me updated."

"Okay."

Melanie shut the door. Justin closed the gas cap and came around to where Melanie stood. Olivia couldn't hear what they were saying, but she could see them in the side mirror. They ended the short conversation with a tight embrace and a quick kiss. Then Melanie knocked on the window, blew Olivia a kiss, and walked away.

Justin got into the car and started it up. "Where to?"

"East Lansing."

He indicated her University of Michigan ball cap. "They let you in there with that?"

"I don't wear it during football season."

"Ah." Justin pulled out of the parking lot and onto I-75 South.

Olivia stared out the window and tried to think of something appropriate to say, but nothing was coming to her. How did you talk to a friend you'd abandoned? How did you talk to the man who'd stolen away your parents and hoped to marry your sister? How did you begin to dig yourself out of a decade of bitterness?

She waited for him to break, to say something first. But he didn't.

"What do you do in Petoskey?" she finally said. Inane, but safe.

"I do custom bodywork on cars. Restore them, soup them up. Engine work. Detailing. Stuff like that."

"You have your own garage?"

"Yeah." He glanced at her. "It's a good living."

She nodded. "I'm sure it is."

The agonizing silence set back in. There was no way to start this conversation. Not without sounding like the prosecuting attorney she was.

"Get to the beach much?" Olivia tried.

"Just say it," Justin said.

"Excuse me?"

He looked at her. "Just say it."

"Say what?"

He looked back to the road. "Whatever it is you've wanted to say to me all these years. Just say it."

Olivia scowled. "What do you think I've wanted to say to you?"

He didn't answer.

"You think I had anything good to say to you? Any words of forgiveness or reconciliation? 'Let's let bygones be bygones'?"

"No."

"Then what the heck do you think I should say to you?"

Olivia sighed and shifted in her seat. Her foot hit something on the floor of the car. The shoebox of memories. Of course Melanie would put it right there where Olivia would see it. She rubbed her forehead and softened her tone.

"I've had a lot of time to be angry. A lot of time to wish things had been different. But they aren't. And there's nothing I can do about it."

She reached into her pocket for the used napkin from her breakfast to blow her nose, but her fingers found something else.

Something hard and round. She pulled it out. Josh's compass. How did that get there?

So you can find your way in the wilderness.

Forgiving Justin had never been part of her plan. She was off the path she'd marked out for her life, slogging through the muck and the underbrush, directionless. She opened the compass. The needle swung around to point north, back where they'd just come from, back where, for a moment at least, Olivia had allowed herself to imagine that there might be a God after all. One who called on people to do justice, love mercy, walk humbly. She'd been all hung up on the first part, had made it central to her identity. But she'd never been very good at the other two.

She flipped the compass closed. Despite all of their missteps and mistakes while hiking, they had made it out alive. More than that, if the doctor was correct, Olivia might have that hiking trip to thank for saving her from cancer. That wasn't really justice. She and Melanie were unfit in the Darwinian sense and should have been eliminated from the gene pool. If it hadn't been for Josh—guiding them along the river, sharing his food and his shelter, dragging her back up the escarpment and out of the woods—they might still be out there. Maybe caught in a forest fire.

Josh had put his own life on the line, for her and for others when he went back in with a search party. The paper had said everyone was accounted for. No one had been left to fend for themselves amid the flames. He'd found everyone he was looking for—including the people who must have been responsible for the fire. He loved mercy.

"Listen, Justin," she began tentatively. "I know it was an accident." She swallowed down the emotion she felt rising in her throat. "I know you lost them too."

Olivia could see his jaw clench beneath his beard. Did he give himself headaches that way like she did? Had he been as tightly coiled all this time?

"I haven't been a very good friend through all of this. Or a good sister." She pushed the reluctant words past her teeth. "I'm going to try to do better."

Justin nodded a little. "It's been hard—knowing you were out there hating me all these years." He glanced her way. "You were my best friend. My only friend."

"I know."

"When you left it really sucked, you know?"

Olivia pressed her lips together. "Yeah. I know."

"And then the accident and everything fell apart . . . and I had no one."

"You had Melanie," she offered, and for the first time she truly understood what her sister had been trying to tell her all those years ago. Justin had needed forgiveness. And Melanie had needed to forgive.

"Yeah, she helped. A lot. I don't think I'd still be around if it weren't for her."

Olivia tucked the compass back into her pocket and took out the napkin she'd been after in the first place. "She told me you asked her to marry you."

Justin looked at her, the question he was afraid to ask written across his brow.

"I'll admit I didn't take it so well," Olivia said.

His face fell.

"But I'm slowly coming around to it. It makes sense."

Relief washed over Justin's face, but it was quickly replaced with concern. "She hasn't told me yes or no."

Olivia smiled. "She told me."

He waited for more.

"It's not my business to say," she said. "And Melanie didn't want this ride to be about the two of you. Though, I don't know what we're supposed to talk about if we can't bring her into it. She's the only thing we really have in common at this point."

Justin passed a semi and returned to the right lane. "We've got practically twenty years of history together, just you and me. That's two-thirds of our lives."

"We did have some pretty good times." Olivia stared at the road ahead. Those times were all behind her now.

Just like the accident. Ten years in the past but still fresh, still raw. Still permanent. Why did that hang on, a parasite on her soul, when the good stuff faded like mist beneath the heat of the sun?

"Melanie said you've been going to church."

Justin nodded.

"You believe all that stuff?"

"Yes, I do."

He tightened his grip on the steering wheel, but his face relaxed so that Olivia saw something there she'd never seen before. It wasn't just happiness like in the old photos in the box at her feet. It was something more. It was peace. It was serenity. In fact, it wasn't unlike Josh's face.

"What do you think they'll say to you if you see them again?" she mused. "Do you think they'll forgive you?"

"Your parents?" He shook his head. "They won't have to. When my life ends, I'll be carrying nothing with me into the next one. No sins, no mistakes, no guilt. There's nothing to forgive in heaven."

"So that's it, then? All the transgressions of our lives on Earth are just gone and no one has to pay? How is that fair?"

"It isn't. Just like it isn't fair that nearly twenty years of friendship can be destroyed by three seconds of reckless driving."

"Careful."

"Just like it wasn't fair that my dad beat me and spent the grocery money on drugs and alcohol," he barreled on. "You've got to stop thinking in terms of *fair*. Fair is the bare minimum of happiness. It's zero. It's not positive, it's not negative, it's just zero. You want to live your life striving to achieve zero?"

Olivia shifted uncomfortably in her seat.

Justin softened his tone. "When has something being fair ever made you happy? When Melanie said it wasn't fair that you took both drumsticks when your dad brought home fried chicken, he took one of them from you and gave it to her. Did *fair* work for you then?"

"It worked for Melanie," Olivia quipped.

"When the two of you couldn't agree whose turn it was to pick the Friday night movie, what happened?"

"Mom picked."

"And what did she always pick?"

Olivia sighed. "*Dead Poets Society.*"

"Which you *hated.*"

"You hated it too."

"What about how angry you used to get because your parents

were so much stricter with you than they were with Melanie? That her curfew was later than yours was at the same age. That she got her kitten when they wouldn't let you get a husky puppy. That you had to get a summer job at an office while she got to babysit kids at the country club pool every day."

"What's your point?"

"That your obsession with things being fair hasn't brought you any joy. All it's produced is bitterness." He glanced her way. "And by the way, I never said that no one had to pay."

Thirty-Four

MELANIE SAT by the stone fireplace in the lobby of the tiny Cherry Capital Airport in Traverse City and watched the spot where she knew Justin would appear. The day before, she'd gotten home, taken a shower, and collapsed into bed. She'd woken up at six o'clock, savored a hot cup of tea, and sat down with a blank journal, thinking she'd process some of the events of the past week. To her surprise, she could not quite bring herself to write anything down.

She relocated to the computer to start working through what she had missed during her time off the grid, starting with the comments on the video from the scene of the motorcycle accident. They were largely what she'd expected—notes of support and declarations that thoughts and vibes were going out and prayers were going up. But there were also a few along the lines of what Olivia had said—that she was using someone else's tragedy to get clicks. Her fingers itched to respond to those comments as she had responded to Olivia's criticism, but she refrained.

Instead, she deleted them. She couldn't do anything about

the thumbs-downs—there were always a few of them—but she didn't have to let false accusations go unchecked. After she finished with that video's comments, she clicked to the previous video she had posted and did the same. It felt good. It felt like scraping the sad remains of a failed recipe from her plate and shoving it down the garbage disposal.

Once she got started, it was hard to stop. Comment by comment, video by video, she rejected every criticism of her or her motives until everyone who disagreed with her was silenced. Then she sat back and looked at the clock. If Justin's flight was on time, she was going to be late. Again.

The drive down to Traverse City was always lovely, but today especially. The rolling green hills had burst into fall color while she was gone. Every tree had become an individual rather than just an anonymous part of the collective. The blue sky was studded with fluffy white clouds playing peekaboo with the sun. Lake Michigan and Grand Traverse Bay sparkled to her right. Lake Charlevoix, Torch Lake, and Elk Lake glittered to her left. Every charming tourist town along US-31 was now empty of its summer traffic snarls. It was for moments like these that she lived Up North.

Plus she was on her way to see Justin. To take him home and tell him she would marry him.

She'd meant to text him the night before to see how everything went, but then she'd fallen asleep so quickly and completely. She'd been a little annoyed when there wasn't a text from him this morning to update her on the situation with Olivia. No text letting her know he was boarding his plane. No text letting her know it had landed.

Now she stood up to check the status of the flight, but as she did people started filtering into the lobby. She spotted Justin immediately. He was talking on his phone, a wide smile on his normally stoic face. Melanie's gut twisted at the sudden thought that perhaps Justin had not stayed at a hotel that night. That maybe he'd stayed with Olivia. But the thought fled when Justin saw her, said "I gotta go" into the phone, dropped his backpack, and pulled her into his arms.

"Oh, I missed you," he said into her neck.

"I missed you too."

He kissed her long and slow, the kind of kiss she'd wanted back in Indian River but hesitated to give him in front of Olivia. He shouldered his backpack and steered her toward the door.

"So how did it go?" Melanie asked.

"Rocky start. But ultimately better than I expected."

"That's good," she said. "What did you talk about?"

"Oh, lots of stuff. We talked about old times. I got her set up at her place. Got us some Chinese food while she took a shower. We watched a movie. Then I took an Uber to the hotel. Took another to the airport, and here I am."

A movie? They'd watched a movie?

Melanie unlocked the car, and Justin tossed his bag in the back seat. "Did you talk about the accident?"

"A bit." He got into the car.

Melanie got in and fastened her seat belt but did not start the car. "What did she say? Did she forgive you?"

Justin scrunched up his brow. "She's not quite there yet."

"But she watched a movie with you?"

"She's on the right path, I think. Give her time."

Melanie frowned and started the car. "She's had ten years."

Justin put his hand on hers where it rested on the shifter. "Don't be like that. This is progress." He sat back. "She seemed like a different person in a lot of ways. And I guess in others she seemed exactly the same."

Melanie put the car in reverse and then studied his face, which seemed lost in a memory that did not include her. Just as all those photos had not included her. Was there a piece of him that would never quite be hers? A piece that would forever belong to her sister?

"What's up?" Justin said.

"What?"

He looked around. "We're not moving."

"I just thought . . ." She put the car in drive. "I don't know what I thought."

She could feel him watching her, but she pasted a smile on her face and headed for the highway.

"So who were you talking to back there?" Melanie said after they'd been on the road for a few minutes.

"Back where?"

"The airport. Before you saw me. Who were you talking to?"

"Oh, that. That was Dale. The guy with the '55 T-Bird I was telling you about a couple weeks ago. Said he might have a couple more cars coming my way this winter. Wants them ready for the summer car shows."

"That's great!" she said, masking her relief that it was not Olivia with extra enthusiasm.

"It'll be good money. Which is great if we're going to be paying for a wedding." He let the word hang there in the air a moment. "So what do you think? Are we going to be paying for a wedding? I kind of got the idea from Olivia that maybe we'd be paying for a wedding."

"Olivia said that?" Melanie snapped. What gave Olivia the right to tell Justin yes or no?

"Not exactly. She said she knew I'd asked you."

"And?"

"And she said she knew what your answer was, but she wouldn't tell me. She didn't seem like she was upset about it or anything, so I kind of thought—I mean, that was your reservation, right? That she'd be angry and you'd have to choose, her or me. But now it doesn't seem like that's the case." He fell silent.

Melanie pulled off to the side of the road. "I can't have this conversation while driving." She parked by a stretch of sandy beach that separated US-31 from the waves on Grand Traverse Bay and swiveled in her seat to face Justin. She reached for his hand. "I've given this a lot of thought since you asked me, but also a lot just this week. And I do want to say yes."

He frowned. "But?"

"I just have to ask—when you were with Olivia yesterday, did any of your old feelings for her pop up?"

"What do you mean?"

"I think you know what I mean. I just have to be sure that when you saw her yesterday, you weren't thinking about what might have been if things had gone differently."

Justin relaxed his face and put a hand on top of hers. "That was a really long time ago, Mel. God led me away from Olivia. And he led me to you. You were there for me. You cared. You showed me love and mercy and friendship. And you're the one I want to marry. Not Olivia. Okay?"

Melanie sniffed and felt a tear escape her eye. "Okay."

"You believe me?"

She nodded. "Yeah. Okay."

He dipped his head and caught her eye. "So will you marry me?"

Melanie straightened in her seat and smiled through her tears. "Yes."

Later that night when Melanie returned home, she sat back down with her new journal. She had lost the record of Justin asking. She would not miss recording her answer. She scribbled away for ten or fifteen minutes, reliving the emotions from the car. But she only chronicled the joy. None of the suspicion or second-guessing would make it into the official record of her life.

Afterward she scanned her emails and social media notifications. So many people looking to her for encouragement and guidance. So many people taking without offering anything in return beyond an ego boost. She scrolled through months of posts and comments, and rather than feeling accomplished as she usually did, she felt mildly irritated. Nothing she said actually meant anything. She had just been saying things that people wanted to hear, feeding their ideas back to them, a slightly shined-up version of what they already believed.

What was the point of it all? Was she even helping anyone? Or had it all been about her all along?

Suddenly she wished she had not deleted all those negative comments. She wanted to think about what they said. Wanted to look herself in the face with a more critical eye, to see if maybe there were some things she was just plain wrong about. But she couldn't undo it.

She got up and searched the fridge for something edible, but she'd emptied it of all but condiments before leaving for the hiking trip. Anyway, it wasn't food she was craving. Not physically, at least. She needed something to nourish her soul. And before that, she needed to detox it.

She turned on every light in the kitchen and dining room, settled into a chair, and picked up her phone. She fixed her hair in the screen, centered herself, then hit record.

"Hello, my Mellies! I'm back from my hiking trip in Michigan's glorious Upper Peninsula, and I have to tell you that I am just filled to overflowing with stories I'd love to share with you. Getting lost and encountering bears and escaping a forest fire—no, really, all of that happened and more!"

She paused, knowing that even now she was putting on a front. She relaxed the practiced smile on her face and took a breath.

"The thing is, I'm not really ready to talk about it. I need some time to process. Some time to think through what this trip really meant to me. For that reason, among others, I'm going to be signing off for a while. It's time to clean my mental house, to reevaluate. Over the next few weeks, you may see content disappearing from my channels as I sort through the kind of person I want to be and the kind of messages I want to send. It may be that I close up shop online altogether and start something completely new. I don't know yet. But there's one thing I do know: life is about more than just being happy or being liked or being self-actualized. It's about more than just me. It's about more than just you.

"Now, I'm not saying I know *what* it's about. But I know it's about *something*. Something bigger. Something real. Something mysterious, yes, but also something that wants to be known. So that's what I'm going to be looking for. You know me: I'm all about the journey. But what's a journey without a destination?

"So goodbye for now, my Mellies. Peace, love, and life to you. And may we all find what we're really looking for."

Melanie blew a kiss at the camera and stopped the recording. A few minutes later, it had been uploaded to all of her platforms. Before she could see any comments, she shut down her computer and uninstalled the apps from her phone. Then she texted her sister.

How are you holding up?

Epilogue

THREE YEARS LATER

OLIVIA PUT THE CAR in park in a handicapped spot in the lot at Tahquamenon Falls State Park and pulled a red knit cap over her short brown hair. She opened the door, slowly turning her entire body to the left before she stepped out of the car. Deliberate movements like this had become second nature to her. She had to be careful not to wrench her new titanium hip, still had to concentrate to stand on her prosthetic without her cane. It had been a long, agonizing road to get to this point, but she was determined to reassert her independence.

This was why she was here. Or at least, that's what she told herself.

The amputation of her right leg from just above the knee had been difficult to come to terms with, though she felt that the recovery from the hip replacement on the other leg was more tedious. The chemo was no picnic either. But she had come through. Next week she'd be back to work full-time. For now, she had just one goal: walk unassisted from her car to the falls.

She drew in a deep draught of the crisp autumnal air. It smelled of pine needles and decay and cedar trees, a welcome relief after so much time breathing the sterile air in hospitals and rehab centers and her apartment. It crossed her mind that her sister got to smell air like this all the time. Perhaps she ought to reconsider Melanie's invitation to come live with her and Justin. But no, she'd only be in the way. Especially since Melanie was pregnant with number two.

She stepped up onto the sidewalk gingerly, giving the task her full attention. When that feat was accomplished, she began to make her way up the paved walk toward the trees. With each step, she felt more confident, more at ease. There were few people there this late in the season, and those who passed by gave her little notice. In long pants it was hard to tell she had a prosthesis. In summer she'd had to contend with staring children and people thanking her for her service. At first she tried to explain that she was not a veteran, merely a cancer survivor. But it got complicated and took forever, especially if the hiking trip somehow slipped in there, so she stopped correcting people and merely made a point to always thank actual veterans and soldiers anywhere she encountered them.

She could hear the crash of the forty-eight-foot falls getting stronger, sneaking past the trees on her left, drawing her down the walkway. At one point the railing by which she'd been hovering—just in case—made a sharp left turn toward an opening in the trees, where she'd be able to see the falls in the gorge far below. Did she follow the rail? Or meet back up with it when it returned to the straighter path in fifteen feet? Perhaps she should have brought the cane after all.

She opted to follow the rail. Safe was better. At the opening in the trees she paused to watch the foam drift away from the basin of churning water. White foam tinged with brown from the tannins that leeched from the cedar trees, like a river of root beer. A little farther and she could see the falls in the middle distance.

She lingered at the rail, trying not to think of anything in particular, trying to experience something without making any plans or doing any mental calculations about time or distance or efficiency. It was a skill that was hard to master, one that had been suggested to her by the therapist she saw during her recovery. When she found herself wondering exactly how much water went over the falls each day, she moved on.

A few minutes later, she stood at the precipice of a very long flight of stairs—the sign said ninety-four—twisting down toward the brink of the falls and broken every ten or twelve steps by landings with benches. She was sure she could get down them if she took it slow. Coming up, though, could be another matter. Yes, she was cleared for normal activity, but this wasn't exactly normal. Given the choice, even an able-bodied person might opt for an elevator rather than climb that many steps. And she was less able-bodied than most.

Disappointed, she slowly retraced her steps toward the car. She'd have to settle for the lower falls today. She drove four miles down a winding road hedged in by forest to another parking lot, repeated the slow ritual of exiting the car, and headed down another long, paved path.

After several minutes of careful walking, she stepped off the paved path and onto a boardwalk leading to a deck she was sure had not been there when her family had visited Tahquamenon when she and Melanie were small. On the other side of the wooden rail, the lower falls tumbled and crashed over rocks and downed trees, eventually ending up at a wide basin downstream. For just a moment, she thought of nothing at all, allowing her basic senses—sight, smell, hearing, touch—to simply receive data without using that data to come to any conclusions.

She felt the reassuring shape of Josh's compass in her pocket and thought of the last time she'd seen a waterfall before today, of that cursed hiking trip in the Porkies that had turned out to be the most bizarre of blessings. She'd tried to dismiss it for a while, but when the diagnosis came in she couldn't deny it any longer. There were too many coincidences, too many times she'd been ready to quit but had been thwarted. The man in the river right where he needed to be, the borrowed campsite, the dry sleeping bag, the fire driving them on, the stumble that cracked her kneecap, the fall off the escarpment. Even that overly warm day in March that started it all. Every little thing pushing her a little further along to where she needed to be in order to save her life.

She took out her phone, snapped a picture of the falls, and examined it to see if the phone's mediocre camera had managed to capture the dynamic movement of the water. It hadn't, but something in the top left corner of the shot caught her eye. A small blotch of blue and olive green standing out against the autumn trees.

Olivia looked at the actual river above the falls where the

blotch had been but saw nothing. She moved to the left and stepped up onto the wood slat at the bottom of the rail to gain a better angle. At first there were only trees and water. But then . . . yes, that was a person up there. A man in a blue shirt and olive waders with a canvas bag slung across his body, waving his fly rod back and forth, back and forth, in what seemed like a familiar rhythm. For the barest moment, he turned her way, and Olivia could swear he looked right at her. Then he went back to his fishing.

With a strange sense of urgency, she made her way to the edge of the viewing platform. There was a narrow path that ran along the river, strewn with rocks and roots. A harder path to take than the wide, paved one that would take her back to her car. But it was, she suddenly knew, the right path.

With nothing in her hands, Olivia set her jaw, stepped off the smooth, man-made platform, and took the hard way. The way that would lead her home.

Author's Note
and Acknowledgments

I HAD BEEN SITTING on my butt for more than a decade when I decided I wanted to do some backcountry hiking with my sister, Alison. With equipment mostly borrowed from my father-in-law, we spent several days and nights in June of 2012 hiking Pictured Rocks National Lakeshore in Michigan's Upper Peninsula. In the years that followed, we hiked the Grand Sable Dunes, Tahquamenon Falls, the Manistee River Valley, the Jordan River Pathway, and Sleeping Bear Dunes. We did start a hike in the Porcupine Mountains that we did not finish due to the miserably high level of mosquito activity (I'm talking, like, eleventh plague on Egypt here). But we've never gotten lost, fallen off any cliffs, or run from a wildfire. We've never even had an argument while out on the trail. We did sleep next to a bear one cold October night. Our hiking trips are chronicled at www.erinbartels.com. Just look for the blog posts in the Travel category tagged "hiking" or click through the Photos page.

Alison and I spent most of our twenties thinking that we were very different people. As it turns out, we're not so different after all. Somewhere along the way, we each took a step toward the other, and eventually our paths met. We have been enjoying each other's company on the journey ever since.

Thank you, Alison, for being game to follow me out into the woods. For the companionable silences. For the conversations we probably wouldn't have had anywhere else. Thank you for never complaining. Thank you for eating disgusting, cold SpaghettiOs on the trail. Thank you for knocking down those insufferable little cairns with me. There is a special kind of contentment I know we both experience when we are far from civilization, ensconced in trees and wind and water and sky. I'm so glad I get to share those blessings with you.

Thank you to my publishing team at Revell for your work on this book. To Kelsey Bowen, Andrea Doering, Jessica English, Michele Misiak, Karen Steele, Gayle Raymer, Mark Rice, and everyone else who has had a part in its journey from concept to contract to completed product. Thank you to WFWA, especially Orly Konig and Jennie Nash for the 2018 writing retreat at Hotel Albuquerque (my home away from home), where the idea for this book went from nebulous to certain. Thank you to my agent, Nephele Tempest, and my husband, Zachary, for reading the manuscript and offering both encouragement and helpful critique.

Most of all, thank you to the God who made this world that I so dearly love, the author of all beauty and wonder, who beckons me to walk the narrow, winding path of life by faith. May you be my compass when I stray, my helper when I stumble, and ever the object of my deepest devotion.

LOVED THIS STORY?
READ ON FOR A SNEAK PEEK OF
**ANOTHER CAPTIVATING STORY
FROM ERIN BARTELS!**

• • •

Coming Soon

One

THE SUMMER you chopped off all your hair, I asked your dad what the point was of being a novelist. He said it was to tell the truth, which I thought was a pretty terrible answer.

"Nothing you write is real," I said. "You tell stories about made-up people with made-up problems. You're a professional liar."

"Oh, Kendra," he said. "You know better than that." Then he started typing again, as if that had settled things. As if telling me I already had the answer was any kind of answer at all.

I don't know why he assumed I knew anything. I've been wrong about so much—especially you.

There is one thing about which I am now certain: I was lying to myself about why I decided to finally return to Hidden Lake. Which makes perfect sense in hindsight. After all, novelists are liars.

"It will be a quiet place to work without distraction," I told my agent. "No internet, no cell service. Just me and the lake and a landline for emergencies."

"What about emailing with me and Paula?" Lois said, practicality being one of the reasons I had signed with her three years prior. "I know you need to get down to it if you're going to meet your deadline. But you need to be reachable."

"I can go into town every week and use the Wi-Fi at the coffee shop," I said, sure that this concession would satisfy her.

"And what about the German edition? The translator needs swift responses from you to stay on schedule."

We emailed back and forth a bit, until Lois could see that I was not to be dissuaded, that if I was going to meet my deadline, I needed to see a lake out my window instead of the rusting roof of my apartment building's carport.

Of course, that wasn't the real reason. I see that now.

The email came from your mother in early May, about the time the narcissus were wilting. For her to initiate any kind of communication with me was so bizarre I was sure that something must be wrong even before I read the message.

Kendra,

I'm sorry we didn't get to your grandfather's funeral. We've been out of state. Anyway, please let me know if you have seen or heard from Cami lately or if she has a new number.

Thanks,

Beth Rainier

It was apparent she didn't know that you and I hadn't talked in eight years. That you had never told your mother about the fight we'd had, the things we'd said to each other, the ambiguous state in which we'd left things. And now a woman who only talked to me when necessary was reaching out, wondering if I knew how to get in touch with you. That was the day I started planning my return to the intoxicating place where I had spent every half-naked summer of my youth—because I was sure that in order to find you, I needed to recover us.

THE DRIVE NORTH was like slipping back through time. I skirted fields of early corn, half mesmerized by the knit-and-purl pattern that sped past my windows. Smells of diesel fuel and manure mingled with the dense green fragrance of life rushing to reproduce before another long winter. The miles receded beneath my tires, and the markers of my progress became the familiar billboards for sporting goods stores and ferry lines to Mackinac Island. The farm with the black cows. The one with the quilt block painted on the side of the barn, faded now. The one with the old bus out back of the house. Every structure, each more ramshackle than the last, piled up in my chest until I felt a physical ache that was not entirely unpleasant.

In all our enchanted summers together on the lake, there had been more good than bad. Sweet, silent mornings. Long, languid days. Crisp, starry nights. Your brother had thrown it all out of whack, like an invasive species unleashed upon what had been a perfectly balanced ecosystem. But he hadn't destroyed it. The good was still there, in sheltered pockets of memory I could access if I concentrated.

The first step out of the car when I arrived at the cabin was like Grandpa opening the oven door to check on a pan of brownies—a wave of radiant heat carrying an aroma that promised imminent pleasures. The scent of eighteen summers. A past life, yes, but surely not an irretrievable one.

On the outside, the cabin showed the effects of its recent abandonment—shutters latched tight, roof blanketed by dead pine needles, logs studded with the ghostly cocoons of gypsy moths. Inside, time had stopped suddenly and completely, and the grit of empty years had settled on every surface. The same boxy green-plaid sofa and mismatched chairs sat on the same defeated braided rug around the same coffee table rubbed raw by decades of sandy feet. That creepy stuffed screech owl still stared down from the shelf with unblinking yellow eyes. On tables, windowsills, and mantelpiece sat all of the rocks, shells, feathers, and driftwood I'd gathered with my young hands, now gathering dust. Grandpa had left them there just as I had arranged them, and the weight of memory kept them firmly in place.

Each dust mote, each dead fly beneath the windows, each cobweb whispered the same pointed accusation: *You should have been here.*

For the next hour I manically erased all evidence of my neglect. Sand blown through invisible cracks, spiderwebs and cicada carapaces, the dried remains of a dead redstart in the fireplace. I gathered it from every forgotten corner in the cabin and dumped it all into the hungry mouth of a black trash bag, leaving the bones of the place bare and beautiful in their simplicity.

Satisfied, I turned on the faucet for a glass of cold water, but nothing happened. Of course. I should have turned on the water main first. I'd never opened the cabin. That was something an adult did before I showed up. And when I went out to the shed to read the instructions Grandpa had written on the bare pine wall decades ago, I found it padlocked.

Desperate to cool down, I pulled on my turquoise bikini and walked barefoot down the hot, sandy trail to the lake. Past Grandpa's old rowboat. Past the stacked sections of the dock I had only ever seen in the water—yet another task adults did that I never paid any attention to because I could not conceive of being one someday. At the edge of the woods, I hesitated. Beyond the trees I was exposed, and for all I knew your brother was there across the lake, waiting, watching.

I hurried across the sandy beach and through the shallows into deep water, dipped beneath the surface, and held my breath as long as I could, which seemed like much less than when I was a kid. As I came back up and released the stale air from my lungs, I imagined the stress of the past year leaving my body in that long sigh. All of the nervous waiting before interviews, all of the dread I felt before reading reviews, all of the moments spent worrying whether anyone would show up to a bookstore event. What I couldn't quite get rid of was my anxiety about The Letter.

Out of all the reviews and emails and tweets that poured in and around me after I'd published my first novel, one stupid letter had worked its way into my psyche like a splinter under my fingernail. I had been obsessing about it for months, poring over every critical word, justifying myself with logical arguments that couldn't take the sting out of what it said.

```
Kendra,
    Your book, while perhaps thought "brave"
in some circles, is anything but. It is
the work of a selfish opportunist who was
all too ready to monetize the suffering of
others. Did you ever consider that antago-
nists have stories of their own? Or that
in someone else's story you're the antago-
nist?
    Your problem is that you paid more at-
tention to the people who had done you
wrong than the ones who'd done you right.
That, and you are obviously completely
self-obsessed.
    I hope you're happy with the success
you've found with this book, because the
admiration of strangers is all you're
likely to get from here on out. It cer-
tainly won't win you any new friends. And
I'm willing to bet the old ones will steer
pretty clear of you from here on out. In
fact, some of them you'll probably never
see again.

                    Sincerely,
                    A Very Disappointed Reader
```

Maybe it was because the writer hadn't had the courage to sign his name — it had to be a him. Maybe it was because it had been mailed directly to me rather than forwarded on from my publisher, which could only mean that the writer either knew me personally or had done a bit of stalking in order to retrieve my address. It hurt to think of any of my friends calling me a "selfish opportunist." But the thought of a total stranger taking the trouble to track me down in order to upbraid me gave me the absolute creeps.

But really, if I'm honest with myself, the letter ate at me because deep down I knew it had to be someone from the small, private community of Hidden Lake. Who else could have guessed at the relationship between my book and my real life?

Whoever this Very Disappointed Reader was, he had completely undermined my attempts to write my second book. I knew it was silly to let a bad review have power over me. But this wasn't someone who just didn't like my writing. This was someone who thought I was the bad guy. He had read my novel and taken the antagonist's side—your brother's side.

Now I closed my eyes, lay back, and tried to let the cool, clear water of Hidden Lake wash it all away. But the peaceful moment didn't last. The humming of an outboard motor signaled the approach of a small fishing boat from the opposite shore. Hope straightened my spine and sent shards of some old energy through my limbs and into my fingers and toes. And even though I knew in my heart that it wouldn't be you, I still deflated a bit when I saw your father, though in almost any other context I would have been thrilled.

He cut the motor and came to a stop a few yards away. "Kendra, it's good to finally see you again. I was sorry to hear about your grandpa. We wanted to make it to the funeral, but Beth and I were out of state."

"Yes, she told me."

He looked surprised at that, then seemed to remember something. Perhaps he knew about the strange email.

I swam to the boat—not the one I remembered—and held on to the side with one hand, using the other to shade my eyes as I looked up into his still handsome face. I didn't ask him where you were that day, and he didn't offer any explanation. More likely than not, he didn't know.

"Beth's in Florida now," he continued. "It's just been me since Memorial Day. I was hoping to catch your mother up here before she put the place up for sale."

"It's not going up for sale."

"No? Figured she would sell it."

"It's mine. Grandpa left it to me."

"That so?" He glanced at my beach. "I can help you put the dock in tonight, around five? I'd help now, but I'm off to talk to Ike."

"Ike's still alive?"

"Far as I know."

I smiled. "That would be great, thanks. Hey, I don't suppose you've heard from Cami yet? No chance she'll be coming up this summer?"

He looked away a moment. "Nothing yet. But I've seen Scott Masters once or twice this month. And Tyler will be up Friday."

He waved and headed out across the lake to Ike's. I tried to separate the thudding of my heart from the loud chugging of the outboard motor that receded into the distance.

Of course Tyler would be there. Every paradise needed a serpent.

Erin Bartels is the award-winning author of *We Hope for Better Things*—a 2020 Michigan Notable Book, winner of two 2020 Star Awards from the Women's Fiction Writers Association, and a 2019 Christy Award finalist—and *The Words between Us*, which was a finalist for the 2015 Rising Star Award from WFWA. Her short story "This Elegant Ruin" was a finalist in *The Saturday Evening Post* 2014 Great American Fiction Contest. Her poems have been published by *The Lyric* and the East Lansing Poetry Attack. A member of the Capital City Writers Association and the Women's Fiction Writers Association, she is the current director of the annual WFWA Writers Retreat in Albuquerque, New Mexico.

Erin lives in Michigan, a land shaped by glaciers and hemmed in by vast inland seas, where one is never more than six miles from a lake, river, or stream. She grew up in the Bay City area, waiting for freighters and sailboats at drawbridges and watching the best Fourth of July fireworks displays in the nation. She spent her college and young married years in Grand Rapids feeling decidedly not-Dutch. She currently lives with her husband and son in Lansing, nestled somewhere between angry protesters on the capitol lawn and couch-burning frat boys at Michigan State University. And yet, she claims it is really quite peaceful.

"A story to savor and share.
I loved every sentence, every word."

—BARBARA CLAYPOLE WHITE, bestselling author of
The Perfect Son and *The Promise between Us*

A reclusive bookstore owner hoped she'd permanently buried
her family's sensational past by taking a new name. But when
the novels she once shared with an old crush begin appearing
in the mail, it's clear her true identity is about to be revealed,
threatening the new life she has painstakingly built.

Revell
a division of Baker Publishing Group
www.RevellBooks.com

Available wherever books and ebooks are sold.

THE PAST IS NEVER AS PAST AS
We'd Like to Think

In this richly textured debut novel, a disgraced journalist moves
into her great-aunt's secret-laden farmhouse and discovers that
the women in her family were testaments to true love and courage
in the face of war, persecution, and racism.

Я Revell
a division of Baker Publishing Group
www.RevellBooks.com

Available wherever books and ebooks are sold.

CONNECT WITH ERIN

Check out her newsletter, blog, podcast, and more at

ErinBartels.com

 @ErinBartelsAuthor    @ErinLBartels   @ErinBartelsWrites